Once Upon a Time . . .

. . . there was a poor widow with two daughters, beautiful as roses — Blanche and Rosamund: Snow White and Rose Red.

Once Upon a Time . . .

. . . the Queen of Faerie had two changeling sons; one was content in his mother's Court, the other yearned to wander through the human lands.

Once Upon a Time . . .

. . . two human sorcerers, in an unwitting alliance with a spiteful spirit, forged an enchantment which trapped a changeling prince, and drew Snow White and Rose Red to befriend him, whatever the cost.

Journey to an Elizabethan England that never was, quite — where human science and faerie magic sometimes meet . . . and clash. Patricia C. Wrede takes a classic fairy tale and gives it vibrant new life.

Tor books by Patricia C. Wrede

Mairelon the Magician
Snow White and Red Rose

SNOW WHITE
A·N·D
ROSE RED

PATRICIA C. WREDE

TOR fantasy

A TOM DOHERTY ASSOCIATES BOOK
NEW YORK

This is a work of fiction. All the characters and events portrayed in this book are fictitious, and any resemblance to real people or events is purely coincidental.

SNOW WHITE AND RED ROSE

Copyright © 1989 by Patricia C. Wrede

Cover painting and design by Thomas Canty. Copyright © 1989, 1990 by Thomas Canty.

A Tor Book
Published by Tom Doherty Associates, Inc.
175 Fifth Avenue
New York, N.Y. 10010

Tor® is a registered trademark of Tom Doherty Associates, Inc.

ISBN: 0-812-53497-2

First edition: April 1989
First mass market edition: July 1990

Printed in the United States of America

0 9 8 7 6 5 4 3 2

This book is for Terri and Val, because without them it would never have happened

✦ Acknowledgments ✦

The author is deeply grateful for the patient assistance of Cordelia Sherman and Pamela Dean Dyer-Bennet in vetting the Elizabethan English in this book. Any egregious errors or deliberate idiocities which remain were committed by the author, and should be dealt with as such.

INTRODUCTION

•FAIRY TALES•

THERE IS NO SATISFACTORY EQUIVALENT TO THE German word *märchen*, tales of magic and wonder such as those collected by the Brothers Grimm: *Rapunzel, Hansel & Gretel, Rumpelstiltskin, The Six Swans,* and other such familiar stories. We call them fairy tales, although none of the above stories actually contains a creature called a "fairy." They do contain those ingredients most familiar to us in fairy tales: magic and enchantment, spells and curses, witches and trolls, and protagonists who defeat overwhelming odds to triumph over evil. J. R. R. Tolkien, in his classic essay, "On Fairy-Stories," offers the definition that these are not in particular tales about fairies or elves, but rather of the land of Faerie: "the Perilous Realm itself, and the air that blows in the country, I will not attempt to define that directly," he goes on, "for it cannot be done. Faerie cannot be caught in a net of words; for it is one of its qualities to be indescribable, though not imperceptible."

Fairy tales were originally created for an adult audience. The tales collected in the German countryside and set to paper by the Brothers Grimm (wherein a Queen orders her step-daughter, Snow White, killed and her heart served "boiled and salted for my dinner," and a peasant girl must cut off her own feet lest the Red Shoes, of which she has been so vain, keep her dancing night and day until she dances herself to death) were published for an adult readership, popular, in the age of Goethe and Schiller, among the German Romantic poets. Charles Perrault's spare and moralistic tales (such as Little Red Riding Hood who, in the original Perrault telling, gets eaten by the wolf in the end for having the ill sense to talk to strangers in the wood) was written for the court of Louis XIV; Madame d'Aulnoy (author of *The White Cat*) and Madame Leprince de Beaumont (author of *Beauty and the Beast*) also wrote for the French aristocracy. In England, fairy stories and heroic legends were popularized through Malory's Arthur, Shakespeare's Puck and Ariel, Spenser's Faerie Queene.

With the Age of Enlightenment and the growing emphasis on rational and scientific modes of thought, along with the rise in fashion of novels of social realism in the nineteenth century, literary fantasy went out of vogue and those stories of magic, enchantment, heroic quests, and courtly romance that form a cultural heritage thousands of years old, dating back to the oldest written epics and further still to tales spoken around the hearth-fire, came to be seen as fit only for children, relegated to the nursery like, Professor Tolkien points out, "shabby or old fashioned furniture . . . primarily because the adults do not want it, and do not mind if it is misused."

And misused the stories have been, in some cases altered so greatly to make them suitable for Victorian children that the original tales were all but forgotten. Andrew Lang's *Tam Lin*, printed in the colored Fairy Books series, tells the story of little Janet whose playmate is stolen away by the fairy folk—ignoring the original, darker tale of seduction and human sacrifice to the Lord of Hell, as the heroine, pregnant with Tam Lin's child, battles the Fairy Queen for her lover's life. Walt Disney's *Sleeping Beauty* bears only a little resemblance to Straparola's *Sleeping Beauty of the Wood*, published in Venice in the sixteenth century, in which the enchanted princess is impregnated as she sleeps, waking to find herself the mother of twins. The Little Golden Book version of the *Arabian Nights* resembles not at all the violent and sensual tales actually recounted by Scheherazade in *One Thousand and One*

Nights, shocking nineteenth-century Europe when fully translated by Sir Richard Burton. (*"Not* for the young and innocent . . ." said the *Daily Mail.*)

The wealth of material from myth and folklore at the disposal of the story-teller (or modern fantasy novelist) has been described as a giant cauldron of soup into which each generation throws new bits of fancy and history, new imaginings, new ideas, to simmer along with the old. The story-teller is the cook who serves up the common ingredients in his or her own individual way, to suit the tastes of a new audience. Each generation has its cooks, its Hans Christian Andersen or Charles Perrault, spinning magical tales for those who will listen—even amid the Industrial Revolution of the nineteenth century or the technological revolution of our own. In the last century, George MacDonald, William Morris, Christina Rossetti, and Oscar Wilde, among others, turned their hands to fairy stories; at the turn of the century lavish fairy tale collections were produced, a showcase for the art of Arthur Rackham, Edmund Dulac, Kai Nielsen, the Robinson Brothers—published as children's books, yet often found gracing adult salons.

In the early part of the twentieth century Lord Dunsany, G. K. Chesterton, C. S. Lewis, T. H. White, J. R. R. Tolkien—to name but a few—created classic tales of fantasy; while more recently we've seen the growing popularity of books published under the category title "Adult Fantasy"—as well as works published in the literary mainstream that could easily go under that heading: John Barth's *Chimera,* John Gardner's *Grendel,* Joyce Carol Oates' *Bellefleur,* Sylvia Townsend Warner's *Kingdoms of Elfin,* Mark Halprin's *A Winter's Tale,* and the works of South American writers such as Gabriel García Márquez and Miguel Angel Asturias.

It is not surprising that modern readers or writers should occasionally turn to fairy tales. The fantasy story or novel differs from novels of social realism in that it is free to portray the world in bright, primary colors, a dream-world half remembered from the stories of childhood when all the world was bright and strange, a fiction unembarrassed to tackle the large themes of Good and Evil, Honor and Betrayal, Love and Hate. Susan Cooper, who won the Newbery Medal for her fantasy novel *The Grey King*, makes this comment about the desire to write fantasy: "In the *Poetics* Aristotle said, 'A likely impossibility is always preferable to an unconvincing possibility.' I think those of us who write fantasy are dedicated to making impossible things seem likely, making dreams seem real. We are somewhere between the Impressionist and abstract painters. Our writing is haunted by those parts of our experience which we do not understand, or even consciously remember. And if you, child or adult, are drawn to our work, your response comes from that same shadowy land."

All Adult Fantasy stories draw in a greater or lesser degree from traditional tales and legends. Some writers consciously acknowledge that material, such as J. R. R. Tolkien's use of themes and imagery from the Icelandic Eddas and the German *Niebelungenlied* in *The Lord of the Rings* or Evangeline Walton's reworking of the stories from the Welsh *Mabinogion* in *The Island of the Mighty*. Some authors use the language and symbols of old tales to create new ones, such as the stories collected in Jane Yolen's *Tales of Wonder*, or Patricia McKillip's *The Forgotten Beasts of Eld*. And others, like Robin McKinley in *Beauty* or Angela Carter in *The Bloody Chamber* (and the movie *The Company of Wolves* derived from a story in that collection) base their stories directly on old tales, breathing new life into them, and presenting them to the modern reader.

The Fairy Tales series presents novels of the later sort—novels directly based on traditional fairy tales. Each novel in the series is based on a specific, often familiar, tale—yet each author is free to retell that story in his or her own way, showing the diverse uses a modern story-teller can make of traditional material. In the previous novels of the Fairy Tale series (published by Ace Books), Steven Brust uses a folk tale from his Hungarian heritage to mirror a contemporary story of artists and courage and the act of creation in *The Sun, the Moon, and the Stars*. In *Jack the Giant-Killer*,

Charles de Lint creates a faery world in the shadows of a modern Canadian city; as with the Latin American "magic realists," the fantasy in this novel tells us much about the real world and one young woman's confrontation with the secret places in her own heart. In *The Nightingale*, Kara Dalkey turns Hans Christian Andersen's classic story into a haunting historical novel set in ancient Japan, a tale of love and magic and poetry which evokes the life of the Japanese imperial court as deftly as did the diaries of the imperial court ladies, written so many centuries ago.

The novel you hold in your hand, the fourth in the Fairy Tales series (now published by Tor Books), comes from one of the most beloved writers to emerge in the fantasy field in the last decade, Patricia C. Wrede. Wrede has taken the familiar story of two exceptional sisters, *Snow White and Rose Red* (found in the tales of the Brothers Grimm, and other collections), and set it in an Elizabethan England that is both real and magical, placing actual historical characters, such as the Queen's astrologer John Dee, alongside the imaginary denizens of the lands of Faery. It is a lovely novel, and a splendid reworking of the original story.

Forthcoming in our series is a novel that mixes the *Sleeping Beauty–Briar Rose* legend with the modern horror story of the Holocaust; a retelling of the Scots ballad-fairy tale *Tam Lin* (as recorded by the folk-rock band Fairport Convention); and other novels by some of the most talented writers working today, retelling the world's most beloved tales, in editions lovingly designed (by the award-winning artist/illustrator Thomas Canty), as all good fairy tale books should be.

I hope you'll enjoy them all.

—Terri Windling
Editor, the Fairy Tales series
The Endicott Studio, Boston
December 1988

CHAPTER · ONE

*"Once upon a time there was a poor widow who lived in a
tiny cottage near a lonely forest. In front of the cottage were
two rosebushes, one white and the other red. The widow had
two girls who were like the two rosebushes; one was called
Snow White and the other Rose Red."*

THE WIDOW ARDEN AND HER TWO DAUGHTERS LIVED
in a one-room cottage just outside the village of Mortlak, less than
a mile from the river Thames. The walls of the cottage were wattle
and plaster, with two small cloth-covered windows to let in the
light, and the floor was of rough-hewn planks. In a fit of prosperity,
the previous owner had built a hearth and chimney into the west
wall, which reduced the risk of setting the thatched roof afire and
added greatly to the winter comfort of the inhabitants.

The cottage lay hard by the forest, separated from Mortlak by
fields and commons, and the villagers were content to have it so.
For the Widow Arden was considered, at best, eccentric; some
spoke openly of madness. A few of the townsfolk hinted at still

darker things and professed themselves grateful that the parish church stood between their comfortable homes and the Widow's tiny dwelling.

These latter rumors were given little credence by most of the villagers. Perhaps this was because the Widow Arden's piety seemed too great to allow the possibility of witchcraft. Did she not bring her family to service every Sunday, morning and evening, without fail? Her dress was always modest and neat, if much mended. Her daughters knew their catechism with a thoroughness that was the envy of every youth and maiden the minister called on to recite during the instruction. If she eked out the pittance her late husband had left her by selling herbs and simples to her neighbors, who could blame her? She was not the only woman to do as much.

Those who bothered to concern themselves with such things felt that the real root of the unpleasant rumors was simply envy. The Widow Arden was a comely woman and not even the most censorious could call her daughters anything but lovely. Rosamund, the younger of the two girls, had inherited her mother's rich, chestnut-colored hair and brown eyes. The elder sister, Blanche, had grey eyes and her hair was a much lighter brown. Both had perfect complexions, arched brows, and white, even teeth; both had slender figures and moved gracefully. It was not surprising that relatives of less fortunate girls murmured. The wonder was that talk was not more common.

The persistence of the rumors was due in part to the Widow's supposed dislike of marriage. Had the Widow merely shown no inclination to remarry the villagers might have accepted it, but she had also rejected several flattering offers for her daughters' hands. The younger girl was now rising sixteen and neither she nor her sister was so much as betrothed, which many felt went beyond the bounds of reason. There was also the uncomfortable fact that the Widow and her daughters could read and write, and not only honest English, but Latin as well. Such learning was appropriate for the Queen (God save her), but in lesser women it smacked of presumption. It was certainly not something any of the villagers wished to encourage in their own families.

"Your daughters shall ne'er be wed, an you continue in this froward fashion," Mistress Townsend told the Widow one clear fall afternoon.

"There's time and plenty to fret," the Widow Arden replied peaceably.

"You should think on it!" Mistress Townsend said. Mistress Townsend was a stout, grey-haired woman, widely known for her piety and good works. It irked her that the Widow Arden seemed unconscious of any need for charity, though she was all but penniless. She had therefore formed the custom of calling at the Widow's cottage, in a subtle attempt to bring her to acknowledge the difficulties of her situation and so provide an opening for Mistress Townsend's beneficence. Since the Widow politely declined to accept her services, Mistress Townsend had resorted to proffering advice. So far, the change in approach had not been notable for its success.

"Why is that, Mistress Townsend?" the Widow asked in a tone of mild curiosity as she carefully measured a length of thread.

"Because you've cause and more to be uneasy. Look you, 'tis no simple thing to find a husband for a dowerless girl, be she never so comely, and I fear your daughters have greater defects than lack of dower. I hope you'll not take my plain-speaking amiss."

The Widow looked up from her mending. "Pray, say on."

"Blanche and Rosamund are overlearned for most men's taste," her companion said, pursing her lips as if the very words were distasteful. "Nor is Rosamund so mild-spoken as she belike should be."

"And is that the sum of your complaint?"

"That and their lack of dowry must concern you first and most chiefly, yes," Mistress Townsend said judiciously. "But were they my daughters, I'd fear as well their heedless wanderings in the woods. 'Tis danger enough to live near the forest's edge, but you let your children walk there as if they were armed and weaponed as the

Queen's guard! I tell you, harm will come to them one day; that, or . . ."

"Or what?" said the Widow.

Mistress Townsend lowered her voice to a dramatic whisper. "Or there'll be those who speak of witchcraft, and not softly."

"I see." With meticulous care, the Widow folded the foresmock she had been mending. She set it aside and turned a level gaze on Mistress Townsend. "And what would you have me do?" she asked in a gentle tone.

"Why—why stop them," Mistress Townsend replied, momentarily disconcerted by the Widow's steady regard. "Keep them at home, if you'll not see them wed as yet, or find them places in some gentle household, where they may earn their own way. I know of several London merchants who would—"

"I'd strangle my daughters with my own hands before I'd send them to that vice-ridden plague pit!" the Widow interrupted. "You've said enough, Mistress Townsend, and more than enough. Blanche and Rosamund go into the forest because I send them, to gather the herbs I need. They know the forest well; if I've no fear for their safety, you need have none either. As for their learning, if it keeps them from bad husbands I'll thank Heaven and wish them twenty times as wise! Now I must go to tend my bees, and so I give you good day, Mistress."

Mistress Townsend found herself ushered gently but firmly to the door. So stunned was she by this unaccustomed turn of events that she did not think to resist until she was outside the cottage. Muttering balefully, she lifted her skirts and began the walk back to Mortlak. The Widow Arden stood at one of the windows, peering through a hole in the cloth covering, and watched the other woman out of sight. Then she shook her head, and went out to tend her bees and wait for her daughters' return.

The two girls were not long in making their appearance. They came into the kitchen garden from the forest, just as the Widow finished inspecting the straw shelter by the chimney that was to house the bees for the winter. Rosamund ran ahead, as was her custom; she held her willow basket carefully to keep from spilling its contents. "Mother!" she called. "Look! We found elderberries and wild onion."

"Well done," the Widow said. "Yet thou shouldst not shout thy news from half a mile away, nor run so heedlessly about. Thy harum-scarum ways will bring thee rue, my Rose."

Rosamund blinked at her mother in surprise. Then she set her basket on the ground and sank into an exaggerated court curtsy, her eyes demurely lowered. "I pray you, pardon, Mother," she said in dulcet tones.

"Wretched child!" the Widow said, laughing. "Cease thy foolishness and tell me where thy wandering feet have taken thee today, that thou hast returned with such uncommon treasures."

"We went into the forest, Mother," Blanche said, coming up beside her sister. "Westward and south a little, along the brook where the rushes grow."

"You did not cross the Border?"

"At this season?" Rosamund said indignantly. "We're not so foolish."

Blanche studied her mother, and a small line appeared between her eyebrows. "Mother, why so many questions? Is something amiss?"

"I fear it," the Widow replied, "though I am not sure. It may be but the knowledge of my own folly which makes me so uneasy."

"What folly's that?" Rosamund asked in a skeptical tone as she picked up her basket.

"Mistress Townsend called today."

The girls looked at each other. "That one!" Rosamund said disapprovingly. "Thou shouldst not listen to her gloom."

"She meaneth good," Blanche said with a reproving glance at her sister, "but thou shouldst not let her overset thee, Mother."

"'Tis not Mistress Townsend's tongue that's broken my peace, but my own," the Widow replied.

"Hast sent her off at last?" Rosamund said, looking up with a hopeful expression.

"I have, and with such words as must ill please her. And so I think that for some little while you must do your berrying in the meadow and not the wood."

"But Mother!" Blanche said in shocked surprise. "The coriander jar is barely a quarter full; it will not last the winter! And thy supply of more uncommon herbs is lower still."

"What matters that, an thee and thy sister are taken up for witchcraft?" the Widow retorted. "You've work enough outside the wood to occupy your fingers. 'Tis not forever," she added, seeing her daughters' downcast expressions. "I only wish it seen that you are busy with other things than herbery. There'll be time for gathering ere winter comes."

"A pox on Mistress Townsend and her tongue," Rosamund muttered.

The Widow frowned. "Rose! Thou'lt spend an extra hour with thy prayer book tonight for thy ill-wishing. And in the future, set a better guard upon thy tongue."

"But, Mother—"

"Do as I bid thee! Take thy basket inside and sort it carefully, and in the future stay away from the forest until I give thee leave."

Rosamund's lips set into a stubborn line. Blanche touched her elbow and motioned toward the cottage. Rosamund looked at her sister for a moment, then sighed and picked up her basket. Together, they disappeared into the cottage.

The Widow watched until the door closed behind them, a tiny wrinkle between her eyebrows and her eyes dark with trouble. She had good reason for her concern. Women had been taken to the ducking stool or worse for words as casually spoken as Rosamund's had been. The Widow Arden had set on her daughters the most powerful protections she knew, but her skill had no power over the wagging tongues of mortal women. However vague or idle Mistress Townsend's words had been, the Widow Arden could not afford to take them lightly; the line she and her family walked was already all too narrow.

For in the forest that backed the Widow's cottage lay one of the shifting borders of Faerie, and it was in that strange and shadowed land that Rosamund and Blanche gathered the rarest of the herbs their mother needed. Because the girls were maidens and still young, they could cross the border into Faerie with relative safety, but the Widow had charged them not to wander too far on the other side.

The girls, well aware of the perils of extemporaneous exploration, had always obeyed this stricture implicitly, and it was as well that they had done so. Less than a league from the border they so often crossed, in a stand of ancient oaks, stood the palace of the Faerie Queen herself, and there were those among her court who were not pleased with its proximity to the mortal world.

❖   ❖   ❖

"I swear the forest stinks of humans all about," said a narrow-faced man in a short white ruff and a grey velvet doublet. From his sleeve he pulled a handkerchief, edged with pointed lace and smelling of crushed moss and new ferns, and waved it through the air in front of his face for emphasis.

"You must be newly come to court," the woman beside him said, smiling slightly. Her gown was the same rusty color as maple leaves in autumn, and she rested one hand against a pillar of ice-blue marble to better display the gold lining of her sleeves.

"I am," the first speaker admitted. "But if you mean that I'll become accustomed to the reek, I doubt 'tis possible. Can the Queen do nothing?"

A tall woman standing close by, black-haired and beautiful, looked at him with interest, and the green-gold silk of her gown whispered against the marble-inlay floor of the Queen's Great Hall as she turned.

"Say, rather, that she will not, and if you would be wise you'll say it softly," the man's companion replied in a low voice. "The Queen's sons are one-half mortal, and the younger's much at court."

"I take your point, and likewise will take care to watch my tongue," the man in grey said thoughtfully. "If 'tis the Queen's will, there's no more to be said."

Nearby, the black-haired woman curled her lip and turned away, her curiosity at an apparent end. She had taken barely two steps when an overly ingenuous voice said, "What is't that ails thee, lady? Belike an inflammation of the liver, or else a colic, or a rheum? For surely 'tis not temper that doth make thee look so black."

The woman stiffened and turned to face the wiry youth who had spoken. Her expression became still more disdainful. "Be wary, Robin, lest 'tis thyself thy tongue dost cut."

The youth lowered his chin and peered at her through a fringe of unruly black hair. "Did I say aught amiss?"

"Go to," the woman said contemptuously. "Thou'rt near as worthless as a mortal man. Find someone else on whom to whet thy wits; an thou dost provoke me again, thou'lt rue it." She turned and swept away.

The youth stood motionless, looking after her with narrowed eyes, and the corners of his mouth turned very slightly upward. "Will I so?" he murmured. "Will I, indeed?"

◆   ◆   ◆

On the opposite side of the Widow's cottage, in the village of Mortlak, lived Master John Dee, commonly called Doctor Dee. He and his family occupied a three-story, half-timbered house on the river Thames. Though Dee was welcomed in the homes of the educated and well-to-do (he was, after all, Queen Elizabeth's astrologer), ordinary folk disliked and feared him. Fishmongers, joiners, and even the men who pulled the dustcarts wore hawthorn twigs in their caps whenever they had to pass Dee's house, or carried crosses tucked inside their jerkins. For John Dee was widely known to be a sorcerer, and all his connections at the court could not make him acceptable to his neighbors.

Dee was well aware of the town's hostility. He had faced accusations of witchcraft and sorcery at least twice, though the charges had come to nothing. For a long time thereafter he had kept quiet about his interest in things magical, but in recent years he had begun to experiment once more. He was aided in these activities by a like-minded friend, one Edward Kelly. For over a year, the two men had worked in the high-ceilinged study on the second floor of Dee's house, and now Kelly had proposed a new and ambitious enterprise. He was taken aback, and somewhat disgruntled, to discover that Dee was less than enthusiastic.

"There is great profit in't, can we but discover a means to secure the power to our requirements," Kelly said persuasively. He was a short, bearded man in his late twenties. A fringe of brown hair showed around the edges of the close-fitting black skullcap he always wore. His smooth voice had the accent of a well-educated man, and he wore the black robes of a scholar.

"I cannot like it, Ned," Dee replied, frowning. He was nearly twice his companion's age and his long beard was quite grey, but his face was handsome and well bred. He, too, wore a scholar's robes, but they seemed more appropriate to his dignity than to the younger man's restless energy.

"Why say you so?" Master Kelly demanded. "We may have within our grasp the secret of the philosopher's stone or the Elixir itself, and yet you hesitate!"

"The angel of the stone hath not confirmed our purpose," John Dee replied, waving at a square table in the center of the room. The top of the table was covered with symbols, and in the center rested a sphere of polished quartz.

"Nor hath the angel condemned it," Kelly shot back. "And how should he? Think, John! The hosts of Heaven have naught to do with those of Faerie."

"That is my point precisely," said the older man dryly.

"You are unreasonable!" Kelly said, schooling his face into a wounded expression. "You twist my words all out of sense. I meant but this: if Heaven hath no communion with Faerie, then the angel who speaks through yonder stone shall ne'er make protest of our intended enterprise."

"Faerie is an un-Godly power, Ned," the other man soberly.

"An our ends be Godly, what need we fear?" Kelly retorted. "Why was it that you came to Mortlak, if not for Faerie's nearness?"

"The lure of Faerie drew me here, so much is true," Dee answered, but his expression was troubled. "Yet I'd thought but to study it, not snatch at Faerie power for my own."

"What, will you ask politely for some sprite to join you here, that you may make inquiries of it?" Kelly said sarcastically. "Or in your own person brave the gates of Faerie, or how?"

"Nay, Ned, you need not mock at me," Dee said with dignity. "Your talents may be more than mine, but your knowledge is not greater."

"Not in all things, certainly," Kelly said. "But in this I think I must claim precedence, since Faerie and all other occult matters have been my especial study."

"I did not mean to call your knowledge into question," Dee said, his troubled frown returning. "You've proved its worth and twelve times over, this past year. Yet to directly outface Faerie is a chancy thing, at best."

Kelly chuckled. "You fright yourself with ill-chosen words, to speak of 'directly' when we'll not so much as step o'er the border twixt our land and that other. But if you've no stomach for't, I'll to the woods at All Hallows' Eve, and make the attempt alone."

"Nay, I'll not let you risk all while I stay safe," Dee said quickly. "An you're determined on't, we'll brave the gates of Faerie together, or not at all."

"'Tis decided, then," Ned Kelly said with a barely audible sigh of relief. "You'll not regret it, John."

Dee made an ambiguous gesture that might have been indicative of either assent or doubt. "Can you and I, unaided, carry all that will be needed? 'Twould be unwise indeed to bring another into this affair."

"We can manage. But is it certain that we must?"

"In this I'll not be moved, Ned," Dee interrupted. "No one save you and I must know of this."

"You fear a witch-hunt?" Kelly said, a barely audible note of disdain in his voice.

"Aye," Dee said sharply. "And so would you, an you'd faced the Star Chamber's questioning or been twice imprisoned on a charge of sorcery." He closed his eyes briefly, and so did not see the cold expression that stiffened Kelly's face, nor notice Kelly's hand rise to touch the edge of his black skullcap where it covered his right ear. "There's rumor enough i'the town," Dee said more gently. "Let us not add to it."

"As you wish," Kelly said, forcing a smile. "I'll begin creation of the spell; do you do likewise, and we'll use the better of the two."

"An you insist, I'll do't." Dee returned Kelly's false smile with a genuine one. "But I've no doubt you'll best me. You've a rare talent for such things, Ned."

Kelly stroked his beard, not at all displeased by Dee's remark, but all he said was, "Nonetheless, let's both prepare. To capture Faerie power will be no easy task; 'tis best that both our minds be set to't."

"Very well," Dee said. "Until the morrow, then."

♦   ♦   ♦

In the twilight garden beside Master John Dee's house, a silver-grey shadow slid down from the window that gave onto the study where Dee and his friend had been conversing so earnestly. Moonlight glinted briefly from pointed teeth, bared in a fierce parody of a smile; then the shadow drifted across the garden to the water gate and down the stairs to the Thames. A swan, swimming late on the river, was startled into flight when the shadow-creature entered the water, and the ripples of the bird's hasty leave-taking hid whatever traces there might have been of the shadow's passing.

CHAPTER · TWO

•

"Snow White was the quieter of the two girls; she liked to sit at home with her mother and read. Rose Red preferred to run through the fields and forests, looking for flowers."

•

ROSAMUND AND BLANCHE DID NOT GO NEAR THE forest for a week. This curtailment of their rambles affected Blanche very little. She had always enjoyed her walks with her sister, but it must be confessed that at times she found Rosamund's more adventurous spirit rather trying. Though she would not for the world have hurt her sister by saying so, Blanche was relieved to be spared, for a time, the necessity of curbing Rosamund's whims. She was happy to be at home, polishing the treasured copper kettle and measuring out herbs for her mother's simples.

The Widow's ban was far harder for Rosamund to accept. She loved the forest, and she missed it deeply. But more than the forest, she missed the sharp clarity of the air of Faerie and the sudden strangeness of its trees and flowers, the scents of a mingled spring and summer that never faded, the piercing calls of birds unseen and unafraid. She missed the care and caution that were necessary within that other land, and the feeling of triumph that came with a safe return. She even missed the long, sometimes fruitless search for the constantly shifting border of Faerie.

Rosamund tried not to be foolish. She and Blanche had never traveled regularly in Faerie; they seldom visited more than once or twice a month in summer, and not at all during winter. Rosamund had often gone for long periods without so much as coming near the border of Faerie, for certain seasons were particularly hazardous for mortal dealings there. The weeks immediately prior to All Hallows' Eve were among these dangerous times, and Rosamund and Blanche had always been careful to avoid the fringes of Faerie then. Deprivation had not bothered her before; indeed, she had thought nothing of it. But all Rosamund's reasoning made no impression on the stubborn longing of her heart, and she continued to pine for the forbidden walks.

The Widow Arden was not blind to her younger daughter's difficulty, and she tried to help as best she could. She assigned Rosamund the more active tasks, especially those which would take her out of the cottage and away from the forest that brooded behind it. When there were errands to run in the village, she sent Rosamund; when a tincture or potion was finished, Rosamund delivered it. If all else failed, the Widow sent the girl to gather rushes for Blanche to plait into winter coverings for the floor.

None of these measures did much to ease Rosamund's mind. She could see what her mother was trying to do, and she was grateful for it, but struggling down the muddy path to Mortlak was not an adequate substitute for walking across the spongy moss that covered the forest floor. Nor was watching the swans floating on the river Thames a satisfying alternative to catching the merest glimpse of a strange, bright-plumed bird sailing through the forests of Faerie.

Rosamund did not voice any of this. She gritted her teeth and went about her work with fierce determination, hoping all the while that her mother would relent before winter closed in and adventuring in the woods became impossible. She took to spending as much of her time as she could away from home; if her mother had no errands for her, she would wander through the meadow, gathering herbs and sometimes chatting with the laborers working in the fields. When the sun began to sink toward the west, she would find a footpath and make her way home, swinging her basket and humming with stubborn cheerfulness.

Late one afternoon, Rosamund was heading homeward when she saw a flash of red among the branches of a hawthorn bush beside the path. She stopped and looked more closely, then smiled. Some berries still clung determinedly to the spiny branches near the center of the bush. Rosamund set her basket on the ground, then knelt and insinuated her arm carefully into the spaces between the thorns. So intent was she that she did not notice a man approaching from the direction of Mortlak.

The man slowed as he came up behind her, and commented in a mellow voice, "A curious task for such a pretty maid."

Rosamund started, then exclaimed as the hawthorn scratched her hand. She turned, frowning. "The task is common enough, and better done had you not interrupted."

"Why, here's a lively tongue!" the man said, his eyes dancing. His face was shadowed by a soft, broad-brimmed hat; a large canvas sack was slung over one of his shoulders, and he had to lean to the other side to balance its weight. His clothes were patched and worn, and dusty with much traveling. He was the very picture of a wandering peddler.

Rosamund tried to meet the peddler's eyes sternly, but after a moment she was forced to drop her gaze to her scratched hand. This irritated her more than ever, and she said crossly, "Go your ways and let me work, discourteous man."

"In what courtesy have I failed so sorely?"

"You might have given better warning of your coming, goodman," Rosamund said. "Or waited, at the least, until I'd withdrawn my hand. Now I've scratched myself and my berries are scattered, and all for your foolish lack of thought."

"Why, then, I'll make amends," the peddler said. He lowered his sack to the pathway. Before Rosamund could protest, he was crouched at her side, reaching delicately among the hawthorn branches with long, slender fingers.

Rosamund studied him with interest, and a few misgivings. She did not feel afraid, though the Widow had often warned her daughters against the vagabonds and rogues who sometimes haunted the byways of the countryside, but she did not feel at ease with the man either. He was too contradictory; his actions and his hands were more those of a gentleman than a rogue, and they gave the lie to his pack and ragged clothing. Rosamund leaned forward slightly, hoping to catch a better glimpse of the peddler's face.

The peddler turned, and held out his cupped hands. "Bring your basket hither," he commanded.

Rosamund did as she was told. The peddler's eyes smiled at her from the shadow beneath his hat; then he tilted his hands and poured a stream of hawthorn berries into the basket.

"Is that enough to quit me of your displeasure?" he said, dusting his long fingers. "Or will you demand the golden apples of the sun, or three feathers from the firebird, before you let me go?"

"I had not thought that bush held so many berries," Rosamund said, staring at the shiny red pile that lay atop the herbs she had gathered earlier.

"Oh, I'm well versed in finding the nooks and crannies where such things hide," the peddler said in a careless tone. "But am I quits with you?"

"Aye, and I must offer you my thanks as well," Rosamund said. "Alone I'd never have gleaned so much."

The peddler winced and rose quickly. "Then I'll go along my way. Fare you well, sweet maid."

"I am named Rosamund Arden," Rosamund said as the peddler stooped to shoulder his pack. She felt she had misjudged the man, and, wishing to make amends, she added, "My home is just ahead, there by the forest. I'm sure you'd be welcome if you wish to stop and show your wares, though we've little coin with which to buy."

For a moment, the peddler hesitated; then he shook his head. "I'll walk along with you a little way, but I've too far to go tonight to break my journey now."

"You are a most uncommon peddler," Rosamund commented as she picked up her basket and fell into step beside the man.

"How say you so?" the peddler said, giving her a sharp look from under the brim of his hat.

"Why, because I've never known a peddler who refused to show his wares," Rosamund replied lightly, though she was still thinking of the man's speech and manners.

"Then I must answer that you're as uncommon as I," the peddler returned. "For, setting aside the fairness of your face—and, Rosamund, you are uncommon fair—I've never met a maid who did not blush and run from wayfarers of my ilk, unless a table spread with ribbons lay between."

Rosamund, who was by this time blushing furiously, looked down at her basket and said nothing. She was not unaccustomed to hearing her charms made much of by the hopeful youths of Mortlak, but the peddler's praise, dropped so casually into the middle of another subject, seemed more truthful and more serious than the exaggerated flattery of her would-be suitors.

"What's this? Struck dumb?" the peddler said. "I cry you pardon, Rosamund." His tone was half teasing, half serious, as if he meant more than he was willing to admit, even to himself.

"You make yourself too free of my name," Rosamund said tartly. They had almost reached the two rose trees that stood on either side of her mother's gate, and she felt that the peddler's boldness deserved some rebuke before she had to leave him.

"Why, then, I'll make you free of mine," the peddler responded, and then his eyes widened, as if he had said far more than he had intended.

"You need not, an it would discomfit you," Rosamund said

quickly. "Or else I'll give my promise not to speak of it, save to my mother and my sister, Blanche." It had occurred to her that the peddler's evident reluctance to give his name might be due to fear of the Queen's justice.

The peddler looked at her as she stood at the gate between the two rose trees, her expression a blend of curiosity, concern, and kindness. His lips twisted in a smile full of self-mockery. "Nay, I'll not ask it of thee, Rosamund. I am called John, though I was baptized Thomas."

Rosamund's cheeks reddened once more at the peddler's use of the intimate "thee," but all she said was, "Will you not come in?"

"The offer's kind, but I fear I must refuse it," the peddler said. He studied Rosamund a moment longer, then leaned forward and broke a twig from the rose tree beside her. He bowed awkwardly, hampered by his heavy pack, and held out the rose, full-blown and richly crimson. "Yet pray accept a token of my gratitude."

"Fie, rogue, to offer me my mother's roses! Have you no shame?" Rosamund said, but she took the flower from the peddler's hand and laid it gently in her basket.

"Little enough," the peddler replied cheerfully. "Farewell, gentle Rosamund."

"Farewell," Rosamund said. As he started down the path toward the forest, she whispered under her breath, "And God go with thee, John."

The peddler's step faltered, and Rosamund feared that he might have overheard her whispered words. He straightened almost at once, however, and continued toward the forest without looking back. Rosamund gave a little sigh, and turned to go into the cottage, glancing down at the rose tree beside the gate. The leaves were limp and darkening toward winter dormancy, and where the full-blown roses had hung in midsummer there were now only the small, hard knobs of the rose hips.

Wide-eyed, Rosamund looked from the rose tree to the crimson flower nestled in her basket. Then she turned a thoughtful gaze toward the forest. The peddler was already out of sight among the trees.

●　　　　●　　　　●

Within the forest, the peddler's stride lengthened. By twilight he had reached a small stand of young beech trees, near the brook where Rosamund and Blanche had found wild onions. There he paused. He swung his sack to the ground and opened it, then began to strip off his ragged clothing. The fading light showed him to be a much younger man than he had seemed in his peddler's garb; he looked to be in his mid-twenties, and well formed.

From his canvas sack, he drew a doublet and breeches made of brown velvet, a starched white ruff, silk hose, and a pair of narrow shoes with pointed toes. Swiftly, he donned the finer clothes, shoving his tattered rags and broad-brimmed hat into the sack in their place. When he had finished, he rose and shouldered the sack once more. Whistling through his teeth, he left the stand of trees and crossed the brook.

A breath of warm air greeted him as he passed under the boughs of the first great oak tree, just outside the copse. He smiled, noting the crystalline quality of the twilight and the sudden absence of the signs of coming winter. Heaving a deep sigh of satisfaction, he glanced around to choose his path.

Under the next oak, a figure moved out of the shadows. "Welcome, John," said a clear, cold voice. "How went thy travels?"

The man called John turned. "Hugh!" he said in a tone of pleased surprise. He dropped his canvas sack to the ground and embraced the other man. The two were nearly of an age, and they shared the same high forehead and dark, wavy hair. Their heights were identical, too, and both men had wide-set brown eyes and square, determined chins. But Hugh's eyes and smile held a coolness that set him apart from John, despite their physical resemblance, and the unearthly composure of Faerie was present in his expression and his stance.

"'Tis good to see thee, brother mine," John said, smiling warmly.

"It's good to have thee home at last, and safe," Hugh said. He returned the smile, and though it could not be described as warm his expression came closer to it than anyone familiar with the denizens of Faerie would have expected.

"What brings thee out to wait for me?" John asked.

The vestige of warmth left Hugh's face. "Ill tidings. Yet I'd not have thee hear them from another tongue. Thou art aware that Faerie's Queen hath long been little pleased by all thy wanderings?"

"I am."

"Her patience hath now reached its end," Hugh said bluntly. "She hath decreed thou mayest not, for any cause, depart from Faerie more."

A black and yellow bird sailed across the sky above, its wings gleaming golden in the setting sun. John blinked, as if he did not believe what he had just heard. "How if I should turn this instant and cross back to mortal lands?"

"The border would not be there for thee to find," Hugh said with visible reluctance. "She hath bespelled it against thee, that thou mayest not discover it without aid. And there's none in Faerie that will aid thee 'gainst the Queen's command."

John stared blankly for a long moment; then his lips thinned. "Why has our mother done this?"

"She is Queen, and fears for Faerie and for thee," Hugh replied. "If she hath another reason, I know it not." A breath of cool air stirred the leaves of the oak above him, and their rustling sounded loud and foreign in the clearing.

"Does she mistrust me?" John said in a tight voice.

Hugh shrugged. "It's possible. There are those among her councillors who'd gladly urge her to it. Thy travels in the mortal world have not endeared thee to the greater part of Faerie, and there are many who mislike thy human blood."

"Thou hast as much of mortal blood as I!"

"Thou speakest truth, yet thy ties to humankind are greater,"

Hugh said. His pale face was inhumanly calm. "Our father had thee baptized."

"Yet I chose Faerie freely," John said angrily. "I've given no one cause for this harsh treatment!"

"Calm thyself," Hugh advised. "The court meets for revels three days hence, on the Eve of All Hallows'. Thou mayest then lay thy case before the Queen."

"And if she denies me?"

"Why, then, thou'lt spend the winter here, as thou hast always done, and speak to her again at May Eve," Hugh responded. "It's not so great a matter, after all."

"Belike it seems not so to thee," John said. "In me, it rankles." He sighed and picked up his sack, then paused and looked at his brother. "Yet I am glad thou wast the bearer of these tidings, however ill they sit."

Hugh gave a small, dispassionate smile of acknowledgment, and the two brothers, one more fay than mortal, the other far too mortal for Faerie comfort, walked side by side into the deep woods.

◆　　　◆　　　◆

The shadows beneath the great oak tree remained empty as the twilight deepened. The stirring of the air ceased, and all was still, dark, and silent. The only movement was the all but imperceptible blending of the evening shadows with the growing gloom of night.

Shortly after moonrise a shiver ran through the leaves of the tree. A gnarled figure dropped into the open space below the boughs. He was short and twisted, with skin like wrinkled brown leather; his hair and beard were stiff and wiry, and several shades darker than his skin. His loose tunic was made of oak leaves stitched together, and he wore a red cap shaped like a toadstool. The smell of crushed moss rose strongly from beneath his flat, splayed feet, but he seemed not to notice. He glanced about him, snorted once, and leaned back against the tree, grimacing ferociously.

His wait was brief. A second figure joined him almost at once. It, too, was small, but there its resemblance to the first creature ended. Moonlight shone silver on its slick, scaly skin, and its mouth was wide and full of sharply pointed teeth. It was completely hairless, and there were webs between its fingers. A close-fitting garment of grey silk was wrapped about its loins; otherwise its skin was bare.

"Am I late?" the scaly creature asked without preamble.

"Madini's later," the first being growled.

"Didst thou suppose she would be otherwise? But check thy anger; see where she comes."

As the second creature spoke, a tall, black-haired woman stepped into the circle of moonlight. She moved with unearthly grace, and the beauty of her face was the cruel, sharp-edged beauty of the great ones of Faerie. Her eyes were dark, and her lips were very red. She wore an elegant green gown of shot silk embroidered with gold sequins. "Wherefore hast thou summoned us, goblin?" she said imperiously.

"An thou'dst learn it, call me not goblin,'" the brown-skinned dwarf replied, scowling. "Thou knowest my name."

"Thou'lt waste away to nothing, ere thou gettest aught of courtesy from Madini," the silver-scaled creature said. "Come, Bochad-Bec, speak thy news."

"The Queen's eldest bastard is back," the dwarf replied.

"John has returned?" snapped the woman called Madini. "Has he had speech with his brother?"

"Aye, beneath this very tree," Bochad-Bec said with sour satisfaction. "So he's warned of the Queen's displeasure. He'll speak to her at All Hallows'."

"Devils take him and tear out his tongue!" Madini said violently. "He'll throw my plans awry."

"Our plans, surely?" said the silver-scaled creature delicately. It paused and waited, but Madini said nothing. "I see but little reason for thy low spirits," it went on. "To postpone our work will do no harm."

"Thou'rt wrong in that," Madini snapped. "The land of Faerie's balanced like a juggler's plates; the longer we must hold our hands, the greater grows the chance that, by some accident or careless spell, that balance will be overset, and Faerie sent sliding toward the mortal world." She wrinkled her nose in distaste at the thought.

"Then, if thou'rt set on it, why can we not proceed as we'd intended?"

"And have those foolish humans catch John's power before the whole of the Queen's court?" Madini said scornfully. "Thou'rt a fool, Furgen."

"How so?" Furgen said, flashing its pointed teeth in the moonlight. "Or are there none at court who dislike John and mortals?"

"None who would cross our Queen's most slender whim to say so," Madini retorted bitterly. "Her fondness for her sons is known."

"What boots it? Will we, nil we, the human sorcerers will send their spells to seek for Faerie power on All Hallows' Eve. If we do not guide those spells, they must still find something. If—"

"Hugh's the greater menace," Bochad-Bec interrupted. The dark boughs of the oak creaked overhead as if in agreement. "He's human, and at court."

"Thou'st told us that till we have tired of hearing it," Madini said. "Hugh's blood is but half mortal, and his mind is wholly Faerie. 'Tis John whose wanderings keep our land close-tied to the mortal world."

"If I may finish?" Furgen said. Madini nodded, and Furgen went on. "If we guide the human's spells, as we had planned, then John will be struck helpless. What matters it that all the court may see? They'll blame the humans, Dee and Kelly, and not think of us."

"Thy point's well taken," Madini said, looking suddenly thoughtful. Her lips widened in a slow smile. "Yes, 'tis well indeed; I'll do't. All Hallows' Eve shall be John's bane."

"It's easy to say," Bochad-Bec muttered.

"'Twill be easy, too, to do, an ye follow my direction," Madini said. "Keep watch on the human wizards, Furgen, lest our preparations fail through some mischance of theirs. We'll meet again All Hallows' Eve."

"If thou'lt have it so," Furgen murmured.

Madini nodded regally, and departed. The remaining two conspirators peered through the darkness after her for a moment; then Furgen said, "That one's ambition may soon reach so high that she'll too easily forget those who aided her."

"Then we must remind her," Bochad-Bec said, scowling. The two exchanged glances of perfect understanding, then faded into the silent, moonlit forest of Faerie.

The Word of God

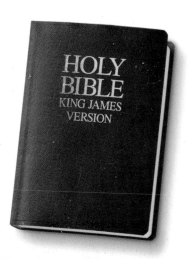

Please accept a free copy as our gift.

Call 1-888-537-1212.

THE CHURCH OF
JESUS CHRIST
OF LATTER-DAY SAINTS

CHAPTER · THREE

◆

"The two girls were very fond of each other, and always went out together. Sometimes Snow White would say, 'We will never part,' and Rose Red would answer, 'Never, as long as we live.' Their mother encouraged them in this, and always added, 'You must share whatever you have with each other.'"

◆

THE WIDOW ARDEN ACCEPTED ROSAMUND'S STORY, and the unseasonable rose she carried, with outward calm. Inwardly, she was seriously unsettled. Like her daughter, the Widow strongly suspected that the "peddler" had been more than mortal, and she knew that Faerie folk seldom showed themselves to mortals, even within their own borders. The peddler's unexpected visitation, therefore, made her profoundly uneasy. Unfortunately, there was nothing she could do to turn away Faerie interest in her daughter, or so she told herself.

This conclusion was not, in the strictest sense, correct. Though the townsfolk called her "wisewoman" because of her knowledge of herbs, the Widow had more right than they knew to be so named.

She seldom made use of her knowledge of magic, and when she did it was the lesser spells of scrying or protection to which she turned. Even then, she kept her proceedings carefully hidden. The Widow had no mind to be among the women hanged each year as witches.

The thought of using a scrying spell to seek the truth of Rosamund's encounter certainly crossed the Widow's mind. She dismissed it at once. If the hosts of Faerie so much as suspected that she might try to spy on them, she would be in even greater trouble than if she were caught in mid-spell by a church informant. The Widow had gone to great lengths to remain, if not on good terms with her unearthly neighbors, at least in a position of neutrality. She was not willing to endanger that neutrality out of unproven fear.

She could, however, explain those fears to her daughters, and warn them to take more care than usual. On the morning after Rosamund's encounter with the peddler, the Widow did just that, while the uncanny and impossible rose nodded at them over the edge of a tin cup in the center of the table.

The girls listened closely, and when she finished, Rosamund asked, "Thinkest thou that the peddler would try to carry me off to Faerie, then?"

"Belike," the Widow replied. "Thou hast what safeguards I can give thee, yet that may not suffice to turn a determined attempt. And 'tis not for thyself alone I fear."

"Blanche?" Rosamund paled, more disturbed by a threat to her gentle sister than by one to herself. "Thou thinkest they might take her in my stead?"

"An they're minded to," the Widow said. "Wherefore, I counsel you both to keep a watch upon each other. When you go out, go together, and do not stray from each other's sight. The folk of Faerie work most often by trickery and guile, and 'tis easier to befool one pair of eyes than two."

"We'll stay together, Mother," Blanche said with quiet determination. Then she smiled. "'Tis no great hardship." Rosamund nodded her agreement.

"You may prove your promises now," the Widow said, rising from the three-legged stool where she sat. "I'll bring you both with me into Mortlak this morning, and you shall practice your watchfulness."

The girls scrambled to their feet, and for a few moments the cottage was a whirl of locating baskets, straightening linen caps, donning extra petticoats, and tucking up the top layer of their skirts to keep the hems out of the dirt.

They set out as soon as the girls had finished. The Widow led the way along the narrow footpath. Rosamund and Blanche followed, side by side as they had promised. The day was grey and rainy, and by the time they reached Mortlak all three women were half covered in mud. The Widow sent her daughters to the apothecary, to try and trade some of their extra herbs for tooth-soap.

The girls departed happily enough, and the Widow was left to pursue her own errands. She began by stopping at one and another of the tall, half-timbered shops and houses to deliver various mixtures they had requested, then went on to make brief calls upon some of the women who had not made orders. At each house, the Widow found an excuse to open the subject of her daughters, then probed delicately for misgivings on the part of her companion. In several places, she led her listeners to the subject of witchcraft, and joined with them in deploring the existence of such a vile pursuit.

The results of this haphazard examination reassured the Widow greatly. Everyone spoke highly of Blanche and Rosamund, and though one or two remarked Rosamund's "high spirits," the comments were plainly meant to be kind. No one seemed more concerned than usual with witchcraft, though there were the usual grumblings about the presence of Master John Dee in the town. It was all very well to call him the Queen's Astrologer and to point out that Her Majesty had actually ridden into Mortlak several times to visit him, one disgruntled taverner told the Widow, but the man was still nothing less than a sorcerer, and no honest man would deal with him. And that friend of his, Talbot or Kelly or whatever he called himself, was no better than a common thief and lecher. Why, word was that Joan Cooper of Chipping Norton had *had* to marry the man last spring, and she a good, respectable girl until Kelly had taken up with her!

As the Widow was not at all concerned with Master Dee's affairs, much less Edward Kelly's, she greeted these grumblings with well-concealed relief. So long as the rumors of magic named anyone but her family, they did not disturb her. It was with a much lighter heart that the Widow went to meet her daughters for the trip home.

The girls were already waiting just outside the church when the Widow arrived. Rosamund was in a state of high excitement, and she burst out almost at once, "Mother! One of Master Hinde's ewes has borne twins, and will not feed them both, and he said that he'll give us the other lamb, if we think we may save it."

The Widow's eyes widened and her face took on a thoughtful expression when she heard this. Since her husband's death, she had steadfastly refused to accept charity from anyone, but Master Hinde's offer, strictly speaking, was not charity. A lamb born out of season and rejected by its mother would die without careful tending, and neither Master Hinde nor his servants had the temperament for such work. If the Widow did not take it, the lamb would probably die and do no good to anyone. On the other hand, if the Widow took it and could manage to save its life, her trouble would be well repaid. The lamb would grow to provide wool for her and her daughters, and if it was female, it would give milk and bear other lambs that could be sold or kept to increase a flock.

"I'll look at it, and see what may be done," she said. "There's no reason to carry the creature home, an the effort's to be wasted."

"Thou canst save it, Mother," Blanche said with confidence. "Thou didst as much for Goodman Garret these two winters past."

"Goodman Garret's sheep suffered of the scab," the Widow cautioned. "This task is not so simple." But she allowed herself to be swept along with Rosamund and Blanche in the direction of Master Hinde's.

*   *   *

Master Hinde had gone out, but he had left instructions with his man. The Widow and her daughters were taken to see the rejected lamb. It was a sickly-looking creature, and the Widow was not surprised that Master Hinde did not wish to expend the effort it would take to keep it alive. After a close inspection, however, the Widow pronounced herself satisfied that she could indeed save the tiny creature's life. As she was unwilling to wait for Master Hinde's return, she left a message expressing her profound thanks and gratitude, and she and her daughters were soon on their way back to the cottage. The return journey was even more uncomfortable than the trip into town. The rain had not stopped, and now the wind was in their faces. Blanche and Rosamund had to take turns carrying the lamb and trying to shield it from the cold.

They were all glad to reach the warm shelter of the cottage. Their first concern was with the lamb. The girls dried it, wrapped it in their oldest blanket, and set it near the fire before they removed their own wet and chilly clothing. The Widow set to work at once to brew a posset for Blanche to feed the lamb, while Rosamund hovered solicitously in the background. Finally, the Widow told Rosamund rather sharply that she would be of at least some use, did she go through the jars of herbs and set aside those that would be needed.

Rosamund took the reproof in good part, and set to work with a will. The Widow made an enormous kettle of vile-smelling liquid, and Blanche and Rosamund took turns coaxing the lamb to suck on an old dish-clout that had been soaked in the brew.

These efforts continued throughout the night and into the following day. At last the Widow announced that the lamb was in no immediate danger of dying, and that she would assume temporary responsibility for its care while Blanche and Rosamund caught up with some of their neglected chores. The girls were jubilant, and their good spirits carried them quickly through the worst of their tasks. Still, they were glad when they could finally settle themselves by the hearth with their mending.

"Thou'rt certain the lamb is well, Mother?" Blanche asked, looking across at it with a troubled expression. "It lies so still."

"'Tis sleeping, Blanche," the Widow said. "Young creatures must do so a great part of the time."

"I know, but—"

Blanche's reply was interrupted by a knock at the cottage door. The Widow smiled reassuringly at her daughter, then went to open the door herself. Standing on the step outside was Joan Bowes, a sharp-eyed, ruddy-cheeked young woman of eighteen who had lately hired herself to Mistress Rundel as a serving-girl.

"Oh, Widow Arden, I'm so glad you're here," Joan said as soon as she saw the Widow. "'Tis Elanor, Mistress Rundel's youngest; she's taken with a fever and the rheum. Mistress Rundel's half frantic. She sent me to beg that you give her a soothing draught as quickly as may be."

"Calm yourself, Joan," the Widow said. "Come in and warm yourself a little, and as you do you may tell me more, and in better order. I'll do what I can, but I must be certain what to send."

Joan had had a long, cold walk from Mortlak to the cottage; she accepted the Widow's suggestion with alacrity. As she walked slowly to the hearth, her eyes darted around the room, but she found very little to hold her interest. With a disappointed sigh, she seated herself on the stool by the fire and began answering the Widow's questions.

"I believe I have something that will help Elanor," the Widow said at last. "I've only a little here at hand; I'll give you that, and send Rosamund and Blanche with more tomorrow." She reached up to the shelf where she kept her remedies and took down a tiny vial, sealed with beeswax. "Tell Mistress Rundel to give the child a few drops of this, but no more than five at once, and no more frequently than every third hour."

"Thank you, Widow," Joan said, taking the vial. "I'll keep it—oh!" She jumped and nearly fell over the stool as the lamb, awakened by all the activity and conversation, struggled out from under its blanket, bleating piteously.

Blanche hurried to comfort the little creature, while the Widow caught Joan's arm just in time to keep her from losing her balance completely. "My apologies, Joan; I should have warned you," the Widow said. "'Tis but a winter lamb whose mother will not keep it."

"O-of course," Joan said, eyeing Blanche and the lamb doubtfully. She rose and backed toward the door, clutching the precious vial in one hand. When she reached the door, she hesitated visibly for a moment, then took a deep breath and said to the Widow, "I've done my errand for my mistress, but I've one of my own to you, an you'll hear me."

"Surely I'll hear you," the Widow said gently. The girl's circumspection did not surprise her; she'd had enough customers with various kinds of women's complaints to know that they rarely came directly to the point. The Widow nodded encouragingly to her visitor.

"I want—I have heard— 'Tis Master William, you see," Joan said all in a breath.

"William Rundel?" the Widow said, puzzled.

"Aye," Joan said eagerly. "Can you give me something, some potion for him? I can pay you well."

"He's not sick as well!" the Widow said. "Why didn't you say so at once? I could—"

"No, no, he's not ill," Joan said. She kept her voice low, despite her evident impatience. "'Tis I who am ill for wanting him, yet he sees it not. He has eyes only for his whey-faced wife. So I have come to you for a love-draught, to bring him to my bed at last."

"Go home, girl," the Widow said coldly. "I mix no potions of that kind, nor ever have, nor will."

Joan looked at her with an expression of shock that changed quickly to anger. "You'll not help me, then?"

"No," said the Widow implacably, "I shall not. And if you've any wisdom in you, you'll go home and pray on your knees that God will forgive your wicked thoughts. Now leave."

With a backward look of hatred, Joan left. The Widow shut the door behind the girl with unnecessary vehemence and latched it, then turned to her wide-eyed daughters. "Neither of you will speak of this to anyone," she commanded. "Not even to each other."

"Yes, Mother," Rosamund said in a subdued voice. Blanche could only nod.

The Widow went back to her shelf of herbs and began taking down various jars with hands that still shook a little. Blanche and Rosamund exchanged glances and returned silently to their mending. After a time, the Widow said, "Is this all of the elecampane we have put by?"

"Yes, Mother," Blanche said. "'Twas all the second-year plants that survived the frost last spring. Is't not enough?"

"'Tis not even enough to make more syrup for little Elanor," the Widow said, sounding much disturbed. "These roots are rotting; they must not have been well dried."

"There are one-year plants still in the garden," Rosamund offered doubtfully.

"An we harvest those now, where shall we get our elecampane next fall?" the Widow said. "And first-year roots are small." She shook her head. "No, I fear you must go to the forest tomorrow and search out a wild clump, if such there be."

Rosamund's face lit up. "The forest?"

"But thou hast warned us against it, Mother," Blanche said, frowning slightly.

"And shall I say to Mistress Rundel that I've naught to give her daughter because I fear to let mine own go walking in the woods?" the Widow snapped, as much to persuade herself as to convince her daughter. "And shall I say the same to all who sicken of a cough this winter, or to those who're short of breath?"

"Nay, Mother, I see the necessity," Blanche said in a tone that clearly indicated her surprise at the strength of her mother's response.

The Widow sighed and said more gently, "I know thou dost, and I know likewise that I have no choice but to send thee and thy sister for't. Yet I like it not. Tomorrow eve's All Hallows'; 'tis like the fay will be at their mischief."

"Oh, we'll be wary, Mother," Rosamund said with buoyant confidence. "We'll not go near the Faerie lands, and we'll be home by dusk."

"With thy assurance I must rest content," the Widow said, but her frown did not lighten as she turned back to her jars of herbs.

◆   ◆   ◆

The Queen of Faerie's elder son was as concerned with leaving Faerie as the Widow Arden was with keeping her daughters from entering it. His face showed little of his disquiet; in the two days since John's return to Faerie, his expression had grown less revealing, making his Faerie heritage more plain. Even so, something in his stance and gestures, something in the very air about him, proclaimed his difference from the other inhabitants of his mother's palace. Only in his brother's presence did he seem well suited to his company, and he remained restless even there.

"Thou hast no need for such disquiet," Hugh said soothingly as he watched John pace the length of the palace library. "She'll speak with thee tomorrow."

John paused and looked at Hugh, who was lounging elegantly against the carved rosewood paneling between two windows. "And that's not cause for care?"

"If thou dost not demand too much of this reunion, no," Hugh answered in a serious tone. "She's Queen, remember, and not our mother only. 'Twill be enough if her manner with thee's not reserved."

"Enough for thee," John said, exasperated. "Thou art not banned from thy diversions for small cause, or none."

Hugh's eyebrows rose toward his hairline in a parody of polite incredulity. "Thou dost not find the court diverting?"

John's answering laugh lacked humor. "Thy antics distract, certainly, but 'tis a temporary thing. And do not tell me again that 'tis my custom to spend winter here, and sometimes longer. 'Tis lack of choice that frets me, not my presence here."

"There's a mercy," Hugh commented. "I think—"

The muted sound of the latches at the library door resonated through the room, interrupting Hugh in mid-sentence. As the two men looked up, the double panels swung open to reveal a wiry youth with an unruly fringe of black hair above dancing black eyes. His doublet was brown and badly rumpled, as if it had been slept in, though his ruff was as stiff and white as if it were made of porcelain.

"What's this?" the youth said with mock sternness. "Laughter, in the Queen's library?" He studied John's face a moment, then nodded in satisfaction. "I thought it could not be. 'Tis the planning of a funeral, by the look on't. Shall I stay and give you guidance?"

This time John's laugh was clear and unconstrained. "Indeed thou shalt, Robin; thy wit's a welcome change from Hugh's sermons."

"Sermons?" Hugh said, affronted. "I but wish to explain to thee what pleasures thou mayest find at court."

"What pleasures, indeed!" Robin said enthusiastically. "Fresh and fair as morning, every one; 'tis what's expected in the Queen's companions."

"'Twas not the Queen's ladies that I was speaking of, thou panderer," Hugh said.

"Oh?" Robin said in the tones of one eager for enlightenment. "Hast thou spent time with others of the court when my attention's elsewhere?"

"Enough, Robin," John said, though he could not help smiling at Hugh's disgruntled expression. "The Queen's ladies are but small temptation to me."

"Ah, but thou hast not yet seen Selena," Robin said wisely. "She's small enough to suit thee, I'll be bound. And there are others, who've appeared since thy last visit, who may alter thy opinions as to height. Tallis, and Marvenna—"

"And Madini," Hugh put in, giving John a sly look. "Though I must tell thee that she's made it plain she finds no pleasure in my company; belike thou wilt have better fortune."

"Nay," Robin said, suddenly serious. "Look not to that lady, or if thou dost, have one hand near thy dagger. 'Tis not alone thy company that she mislikes; 'tis the half thy blood that's mortal. She'll be no fonder of thy brother, for it seems he has the greater liking for the mortal world."

"Have done," John said sharply. "I've told you, I've no interest in these ladies; turn your tongues to other things, if you've no wish to bore me."

Hugh and Robin turned to stare at him with identical looks of patent disbelief, and in spite of himself John laughed. His dislike of the topic, and of the ladies of the Faerie court, was, however, quite sincere. The beauty of the fay was undeniable, but somehow in its precise and icy perfection it had always left some part of him unwarmed. Then, too, the Faerie court was far more conscious of John's mortal heritage than of Hugh's, and there had been slights enough to make John hold himself aloof for the most part. For all that John loved his mother's land, he had few real friends there.

"Dicing," Robin said with fastidious distaste. "He'd have us speak of dicing, or of cards, when we could praise the fairest flowers at court instead."

"A week ago thou wast not too proud to speak of dicing, when thou hadst a case of Spanish wine and Lord Branden's favorite horse on the fifth throw," Hugh pointed out.

"Ah, but then I won," Robin said smugly.

"Thou?" John said incredulously. "Thou, win at dice? It passes comprehension."

"'Tis true," said Robin, "and I've the wine to prove it. Come and sample it, and tell me if 'twas worth the wager."

"A princely offer, I declare, and one I'll not decline," John said. "Willt join us, Hugh?"

"Gladly," Hugh replied, and the three left the library to the dust motes falling through the slanting sunlight.

CHAPTER · FOUR

•

"The girls often went to gather berries in the forest. None of the animals ever harmed them. Rabbits would eat cabbage leaves and clover out of their hands, and the birds sang cheerfully in the branches of the trees above them. Sometimes they even saw deer leaping by them through the bushes."

•

BLANCHE AND ROSAMUND LEFT AT FIRST LIGHT THE following morning. Their mother's misgivings had intensified their own, and even Rosamund was not as carefree as usual. They stayed close together, just as they had promised, and never left each other's sight for even an instant. Nor did they stray far from their accustomed paths.

As the day wore on, the two girls relaxed their vigilance a little. Though they continued to keep close to each other, they began to roam farther afield. For, as Rosamund pointed out, they already knew that there was no elecampane growing near their usual haunts. "We should look nearer the stream," Rosamund said. "Elecampane likes moisture."

"Is't not closer to the border than is wise?" Blanche said doubtfully.

"Wouldst thou rather wander all day and find nothing?" Rosamund answered impatiently.

"It likes me not," Blanche admitted. "But neither do I like the thought of being caught by Faerie folk. Remember what our mother said."

"I remember as well as thou!" Rosamund snapped. "But Faerie folk seldom cross the border at midday; 'tis safer now than later."

"'Tis safer yet if we go not at all," Blanche pointed out. "Seldom is not the same as never."

"An there be Faerie folk about, we'd do best to keep our time here as short as we may. Be not unwisely overcautious, Blanche!"

Blanche rolled her eyes. "I do but try to be a balance for thy rashness, and with small success."

"'Tis not rashness, to try to do our task quickly! Come, Blanche; 'twill not take long to look."

"Aye, and if I say thee nay, thou'lt argue till the sun sets, and belike the moon also!" Blanche shook her head in exasperation. "Well, to the stream, then, but it still likes me not."

The two girls set off in the direction of the stream. To Rosamund's immense and ill-concealed gratification, their change of course was rewarded almost at once. In a shady hollow near the stream they found a large patch of elecampane growing in the rich leaf mold, its tall, unbranching stems rising well above their heads. They fell upon it with delighted relief, scraping and prodding at the soil with dead branches to uncover the roots.

It took some time for the girls to gather all the roots they needed. Some were too old and tough; others were too small; still others had been damaged by grubs or other insects. Blanche sorted carefully through the roots while Rosamund dug. As soon as they had a sizable pile of likely-looking specimens, the two girls took the roots to the river and carefully washed them. They set the roots in a patch of sun to dry and returned to the hollow, where Blanche took her turn at digging while Rosamund sorted.

They were at the stream, washing their third batch of elecampane roots, when Rosamund noticed a small hare crouched among the bushes on the opposite bank. She nudged Blanche and whispered, "Look there, on the other side of the stream."

"'Tis frightened of us, poor thing," Blanche said.

"Nay, not of us, I think, or it would run," Rosamund replied, craning her neck to look over the bushes. "See over there, among the trees. Is it not a fire's glow?"

"Perhaps," Blanche said cautiously. "'Tis not easy to be certain in the day and at this distance."

"Then we must go nearer," Rosamund said with determination. "An it be not to cook some tinker's dinner, we must warn Mother, and the town."

Before Blanche could answer, there was a crackling sound from the far bank. An instant later a large stag leapt over bushes and stream together. It landed gracefully, rolled its eyes at the girls in terror, and bounded off into the woods once more.

"See there!" Rosamund said. "'Tis not the hare alone that's frightened."

"I suppose we must go," Blanche said reluctantly. A forest fire was unlikely at this season, but it was not impossible, and should one occur it could easily become a major disaster for the town. The last of the hay still drying in the fields would burn easily; so would the thatched roofs of the poorer cottages and homes. Once begun, such a blaze could sweep through Mortlak with little hindrance, for few of the buildings were of stone and over half the citizens who should have kept hooks and leather buckets ready for fire-fighting ignored the law that required such preparation.

Rosamund jumped to her feet at once, but Blanche insisted on packing the latest batch of elecampane roots into their baskets before they left. "If thy fears prove well founded, then we must speed home quickly, and I'll not have our labor wasted," Blanche said firmly when Rosamund objected. "There; that's the last. Come now, but have a care."

Crossing the brook was not difficult; it was a mere trickle of water, less than three feet wide and only a few inches deep. The girls found a spot where the opposite bank was almost clear of brush and jumped the stream. Then they headed back toward the area where Rosamund thought she had seen the fire.

They had gone only a little way when Blanche held out a hand to stop her sister. "What now?" Rosamund said crossly.

"I feel an evil in the air," Blanche said in a low voice. "Dost thou not sense it?"

"'Tis only that we draw near the border of Faerie," Rosamund said with some impatience.

"Nay, 'tis more than that," Blanche said. "The crossing into Faerie ne'er made my flesh creep. Be still a moment, and listen."

Rosamund did as Blanche suggested, and for a long moment the two girls stood like deer tasting the air for a scent of strangeness. "'Tis nothing," Rosamund said at last, with rather too much firmness. "Come, we must see about that fire."

"Perhaps we should not; perhaps we should go home and tell Mother," Blanche said, but there was more hope than conviction in her voice.

"Nay, if we do that, we'll never learn what's toward," Rosamund replied. "We'll go on, but with caution."

"Thou art a stubborn mule," Blanche muttered, too low for Rosamund to hear. Sighing, she tucked the linen cloth that covered her basket more tightly into place and followed at her sister's heels.

They reached a fringe of bushes that partially screened the place where Rosamund had seen the fire. Rosamund stopped short. When Blanche started to ask why, Rosamund gestured her to silence. A moment later, Blanche heard the low rumble of men's voices ahead of them. The two girls exchanged a long look; then Blanche sighed again and slipped her free hand into Rosamund's. Clutching each other tightly, they crept closer, looking for a place where they would be able to see the fire clearly.

♦　　　♦　　　♦

The fire had been burning since shortly after daybreak, when John Dee and Edward Kelly had begun their secret spell-casting. The two men had, with much effort (and a fair amount of complaining on Kelly's part), carried their carefully prepared tools into the forest before it was quite light, to avoid being seen by the villagers. It had taken them some time to find a suitable place for their work, and the men's long robes were somewhat the worse for their long trek through the forest. Burrs and twigs had caught on their sleeves, and an oak leaf protruded from the back of John Dee's collar.

Neither man bothered to correct his dishevelment. They set to work at once, first spreading a large square of red silk out on the forest floor, then placing an iron brazier in the center of the silk and lighting a fire within it. Kelly had tended the fire for some hours, while Dee laid out, in careful order along one edge of the silk square, their remaining tools: two wax tablets bearing inscriptions in Hebrew, a tarnished silver bowl partially filled with wine, a slim dagger, a clay dish of herbs, and an unlit lamp. And as they worked, each of the men kept a sharp eye on the shadows at the far side of the brazier, just beyond the edge of the silk cloth—the shadows whose distorted clarity marked the border between the lands of Faerie and the mortal world.

Now the two men stood half-crouched over the brazier, chanting steadily in low voices. Suddenly, John Dee straightened, then bent backward and seized the two wax tablets. Without pausing in his chanting, he handed one of the tablets to his companion. Then he held his own above the brazier and called in a strong voice, "Omnia in terra tradita sunt in manus nostros; all things on earth are given into our hands." In a single, smooth motion, he dropped the tablet into the brazier and leaned back to pick up the bowl of wine.

The flames in the brazier flickered and seemed to die, then suddenly shot upward in a long, ruddy tongue. "Hic est verus ordo orbis terrarum," Kelly said, holding up his own tablet. "This is the proper order of the world."

A second tongue of flame reached up from the brazier as Kelly dropped the square of wax onto the coals. Dee lifted the silver bowl. "Animae aetheriae invocamus vos ipsos," he said.

"Invocamus vos ipsos perferre volutatem nostrum," said Kelly. "We summon ye to work our will." He dipped his fingers in the wine and scattered droplets into the coals below, being careful to let none of the liquid fall outside the brazier's rim. There was a hissing noise as the wine vaporized, and a puff of steam rose from the fire. It did not dissipate, but hovered above the heads of the two men, a barely visible clump of mist. Kelly repeated his action. The mist thickened, and there was a brief, bright gleam from the silver bowl.

Dee handed the bowl to Kelly and picked up the knife. "Sanguinem et vinum donamus vobis," he said. "Blood and wine we give ye." He pulled back one of his sleeves and made a sudden, swift slash with the knife. Blood welled from the cut in his arm and dripped onto the coals. Black smoke rose from the brazier to mingle with the hovering mist.

"Sanguinem et vinum donamus," Kelly repeated, baring his own arm. The knife made another swift movement, and the brazier smoked again.

"Fiat," said Dee, and again Kelly echoed him. Dee turned and picked up the dish of crushed herbs. Lifting it high above the brazier, he cried, "Ferrte et coercete vim ex faeriae in vasem preparatum sibi; bring and bind the power out of Faerie into the vessel that is prepared for it." With a final flourish, he poured the herbs into the fire.

Golden, glowing smoke billowed out of the brazier, briefly hiding the two sorcerers who stood beside it. The air filled with a pungent aroma. The glow touched the small, dark cloud of mist and black smoke that still hung above the brazier, and it began to coalesce. Soon a small, pulsing globe no larger than a man's fist floated above the brazier like a giant will-o'-the-wisp. The air was clear of smoke, and the fire in the brazier had gone out.

Dee looked up. "Ite!" he commanded, and the globe vanished. He sighed heavily, looking suddenly very tired and old, and turned to his companion. "Now we wait."

"How long?" Kelly demanded.

"I know not," Dee replied, staring into the shadows where the border of Faerie lay. "But till the bringer returns, do not leave this protected ground." He waved at the square of red silk on which they stood. Kelly nodded absently, and the two men lapsed into silence.

◆　　　◆　　　◆

Beneath the bushes at the edge of the clearing, Blanche nudged Rosamund and pointed urgently back the way they had come. Rosamund shook her head, her mouth set in a determined line. Blanche gestured again, and again Rosamund mutely refused. Unable to argue lest the sorcerers overhear their whispering, Blanche breathed a sigh, and thought dark thoughts, and stayed where she was.

◆　　　◆　　　◆

The glowing spell-globe flickered through the lands of Faerie. It was neither alive nor intelligent, though Dee would have argued otherwise; the "spirits of air" on whom he had called were far too canny to be so easily entrapped. The spell-globe was simply that: a spell, formed of power and skill and deep desire, shaped and directed by the wishes of the men who had made it. Compared with the might of even the least of the Faerie folk, the globe was a feeble thing, for the skills of the two sorcerers were not as great as they believed. So, for a relatively long time as such things go, the spell-globe found no creature vulnerable to its imperatives, no being whose essence it could steal.

At last the globe reached a glen, deep within the forest of Faerie. There it paused, balanced between the charms that guarded the glen and the potential within that drew it onward. It waited, hidden among the lush foliage of the trees, while a little way beyond the Queen of Faerie conversed with her two sons.

The Queen of Faerie sat on a satin-covered chair in the middle of the glen. Her face betrayed as little as a perfectly sculpted alabaster mask. Her black hair was bound with a diamond-studded net that sparkled and flashed in the late afternoon sunlight. Her black eyes were calm and cold, and her graceful, long-fingered hands lay quiet against a silk gown of the same rich green as the moss beneath her feet. Her ladies stood behind her, near the edge of the clearing where they could see but not overhear. They, too, were all but expressionless, though a close observer might have seen curiosity in a few of the women's eyes. Madini, watching from the farthest edge, showed no emotion at all as the two men she hated most were greeted by her Queen.

"Thou'rt well, John?" the Queen asked.

"As well as may be, Mother," John replied warily. At his side, Hugh shifted very slightly.

"I'm glad of thy return, and in safety," the Queen said, and there was a hint of warning in her tone.

"I was in no danger," John said. "Yet I, too, am glad to be home."

The Queen's shoulders relaxed minutely. A whisper of a breeze passed through the glen, barely enough to make the leaves quiver, and with it came the scent of apple blossoms. "Thou'lt attend our revels this night?" said the Queen.

"I shall indeed. I'd never willingly miss them," John said, smiling. "But shall I still know any of thy court?"

"The greater part, certainly," the Queen said, returning his smile with a cold one of her own. "Yet thou'lt find new faces enow."

"So Hugh hath told me," John said with a quick glance in his brother's direction.

"I've spoken only of the fairest faces," Hugh put in. "Tallis and Selena and—"

"Nay, an you twain wish to turn your tongues to such matters, either you or I must needs depart," the Queen said with some affection.

"We'll leave thee, Mother, if thou'lt permit it," Hugh said quickly.

The Queen nodded and the brothers withdrew. "I think that went off very well," Hugh said softly as the two crossed the springy moss toward the edge of the clearing.

"Perhaps," John said. "Yet I am not easy. She said nothing of those restrictions of which thou hast warned me."

"They are the province of the Queen," Hugh said. "How should she talk of them, when she meets thee as a mother?"

John stepped over the invisible boundary that barred the spell-globe from entering the glen. The spell-globe quivered, barely disturbing the leaves that concealed it, then subsided into waiting once more. "These fine distinctions like me not," John replied. "I fear I was never meant for—Hugh!"

While John had been speaking, Hugh had reached and crossed the boundary at the edge of the glen. The spell-globe quivered once more, then fell like a stone straight down onto Hugh's head. A glowing black cloud enveloped Hugh, pulsed once, and vanished even as John cried his brother's name, leaving only a stink of burning in the air and Hugh's unconscious body sprawled upon the ground.

◆   ◆   ◆

The spell-globe, its primary purpose completed, returned with uncanny swiftness to its makers. Dee and Kelly sensed its coming as it crossed out of Faerie, and their heads came up together like the heads of hunting dogs who scent a stag. The globe, now double its original size and shifting crazily from glowing gold to a dark and smoky blackness, hurtled toward the two men. At the last instant, just before it would have passed over the edge of the red silk square on which Dee and Kelly still stood, the globe veered sharply to the right and plunged down onto the lamp that lay on the bare ground just behind Dee.

The lamp flickered and began to glow with a steady, flameless light. The two sorcerers stared at it for a moment in silence, then Dee's lips turned up in a slow smile. "We've done it, Ned!" he said. "You had the right of it, to make our attempt in daylight."

"'Tis not accomplished yet," Kelly said warningly, but he, too, was smiling. "The power must be drawn into some object more suited to our purposes, and fixed there. That lamp will crumble into dust, an it hold such energy a month."

"True, but the harder task is finished," Dee replied. "We've time and plenty for the rest, God willing."

"So be it," Kelly answered.

The two men picked up the brazier, which was now quite cold, and carefully dumped the dead embers on the ground at one side of the silk square. Only then did they step off the silk. Dee picked up the square cloth and shook it carefully, frowning at the damp stains and streaks it had acquired. "Jane will be angered when she sees this," he said.

"Keep it from her," Kelly advised, laughing. "A month from now, you may have a disembodied servant make it clean as new."

"For shame, Ned!" Dee said. "This power has better uses than to do the washing."

Kelly shrugged, but made no argument. The two men packed up the remains of their spell-casting, then wrapped the glowing lamp in the red silk cloth and set off toward Mortlak.

♦   ♦   ♦

Some time later, two wide-eyed girls emerged from beneath the drooping branches of a holly bush, still clutching each other's hands, and stared around the clearing as if to be quite certain that the sorcerers had gone.

"What have these men done?" Rosamund asked in a shaky voice.

"I know not, yet I think 'tis nothing good," Blanche replied. "Didst thou know them?"

"I've seen their faces in Mortlak now and again," Rosamund said. "But I never learned their names."

"Nor I. Belike Mother will know; let's go home quickly and tell her."

This suggestion found favor with Rosamund, who had no more desire to remain so near the Faerie border than did her sister. Clutching their baskets of elecampane root and casting occasional nervous glances backward, the two girls started for home.

◆　　　◆　　　◆

On the other side of the Faerie border, as the afternoon faded into twilight, the oakman Bochad-Bec met the water creature Furgen in their accustomed place beneath the oak. "Madini's late again," Bochad-Bec grumbled by way of greeting.

"She's in a temper," Furgen said.

"So is she always," Bochad-Bec said in a sour tone.

Furgen's pointed teeth gleamed briefly. "Hsst! She comes."

"Why wait you here?" Madini demanded as she stepped out of the shadows. A sharp breeze accompanied her arrival, as if to give a physical sign of her rage. "Know you not that our plans are blown awry?"

"We agreed to meet here," Bochad-Bec said. "And thou art late."

"Bait me not, goblin!" Madini said in a cold, dangerous voice. "'Tis not thy place to find fault with my ways."

"'Twas thou who set the time of our meeting," Bochad-Bec pointed out, unrepentant. "And 'tis the sun, not I, that proclaims thy tardiness."

"Perhaps thou wouldst give us all the news," Furgen put in. "As yet, we've heard but a portion."

"News! I'll give thee news," Madini said, her eyes kindling with renewed rage. "The wretched mortals have ruined all. Did I not bid you watch them close? Now see what's come of your neglect!"

"Thus far I see little," Furgen replied calmly. "Say on."

"The dull-witted mortals, for what reason I know not, have done their spell-work in the light of day, ere we were ready for them," Madini said. "An you had done my bidding, we might have been prepared. Now the spell has ensnared Hugh; Hugh, not John!"

"They are both too mortal for my liking," Bochad-Bec said. "One or th'other, it's naught to me. Though I've said before that Hugh's the greater danger."

"Hugh can be dealt with at our leisure," Madini said, her voice full of scorn. "Were it not for the Queen's edict, John would be gone again ere now."

"What matter, if he's not in Faerie?" Bochad-Bec said stubbornly.

"Hast thou heard naught of what I've told thee for these many weeks?" Madini said. "His frequent passage back and forth doth stitch our realm more closely to the mortal lands with his every crossing of the border. Until he's stripped of all things Faerie, or he's dead or exiled by the Queen, his absence from the land but draws it further in. 'Tis why I urged the Queen to keep him here, though his mortal blood is an affront I well could do without."

"Hugh is mortal, too, and—"

"Hugh stays in Faerie! His blood, too, binds us, but at least he pulls the land no nearer to destruction. And make no mistake, 'tis destruction Faerie faces if we slide unresisting to some union with the mortal world."

"There's some who'd quarrel with that claim," Furgen commented.

Madini rounded on him. "An thou'rt one, how is it thou art here? Or art thou of a different mind than formerly?"

"I've no great liking for mortals," the water creature answered, unperturbed. "But this quarrel serves no purpose I can see. To return to matter of more moment: can we not turn Hugh's mishap to our benefit?"

"How?" Madini snapped, but her tone was less hostile than it had been a moment earlier.

"Thus: canst thou not whisper i'the Queen's ear that it's John's travels in the mortal lands which have brought down this trouble on his brother's head? For the Queen hath long favored Hugh, and 'twill not please her to think the elder son's the cause of the younger's misfortune."

Madini's eyes narrowed; suddenly she laughed humorlessly. "'Twill serve, for now. But look you, John's disgrace sufficeth not to satisfy me. I'll have him in my power, he and his brother, to do with as I will. They'll learn what follows when they presume to ape the ways of Faerie."

"So thou hast said," Furgen murmured. "But I trust thou'lt not forget our larger aims. Faerie's of greater import than mere punishing of Hugh and John's presumption."

"'Tis the same thing, thou web-footed fool! The mortal blood of the Queen's sons is the last and greatest fetter that binds Faerie to the mortal lands. An they be dealt with, we can loose ourselves forever from the short-lived half-wits and their world."

"So thou sayest," Furgen said, even more gently than before. "I'd rest easier if I were more certain of it."

"Believe it," Madini commanded. "And in the future, keep a better watch upon these humans, that we may know more plainly what they've done. I'll haste to the Queen, to put thy advice to work."

Furgen nodded. He exchanged glances with Bochad-Bec as Madini swept into the forest; then the two lesser fay followed her into the shadows.

CHAPTER · FIVE

·

"Sometimes the girls stayed too long in the forest, and night overtook them there. Then they would lie down side by side upon the moss and sleep until morning. Their mother knew this, and knew, too, that no one would harm them."

·

THE WIDOW WAS GLAD OF THE ELECAMPANE Blanche and Rosamund brought home, but much disturbed by the tale that came with it. Interference with Faerie would, she was sure, bring no good to anyone in or around Mortlak. Furthermore, she suspected the identities of the two sorcerers her daughters had watched in the forest, and she had no more wish to run afoul of the Queen's Astrologer than she had to trifle with the powers of Faerie. The Widow extracted from the girls a pledge not to try to do anything about the spell they had witnessed until they all had a better understanding of what could and should be done.

There the matter rested. The Widow and her daughters heard no rumors of Faerie hosts riding out of the woods to avenge whatever slight had been done them, nor was there more talk of Master Dee in the town than was usual. Still, the Widow kept her daughters close to home for several weeks, for she had learned caution in a hard school.

As November drew on and no portents came out of Faerie, the Widow sent Rosamund and Blanche into the forest once again. Though she remained reluctant to do so, she had little choice if she wanted a stock of Faerie herbs. Winter was drawing on, and with it the closing of the Faerie borders to humankind. Even among the Faerie folk there were few who could cross the border during winter; for mortals it was impossible.

So Blanche and Rosamund pinned hawthorn twigs to their bodices and set out. In addition to their gathering baskets, their cutting knives, and their balls of cord, each of them carried a flask of water and half a loaf of pease-bread, for they knew how dangerous it was to consume Faerie food or drink. They had no intention of joining the ranks of the travelers trapped in Faerie forever through forgetting such a simple rule.

They found the border and crossed it without incident. Rosamund smiled as the grey-brown of the November forest flickered into life and color. Emerald leaves shone sharp and distinct against a cerulean sky; the mottled trunks of beech trees stood clearly defined against the dark oaks that brooded beyond. Bees hummed about a fragrant hedge of lavender that filled a patch of crystalline sunlight, and in the dense shadows beneath the trees the ground was covered with a thick, springy moss the color of malachite.

The girls set to work at once, ranging up and down the boundary in search of the strange plants that grew only in the lands of magic: blue spearmint, crimson-leaved valerian, fairy bedstraw. They also harvested, though more sparingly, the common herbs which had crept over the boundary, for these gained greater virtue from the unusual setting in which they grew. Rosamund was so glad to be in Faerie once again that she roamed farther than was normal, and several times Blanche had to call her back.

The piles of fresh-cut plants grew large and awkward as the day went on, but Rosamund kept finding reasons to delay their departure. Only when the shadows began to darken with the coming evening was Blanche able to convince her reluctant sister that it was indeed time to go. Regretfully, the two girls packed their baskets with the tenderer items, made bundles of the rest, and started for the border.

They could not find it. At first they thought nothing of this; the edge of Faerie was often elusive, and they had never before had to search for it for long. But as the twilight deepened into darkness and still they saw no sign of the way home, they began to grow fearful.

"Dost thou think we've misjudged the time?" Rosamund said at last, voicing the dread that hovered at the back of both their minds. "That perhaps we've come too late in the year, and now must stay till spring?"

"I thought of that," Blanche said in a voice that shook slightly. "But, look you, two years ago we gathered here early in December, and naught befell us. 'Tis now but mid-November; I doubt the border would close so early or so fast."

"Then why can we not find it?" Rosamund said. Now she sounded more cross than afraid.

"I know not," Blanche admitted. "It may be some Faerie trick we've never seen before."

"Well, there's nothing for it but to look further," Rosamund said, hefting her bundles.

"Not now," Blanche objected. She gestured at the indigo gloom around them. "'Tis near too dark to see; if we go on, we'll lose one another in this murk, or wander deeper into Faerie. We must stay here until the morning."

"Until morning! But what of Mother?"

Blanche sighed. "She'll fret, but there's no help for that. Unless thou canst produce a torch, or a path out of these woods," she added with more sharpness than usual. Blanche was tired, frightened, and all too conscious of the responsibility that rested on her as the elder of the two.

An owl hooted twice, and was answered by the slow creaking of a tree branch. "Thou hast the right of it," Rosamund said grudgingly, "though it likes me not."

"Thinkest thou that I'm more fond of this than thee?" Blanche snapped. "Needs must, and there's an end on't."

"Vent thy anger elsewhere," Rosamund said in a tone as cross as her sister's. "This is not my doing!"

Blanche opened her mouth to respond in kind, then closed it firmly. After a moment she said with credible calm, "I know, and I'm sorry for my temper. 'Tis my fears that speak, and not myself."

"Belike tomorrow we'll have better fortune," Rosamund said, trying hard to sound reassuring. "But how shall we sleep safe?"

Blanche frowned into the darkness. "If we say our prayers, no evil in Faerie will harm us," she said with more confidence than she felt. "Also, we've found valerian, and vervain, and herb-of-grace; we'll lay them all around us to ward off Faerie folk. Mother will not grudge us some for such a purpose."

"More likely she'd urge us to use them all," Rosamund said with a small smile, for she was often impatient with her mother's caution. "But 'tis well thought of."

Blanche blinked at her younger sister, then set her basket carefully on the ground and curtsied. "I do thank thee for thy approval, O wise one," she said demurely.

A handful of twigs and leaves showered over Blanche's head. "Goose!" Rosamund said, fixing her sister with a mock scowl. "There's thy approval, if thou'lt make fun of me."

"Not soon again, thou mayest be certain," Blanche responded, brushing bits of plants from her shoulders. "Come, let's lay the circle."

The two girls put their bundled herbs on the mossy forest floor and removed the plants they needed. These they set on the ground around them, placing them carefully to form an unbroken circle. A warm breeze made soft rustling noises in the leaves above them and stirred the strong herb smells into a single, pungent scent. Then they knelt beside their baskets and said their prayers aloud, before laying themselves side by side on the moss to sleep.

♦   ♦   ♦

In the days that followed Hugh's collapse, John remained close to his brother's bedside. At first, Hugh lay motionless, his face a lifeless, waxen mask that by its lack of expression betrayed just how many of his thoughts and feelings had formerly shown through his Faerie manner. Gradually, a flush rose beneath his skin. His long fingers plucked fretfully at the quilted satin coverlet, and soon he was tossing feverishly on his sickbed.

For a week, Hugh lay in an airy, light-filled room, alternating between deep unconsciousness and fits of restlessness. He would take water from his brother's hands, and sometimes a little barley gruel, but even on the rare occasions when his eyes were open there was neither reason nor recognition in their depths. The vast array of Faerie powers that were brought to his aid were helpless; the most that they could do was to still, for an hour or two, the querulous motion of his hands.

"Can you do nothing?" John demanded of the chief physician for the twentieth time.

"Without exact knowledge of the spell that troubles Prince Hugh, my skill avails but little," the healer replied with regret.

"There's the spell; observe it!" John said angrily, waving at his brother. Hugh lay like a marble statue on the bed, the coverlet barely moving with the rise and fall of his chest.

"This have I done, so far as I am able," the healer said carefully. "That is to say, the effects of this enchantment are plain, as you have said. But what of the purpose of this charm? What of the mechanics of the spell? Can you tell me if it was accomplished by words, or by ritual, or by the virtue in specific plants, or with the aid of some object of power? Whether 'twas intended to entrap the Prince your brother, or whether he has accidentally fallen foul of some dire spell intended to work otherwise? Knowing these things, I might begin to fashion a remedy; without such knowledge, I can but guess and hope."

"Then at least tell me what to expect," John said. "What is this enchantment doing to Hugh? How shall this end?"

"It ends in misery and mourning," said a cool voice from behind the two men. They turned as one, and the healer made a deep obeisance. The Queen of Faerie stood in the doorway with her ladies-in-waiting about her. Each of the women wore something that was the white of Faerie mourning—a sash, an armband, the lining of her sleeves. The Queen herself was all in white, from the small hood she wore to her pearl-covered slippers. Her sleeves were edged with ermine, and a ruff of stiff white lace stood out around her neck. White did not become her.

"What meanest thou, Mother?" John said.

"There's naught that can be done for Hugh," the Queen said. Her pale face was bleak as she stared down at the bed where her youngest son lay. "His very essence hath been riven from him; soon he will lose even the outward semblance of a man."

John stood frozen, his eyes fixed on the stiff white brocade of the Queen's wide skirts. "No."

"Yes," said the Queen implacably. "Thou hast but to look at him to see the truth; the change is even now begun."

Slowly, unwillingly, John's head turned to look at his unconscious brother. The clear, pitiless light of Faerie poured through the long windows overhead, relentlessly marking every alteration in Hugh's face. His nose seemed longer, and beneath the shadow of his unshaven beard his jaw was narrower. His lips were thinner, and his forehead sloped slightly backward. His neck had thickened; so had his shoulders and arms. The long fingers were thicker, too, and shorter. Even his fingernails had changed; they were dark and bruised-looking, and hard as horn. There was no longer anything remotely elegant about the figure on the bed, though no one could have claimed with any success that it was not Hugh.

"No!" John said again, just above a whisper. "Not Hugh."

"Yes. And when he is become a beast, he must be cast from Faerie. That is the law, and not even I can change it," the Queen said coldly. "Therefore I and all my court have put on mourning for my son."

"'Tis not too late to stop this spell," John insisted. "It cannot be!" He glanced at the physician for support.

"If we knew more, 'twere not too late," the physician replied reluctantly. "But where to learn what we must know, I cannot say. This spell comes out of mortal lands, I think, and mortal ways are passing strange."

John turned back to the Queen, his expression intent. "Then let me go into the mortal lands and seek a remedy—"

"You!" The cold immobility of the Queen's face made the bitter anger in her voice cut deep. "This abomination is your doing, yet you think only of how swiftly you may evade my edicts and return to your beloved mortals! You care naught for your brother, nor for me, nor for the realm of Faerie."

For a long moment John was stunned into speechlessness. Finally he managed to stammer out, "My doing? I'd never harm Hugh; thou canst not think it!"

The Queen's expression did not change. "You did not cast the spell yourself, but the responsibility is yours nonetheless. Your foolish wandering among the mortals has drawn their attention here. Had you not left our realm, Hugh would not now lie unknowing as he does."

"Thou dost blame me without cause," John said. "Let me prove it. If there's help for Hugh in mortal lands, I'll find it."

"Seek not to repeat your thoughtless folly!" the Queen answered. "You've done enough already; now you shall stay in Faerie. But keep from my sight."

The Queen turned and swept away. John, staring after her, glimpsed a quick, satisfied smile on the face of one of the Queen's ladies, but he was still too dazed to wonder much about it.

In deference to his mother's command, John, too, put on white mourning, though he refused to give up the hope that his brother could be helped. He began spending less time with Hugh; instead, he talked for hours with the physicians, then went to the adepts and the great magicians of the court. He pored over scrolls and tomes from deep in the archives of Faerie. And he became more and more convinced that the solution to Hugh's difficulty lay outside Faerie, in the mortal world from which the spell had come.

When John sought the Queen, to try once again to persuade her to let him leave Faerie in search of a remedy for Hugh, he discovered that he was barred from her presence. The courtiers and officials were polite; he was, after all, the Queen's son. Unfortunately, they were also firm. The Queen would not see him, nor would she lift the spell that hid the border of Faerie from him. John must remain in Faerie.

Enraged, John stormed away from the court and back to his brother's bedside. What he found there was hard to endure. Hugh lay naked beneath the coverlet, for his attendants could no longer fit the linen nightshirts over his enlarged arms and shoulders, and a dark stubble of sprouting fur covered his skin wherever it was visible. His restless tossing was no longer silent; now he made small animallike growling noises, and as he growled his lips curled away from fat, yellow teeth. His nails were black and thick at the ends of stubby, awkward fingers, and the skin on his palms was like black leather. The worst of it was that, despite the mouth and nose that stretched into a narrow snout, despite the sprouting fur and heavy nails, despite all the changes that proclaimed so clearly that this was no longer quite a man, it was still recognizably Hugh who snarled and scratched at the edges of the bed.

John stayed beside Hugh's bed all night, his expression bleak. At dawn, he slipped quietly away, and returned to his own room on the far side of the palace. He spent an hour in various preparations, then lay down to sleep. At noon he arose and dressed in his finest white doublet and hose. He swung a cloak of white velvet across his shoulder and fastened it with a silver chain. Then he picked up a small sack he had left lying beside his bed and went out of the room. He made his way swiftly through silent halls of alabaster and rose-marble, malachite and jasper. No one saw him leave the palace and disappear into the Faerie forest.

♦   ♦   ♦

John quickly discovered that grim determination was not enough to defeat a spell set by the Faerie Queen. For two days he marched doggedly up and down and across and through all the places where he knew the passage out of Faerie ought to be, without finding a single trace of it. On the third day, Rosamund and Blanche arrived in Faerie in search of herbs.

John was not immediately aware of their presence, but early in the night, just after Rosamund and Blanche had lain down to sleep, he stumbled across their resting place. He recognized Rosamund at once. He was at first amused by her presence, but when he saw the ring of herbs surrounding the two girls he frowned. The spell affecting Hugh had come from mortal lands, and it was plain that these two mortals knew far more of Faerie than was comfortable.

For a moment, John was furiously angry. Then he looked more closely at the sleeping girls huddled together for warmth and at their makeshift protection. He frowned once more. Surely two such knowledgeable people would have come better prepared, had they intended to spend a night in Faerie. And if they had not intended to stay . . .

Eyeing the girls thoughtfully, John pulled a wand of peeled willow from the sack he carried. He concentrated briefly, then wrote in the air with the tip of the wand. Glowing letters formed where the wand passed, fading slowly into darkness. John read the odd, curving script and nodded. The girls had been kept from leaving, and by some spell of Faerie. He thought for a moment, then concentrated once again. A second time the wand wrote a golden message on the darkened air. This time John frowned. The spell that kept these two in Faerie was tied to him, not them. For the Queen of Faerie's spell was stronger than she had intended, and it hid the border from all mortal and half-mortal eyes so long as John was seeking it. Since it was John's attempt to leave that had trapped the girls, he felt in some sense responsible for their safety while they remained in Faerie.

His frown changed to a look of intense thought. Suddenly he smiled. A third time he stared in concentration at the wand, then wrote letters made of light. He stared at them until they faded; then, still smiling, he sat down at the foot of a nearby tree to watch over these unexpected visitors until morning.

CHAPTER · SIX

•

"One morning they awoke after spending a night in the wood and found a child in a shining dress of white sitting on the ground near where they had been sleeping. The child rose and smiled kindly at them, then went off into the forest without speaking. When the girls looked around, they discovered that they had been sleeping near a steep cliff; if they had gone any farther in the dark the night before, they would surely have fallen over it."

•

WHEN SUNSET NEARED AND BLANCHE AND ROSA-mund had not returned from their herb-gathering, the Widow began to worry. She set rushlights in each window, to guide her daughters in the growing dark, and peered anxiously out at the forest every few minutes as if watching would call them home. But the last shreds of light vanished without bringing the smallest sign of either of the girls.

The Widow made one last trip to the door and peered out at the dim, ominous wood just beyond her garden wall. She stood for a long time in the chill wind, watching and listening. When she could no longer make out the shapes of individual trees, she bit her lip and carefully closed the door.

Inside, she turned and leaned her back against the door, her face grey with worry. Her eyes roamed restlessly about the room and came to rest at last on the shelves of herbs and crockery above the trestle table. She pressed her lips together firmly and looked away, but her eyes kept returning to the shelf. Finally she sighed and stepped away from the door.

With a decisiveness she had not shown a moment earlier, the Widow moved rapidly around the room. She collected the rushlights and put out all but one; then she partially filled her kettle and hung it on the iron hook above the fire. Finally she pulled the blanket from the bed and draped it over the windows, so that no gleam of light could escape, and no one could see in. This done, she went purposefully to her shelf of herbs.

First she took down a small, flat dish made of tin and set it carefully in the middle of the trestle table. Then she sorted rapidly through the herbs. A small heap of dried and crumbling leaves grew in the center of the tin dish: angelica and juniper for protection from harm; rosemary for life and constancy; eyebright, rue, and yarrow for vision. Then the Widow took up the dish and began carefully reducing the herbs to powder with her fingers, mixing and spreading them in a thin layer across the bottom of the dish. A sharp, penetrating scent rose from the herbs and clung to the Widow's fingers.

The kettle began to boil. The Widow set the tin dish gently on the table. Wrapping one hand in an old rag, she swung the iron hook out and lifted the kettle. She carried it to the table and paused briefly. Then, in a low, clear voice, she said, "Look in thy glass, and tell the face thou viewest, now is the time that face should form another. *Fiat!*" and began to pour.

Boiling water hissed across the powdered herbs, and a heavy, aromatic cloud of steam rose from the dish. The Widow closed her eyes and breathed deeply; then she set the kettle on the end of the table, opened her eyes, and bent over the bowl.

At first the water was a froth of tiny, foaming bubbles that formed around the powdered herbs and swirled in meaningless patterns. Then a ghostly shape coalesced in the steam above the bubbles: a horrible figure, half man and half bear. As the Widow stared grimly at this apparition, it changed to a handsome, dark-haired young man with anguished eyes. Then, slowly, the figure melted and shifted until it became a black bear roaring defiance. But the eyes of the bear were the same as the man's.

The bear vanished suddenly, and the surface of the water cleared. The Widow saw Blanche and Rosamund sleeping, side by side, on the mossy floor of the Faerie forest. At the foot of a nearby tree sat a man dressed in elegant white clothes, gazing at the girls with a thoughtful expression. The Widow stiffened; then she saw the ring of protective herbs encircling her daughters, and she sighed in relief. The breath of air was faint, but enough to disturb the surface of the water. The vision disappeared.

The rushlight had burned nearly down to its holder. The Widow stared at it unseeing for a moment, then shook herself and reached for a replacement. She picked up the kettle and took it outside to empty. When she returned, she lifted the blanket down from the windows and replaced it on the bed. For some minutes she kept herself busy with these commonplace tasks, avoiding another look at the tin dish on the table. Finally she came back and bent once more over the half-full dish of water and herbs.

Her eyes widened in surprise. The swirling water had calmed and the herbs had settled to the bottom, forming a dark pattern against the carefully burnished brightness of the tin. The shape was one the Widow recognized, but not one she had expected; it was the glyph for protection coming out of Faerie.

The Widow stared for a long time, as if she wished to burn the pattern into the backs of her own eyes. At last she picked up the bowl and carried it to the door. She poured off most of the water onto the ground around the rose trees; the herbs she brought back inside and threw sizzling into the fire. Then, assured of her daughters' safety, at least, she sat down beside the hearth to puzzle over the other things she had been shown.

✦   ✦   ✦

The Widow's spell of scrying, carefully guarded though it had been, did not go unnoticed. John, sitting watchfully beside the sleeping girls, felt a shiver run down his arms and knew he was being observed. His head came up, and as the Widow's spell began to fade he spoke a word of warding, then one of knowledge. He learned enough to know that the spell came from outside Faerie.

That knowledge reawakened all his misgivings about the two sleeping girls. Innocent they might be, in themselves—he could not bring himself to believe harm of the dark-haired girl who had blushed rose-red at his teasing, yet had still been able to look him in the eye and answer back—but evil men had made use of innocence before. After the accusations his mother had hurled at his head, John knew he could not afford to take the risk that the girls might mean ill to Faerie, however small he himself might think it.

And so, just as the sun came up, he opened the sack he had brought with him and took out a ring set with three diamonds. One of the diamonds was cracked across its face; the other two winked and shimmered at him as they caught the first rays of the morning sun. John hesitated. The ring conferred invisibility on its wearer, but it could only be used three times. He had already used it once, years before, and if he put it on now, he would have only one use remaining. He was not sure he wanted to waste the ring out of what might, after all, be phantom worries created by his own fears.

His hesitation lasted too long. Blanche stirred, shifted, and opened her eyes. She was staring straight at John, and her eyes widened as she came fully awake and realized what she was seeing. She clutched at her sister, and Rosamund, too, awoke and saw him.

For a long moment, all three remained motionless. Then John smiled with as much pleasant reassurance as he could express, and slipped the ring onto his finger.

Rosamund and Blanche jumped as the white-clad figure vanished. They clung to each other, staring at the apparently empty space where John had disappeared. Finally Rosamund made an heroic attempt to chuckle. "That's an uncommon way for a day to begin," she said. "Perhaps we're in Faerie."

"Doubt it not," Blanche replied, trying hard to sound calm. "Thinkest thou he's truly gone?"

"Why should he stay?" Rosamund said practically. "If he could cross our warding ring, and so wished, he'd have done so earlier. Faerie power waxes in the night and wanes with day, or so Mother says."

Blanche shivered. "Then let's—Rosamund, look!"

Rosamund turned. A few yards farther on, the spongy moss on which they lay gave way to a fringe of low-growing plants and brush. Beyond, she could see the silver ribbon of a stream reflecting the slanting sunlight, and purple mountains far away that rose more sharply and majestically than any range in all of England. Rosamund stared in awe, and only slowly became aware that the stream was below her, like the Thames seen from the top of a distant hill.

"What—" Rosamund started, then stopped and glanced quickly at her sister. Blanche's face was white. Rosamund scrambled to her feet, paused, then stepped over the herbs she and Blanche had scattered and walked forward.

Blanche made a strangled sound and came after. Rosamund stopped where the brush began, staring downward. "It's but a hill."

"But 'tis very steep," Blanche pointed out, and her voice shook despite her efforts to keep it steady. She cleared her throat and tried again. "I think 'tis as well we went no farther last night."

"I do agree," Rosamund murmured.

In a subdued and wary frame of mind, the two girls returned to their bundles and prepared to resume their search for the way home. The herbs with which they had made the protective circle around their sleeping place were withered and useless, and Rosamund scraped them together and piled them under a bush so that they would not attract unwanted attention. The rest of the harvest was wilted, but this was no great cause for concern since most of it was to be dried in any case.

John watched with impatience, secure in his invisibility. At last the girls set off. John stayed close behind them, his mind carefully emptied of any interest in leaving Faerie and any thought of searching for its borders. He concentrated only on his need to follow his unknowing guides.

At Blanche's suggestion, the girls retraced as much of their path of the previous evening as they could recall. It was clear to both of them that the border they sought was nowhere near the unfamiliar cliff where they had spent the night, and they both kept a sharp watch for anything better known to them. Rosamund was the first to cry out in relief and point to a patch of valerian, half of which had been cut back almost to the ground. A moment later Blanche recognized a rowan tree where they had stopped to rest and eat.

Much excited, the two girls hurried on. Soon they reached the place where they had expected to find the edge of Faerie the previous day, and to their surprise and great relief it was there. Blanche and Rosamund smiled at each other and stepped across.

Rosamund stumbled and half turned. "What is it?" Blanche asked anxiously.

"My skirt was caught on something, but it makes no matter; 'tis free now," Rosamund said. "Come quickly. Mother will be greatly troubled."

Blanche nodded, and the two girls headed toward the edge of the forest at a speed just barely less than running.

◆　　　◆　　　◆

Behind the girls, just outside the lands of Faerie, John lay panting, triumphant, and invisible on the leaf mold of the mortal woodlands. His guesses about the Queen's spell had all been right.

He could not find the border for himself, but once he stopped searching he could be shown. Even so, he had almost failed; his grip on Rosamund's skirt had been what finally pulled him out of Faerie, and the effort had exhausted him.

After a time, John regained his breath. He sat up, fingering the ring of invisibility, then rose without removing it. It would look odd indeed for a man clad in finery to walk out of the forest. He had better make his way to London first, where his raiment would attract many thieves but little comment. He sighed, knowing that the walk would take him much of the day. London was a good ten miles from Mortlak, and John was impatient to begin his search for his brother's tormentor. With a smothered groan, he pushed himself to his feet and started off.

◆   ◆   ◆

The Widow greeted her daughters with joy, and insisted that they have something to eat before they told their story. Rosamund and Blanche were nothing loath, though the meal was interrupted several times by the lamb, demanding food and attention. When the dishes were cleared away, the Widow finally allowed the girls to speak. She listened carefully, betraying none of the knowledge she had gained through her arcane labors of the previous night.

"And so we're safely home at last," Blanche concluded. She hesitated, then went on doubtfully, "Yet that . . . creature whom we saw so briefly on arising frets me still."

"How should he fret thee?" Rosamund demanded. "He's in Faerie; thou'rt here."

"Rosamund hath the right of it, I think," the Widow said firmly. " 'Tis not surprising that Faerie folk should be curious at finding mortals in their midst, and thou hast said this creature offered thee no hurt."

"And yet he frightened me a little," Blanche said.

"He seemed familiar to me," Rosamund said. "And he was sad, and his smile was very kind."

"Familiar?" the Widow said sharply. "How should he be familiar?"

"I know not," Rosamund said. "Only that he seemed so to me. I saw him but briefly; perhaps he resembled one of our neighbors. I cannot say for certain."

"This is a strange coil," the Widow murmured. She sat thinking for a moment, then looked up. "An you see this being again, in Faerie or out, do you both offer him some kindness. Methinks he hath watched over your slumbers, and belike kept harm from you."

Blanche and Rosamund stared at their mother in astonishment, but the Widow would say nothing more. They were left to wonder, and to whisper to each other over their chores, while their mother began serenely sorting out the herbs they had brought home.

◆   ◆   ◆

John's absence from Faerie was not noticed for some time. Those who missed him thought at first that he was keeping to himself out of prudence; the Queen was not crossed with impunity. It was not until several days after his departure that a message was delivered to Madini in the flower garden where she sat with the Queen's other ladies.

The message was brief: "The Queen's eldest son hath broke the ban." Madini's lips curved in a cold smile. She glanced at the message again, and spoke a single word. The writing glittered, then vanished from the page. Madini crumpled the now blank sheet of paper and dropped it in a drift of pinks, then went swiftly to find the Chamberlain and request a private audience with the Queen. A short time later, the Chamberlain escorted Madini into the crystal-walled room where the white-robed Queen of Faerie sat.

"Madam," Madini said, sinking into a graceful curtsy as the Chamberlain departed.

"Madini, my dear," the Queen said. "Come nearer; sit and tell me what bringeth thee so urgently."

"Ill news, I fear, Your Majesty," Madini said. She rose from her curtsy and came forward as the Queen had bidden her.

"Then speak it straight, without circumspection," the Queen said, frowning slightly.

"As Your Majesty wills," Madini said. "Your eldest son hath set aside your wise commands and chosen his own counsels in their spite."

"Doth this roundaboution of thine mean that John hath left the realm of Faerie?" the Queen demanded. Her fingers lay pale and motionless on the silk-smooth arms of the birchwood throne on which she sat.

"Even so."

The Queen's calm expression did not alter. "Who gave him aid?"

"No subject of your own," Madini said. "More than that, I do not know. Yet if no one of Faerie aided him, some mortal must have been his help. Your son—"

"Leave us."

Madini swallowed the remainder of her sentence, along with a large measure of chagrin. She had counted on a longer conversation to give her time to feign sympathy and to drop a few more hints regarding John. She was not sure what to make of the abrupt dismissal, but she was far too wise to protest it. Hiding her frustration, Madini curtsied and left the royal presence.

CHAPTER · SEVEN

"Snow White and Rose Red always kept their mother's cottage neat and tidy. In summer, Rose Red took care of the house. Every morning she gathered flowers for her mother, and she always included some of the roses from the two rosebushes in the garden. In the winter it was Snow White who lit the fire and hung the copper kettle on the hob."

THE PUZZLING CONFINEMENT OF ROSAMUND AND Blanche in Faerie and their even more puzzling release troubled the Widow Arden more than she could bring herself to admit in the presence of her daughters. The unexpected results of her sorcerous vision only added to her fears. Something was happening in Faerie, and though it had brushed lightly by Rosamund and Blanche thus far, the Widow doubted that they would continue to be so lucky.

She, therefore, set herself to think out a way of discovering what lay behind these mysterious and intriguing occurrences, that she might be better prepared if the future brought more of them. She could hardly go to Faerie and ask, and she knew better than to make any further use of magic. What she needed more than anything, the Widow felt, was advice.

So, on the Wednesday following Rosamund and Blanche's safe return from Faerie, the Widow Arden left the girls to take care of the house while she herself set off for Mortlak. The day was grey, cold and overcast, a foretaste of the rapidly approaching winter. By the time she reached the village the Widow was thoroughly chilled, despite her wool petticoat, and she was glad indeed to reach Mistress Hudson's house near the edge of the village.

Mary Hudson was of about the same age as the Widow Arden, but where the Widow was tall, dark-haired, and well-figured, Mary was short, greying, and decidedly plump. Neither woman cared in the slightest for these differences, nor for the more important social discrepancy between a poor widow and the wife of a well-to-do gentleman with a large country house and an equally large income from the thriving trade in wines and wool. At their first meeting, the two women had become fast friends, and they had remained so for as long as the Widow had lived in Mortlak.

Mistress Hudson was in when the Widow arrived, and soon the Widow was gratefully warming her hands over a large brazier of sea-coal, while her kindhearted hostess fussed over her.

"Nay, Mary, thou'rt surely kind, but truly I've no need of possets," the Widow said at last, laughing.

"No need! Why, in God's truth thou'rt chilled to the very bone," her hostess replied indignantly.

"I'm not so chilled as that," the Widow said, though she was indeed quite cold. She had had enough of Mary Hudson's heated brews to avoid them when she could. "'Twould take more than a day so mild as this to discomfort me."

"Or belike a better flavor to my drinks?" Mistress Hudson said in a mischievous tone. "Well, I'll not press thee. Thou hast stayed away too long; I'll not give thee cause for more neglect."

"Wouldst have me disregard my autumn work?" the Widow shot back, unabashed.

"Nay, I did but jest. I know 'tis a busy time for thee. So now I ask, what brings thee from thy duties to my doorstep this November day?"

"Great perplexity," said the Widow, and hesitated. She trusted Mary more than she trusted anyone else in Mortlak, but she had never been able to bring herself to speak of the questionable knowledge of magic that added so much to the virtue of her powders, syrups, and potions.

Mistress Hudson gave the Widow a sharp look. "So? Come to my chambers above, and we'll talk; 'tis warmer there—and private."

The Widow nodded, and Mistress Hudson led the way through the long hall and up the staircase with its ornate balusters and carved newel posts. They passed through a maze of interconnecting rooms, some paneled in oak, others hung with tapestries, and came at last to Mistress Hudson's apartments.

The anteroom, where the women stopped, was spacious and comfortable-looking. A bay window, filled with small, square panes of glass, let in light and gave a somewhat distorted view of the fields and the road. On the opposite side of the room was a large fireplace. The elaborate chimneypiece above it bore the Hudson arms on one side and those of the Gilberts, Mistress Hudson's family, on the other. The floor was strewn with sweet herbs that made a pleasant scent as the women's feet crushed them. Loose cushions stuffed with straw lay atop three large, elaborately carved oak chests.

Mary Hudson seated herself on one of the chests and looked at the Widow. "Tell me straight," she said as the Widow took a seat opposite her, "is't money?"

"Nay, 'tis not indeed. I'd never come to thee for such a thing!" the Widow said.

"Thou'rt stubborn to say it, when I've so often told thee thou might," Mistress Hudson replied calmly. "Well, and if 'tis not the state of thy purse that brings thee to me, 'tis thy girls."

"I fear thou hast it, at least in part," the Widow said with a sigh. "Dost thou recall how they roam the woods to gather herbs for me? I have been less than easy about it these two months past, and have kept them close. Yet even so I fear they've come on that which may be a danger to them."

"An thou would have advice, thou must tell me the whole," Mistress Hudson said, settling herself more comfortably on her cushion. "Begin two months agone; what cause hadst thou for thy misgiving?"

So the Widow embarked on a somewhat edited account of her dealings of the previous two months. She began with Mistress Townsend's visit, and the fear of witchcraft rumors that had led her to bar Rosamund and Blanche from the forest. She did not speak of Rosamund's encounter with the supposed peddler, nor of Faerie, nor of her private magic-working, but she gave a detailed description of Joan Bowes's request for a love potion, without actually mentioning the girl's name. She went on to describe in even greater detail the spell-casting that Rosamund and Blanche had watched on the afternoon of All Hallows' Eve.

"And now there seems a strangeness in the forest, and I fear that those wizards may, by their arts, have learned my daughters saw them," the Widow finished. "Nor can I be easy knowing two such men have been at work so near my door. Yet I know not what action I may take, and so I come to thee for thy advice."

"I think thou shouldst begin by paying less heed to Mistress Townsend," Mary said. "Yes, I know 'tis not the question thou hast asked me, yet I say it still. She's like to trouble thee more than a thousand wizards, an thou allow her."

"Belike I was wrong to take her words so much to heart," the Widow said. "Yet I do not see how knowing that will help me now."

"'Twill give thee one less thing to fret about," Mary Hudson replied tartly. "Now, as to the girl who sought a love charm of thee: she'll have no great liking for thee, but she can do thee little harm. Joan Bowes is not much liked in Mortlak."

"How didst thou guess—"

"That it was Joan who came to thee?" Mistress Hudson smiled. "'Tis common gossip in the village that she's smitten with her master. Then, too, I've seen such greedy, conscienceless girls before, and had to deal with them. 'Twas not difficult."

"So thou sayest," the Widow said, returning the smile. "For myself, I think thou'rt uncommon shrewd."

"That's as may be," Mary said. "Still, now thou mayest leave off worrying at that as well. As to thy wizards—"

"Hardly mine," the Widow murmured.

"Intrude not on my sentences, thou hasty pudding, lest I mislay my thoughts! These wizards, by thy report, I think may be Doctor Dee and his friend Master Kelly, who live beside the river."

"So I thought, also," the Widow said unhappily. "But how may I be certain? More, how may I know they'll do no ill to me or mine, apurpose or by accident?"

"Have thy daughters watch for them, that they may tell thee whether Doctor Dee and his friend are indeed the wizards thou dost fear," Mistress Hudson said impatiently. "Then, when thou'rt certain of their names, thou mayest find some stratagem to learn the rest."

"How?" the Widow asked after a moment. She did not entirely approve of her friend's proposal, but she could see the sense in it. She needed to learn as much as possible about the two wizards Rosamund and Blanche had seen; to do so, she must begin by learning their identities.

"I'll think on't," Mistress Hudson said. "There's time to spare; Master Kelly goes up to London tomorrow, and from thence to Blakley. He'll not return inside a fortnight. And until I send to thee, thou must draw a cross i'the lintel of thy door and hang thy house with those herbs that do protect from spells and harm."

"I thank thee for thy counsel," the Widow said, smiling. "I'll follow thy advice. Though, truth to tell, 'twas a relief simply to speak of it. I would not share my worry with the girls."

"Thou mightest be wiser an thou did," Mistress Hudson said. "Still, I can understand thy caution. I'll send to thee within a fortnight to tell thee what's toward, and how we may discover these wizards."

Much cheered by these reassurances, the Widow returned home, while Mistress Hudson went to her embroidery stand to sit and think.

◆   ◆   ◆

In the book-lined study on the second floor of John Dee's home, Dee and Kelly moved urgently about their business. The study windows had been closed, shuttered, and covered with heavy drapes of green silk, so that not even the smallest ray of light could enter from the outside. The room contained neither candles nor rushlights; the only illumination came from the small brass lamp that Dee and Kelly had taken with them into the forest three weeks before.

The lamp stood near the middle of a square table, inside a six-pointed star formed from two equilateral triangles which were inscribed on the tabletop. Though it held no oil, nor any sign of a flame, the lamp shed a pure, bright light over the engravings and inscriptions that covered the table. Beside it, in the exact center of the table, was a large globe of polished quartz, dull and milky in the unnatural glow of the lamp.

Dee and Kelly were engaged in placing four round slabs of wax, each more than two inches thick and carved with mystic diagrams, under the four legs of the table on which the lamp rested. The task required both strength and dexterity, for the table was solidly constructed and therefore heavy, and it stood on the large square of red silk the two men had taken to the forest, making it difficult to locate the wax seals properly without wrinkling the silk.

"Belike we should have been less hasty to put the lamp and crystal in their places," Kelly panted. He, being the younger of the two by over twenty-five years, had the job of lifting the table, one side at a time, gently enough to keep from dislodging the lamp or the quartz globe, yet far enough for Dee to slide the seals into place.

"Nay, they must stand in the diagram from the beginning," Dee said absently. "Therefore have a care to your work."

Kelly grimaced disgustedly at Dee's unheeding back. "Dispatch your own with speed, else I'll not answer for the consequences. I am no carrier, to make light of such a load."

"Peace, Ned; 'tis done." Dee backed carefully away from the table and watched critically as Kelly slowly lowered his side of the table half an inch. The two legs of the table came to rest precisely in the center of the wax seals. Dee smiled and rose to his feet as Kelly, massaging his left shoulder, turned to face him.

"How much time remains?" Kelly demanded.

Dee went to the shelves behind him and peered at a clock standing there. "Minutes only. To your place; we must begin at once."

The two men took up positions on opposite sides of the table and raised their arms. Dee caught Kelly's eye and nodded. Together they began to chant in long, sonorous Latin phrases that seemed to wind around each other and echo in the darkened corners of the room.

At first, the glow of the lamp brightened, but as the chant went on and on the lamp began to dim. No corresponding glow began to grow in the quartz globe, however, and Kelly's eyes took on a wild expression. A bead of sweat rolled down his nose and fell into his beard. Dee seemed almost unaffected, save for a kind of tightening of the skin over the temples.

The chant wove on, and the glow of the lamp continued to diminish. As the wizards reached the final line, a single spark was all that could be seen even in the darkened room. On the final word, the lamp's glow died completely.

There was a moment's silence. Kelly's face twisted, and he opened his mouth to curse. John Dee, standing tall and dignified despite the crushing disappointment, spoke first by the merest instant. "Fiat," said Dee in a saddened tone. "So be it."

Light flared from the quartz globe, blinding the two men's dark-accustomed eyes. Kelly's curse changed on his lips to a howl of mingled terror and triumph. Dee's command of "Silence!" came too late; in another moment they heard footsteps in the hall and someone knocked at the library door.

"Doctor Dee?" a servant called timidly from outside the room. "Did you call?"

"Nay, Anne, I've no need of thee," Dee said loudly. "Go thy ways."

"Aye, Doctor Dee," said the voice, and the footsteps retreated with far greater haste than they had come.

Dee and Kelly looked at each other as the dazzle cleared from their eyes. The quartz globe lay on the table between them, spewing golden light in all directions. "The whole of the household must have heard your cry. You should have greater caution when we work here, Ned," Dee said.

"I am sorry for't," Kelly replied. "But a portion of the fault's yours. I'd made no noise, if you had warned me what was to happen."

"I did not know," Dee said.

Kelly, who had been reaching for the glowing quartz globe, jerked back. "You did not know we'd seem to fail? That the light would die i'the lamp ere it blossomed elsewhere?"

"I did not."

"Then how may we be certain this final step hath been successful?" Kelly eyed the quartz globe uneasily.

"We must make trial of't," Dee replied. "Pull down the silks and open the shutters; we'll do better now in the light of day."

Kelly gave Dee a long look, then did as he had been told. When he finished, he returned to his place by the table. Dee leaned forward, the end of his long beard brushing the tabletop, and touched the quartz with his left forefinger. "Fiat voluntas nostra," he said.

The glow vanished abruptly, as though it had been snuffed out. Kelly gave a gasp of protest, then suddenly leaned forward to examine the quartz more closely. The globe was no longer milky white; it had become clearer than the finest crystal.

"We have done it," Dee said with evident satisfaction. "The

power of Faerie is imprisoned in the crystal, for as long as we so will it, and we may make what use of it we choose."

"Aye, an we discover how," Kelly said, but he sounded far more cheerful than before.

"That portion of the task is chiefly yours," Dee said, smiling.

"Then I fear it must wait upon my return from Blakley."

"Thou needst not scowl so fierce; we've time and to spare now that the crystal's finished," Dee chided his companion. "And I think 'twould not be amiss for both of us to rest. These past three weeks have been a grievous effort."

"An you'll have it so," Kelly said ungraciously, but he did not look unhappy with this resolution. He picked up the dead lamp, leaving the crystal globe in the center of the table. Together, he and John Dee left the library.

♦　　♦　　♦

In the realm of Faerie, a grim-faced messenger sped from Hugh's sickroom toward the Queen's palace. A short time later, eight strong servants carried a large net to the border of Faerie and firmly thrust its contents across into the mortal world. The half-dazed black bear that had once been John's younger brother rolled out of the net, roared once, and lumbered into the forest. The servants watched it go, then folded their net and went sadly back to tell their Queen that the unalterable and inexorable law of Faerie had been fulfilled.

CHAPTER · EIGHT

"On winter evenings when the snow was falling, the mother would say, 'Snow White, go and bolt the door.' Then they all sat around the fire, and the mother read aloud while the two girls sat and spun. A lamb lay close beside them on the floor, and a white dove perched in the rafters with its head under its wing.

"One evening their reading was interrupted by someone knocking at the door. The mother set her book down and said, 'Open the door, Rose Red; it must be some traveler seeking shelter from the storm.'"

THE FOLLOWING DAY, THE SNOW BEGAN. IT STARTED as small specks of white that fell thinly and vanished when they touched the brown grass of the fields. A few of the older residents of the village raised their eyebrows and spoke in hushed voices of the severity of the winter that would surely follow so early a snowfall. Most simply shrugged; a dusting of snow was no cause for concern. The watermen on the Thames and the laborers and water carriers along its banks alike pulled their wool caps down around their ears and went stolidly on with their work.

Shortly before noon, one of the boats, responding to a servant's signal, pulled up at the water stairs behind Master Dee's house. A brief negotiation ensued concerning fees; then Edward Kelly emerged from the house, called a casual farewell over his shoulder, and hurried down the stairs to the waiting boat. A moment later the boatman pushed off and the boat started eastward on its ten-mile journey downstream to London.

The boat reached the city just before the turning of the tide. As Kelly disembarked, a similar boat pushed off from a wharf just above the London bridge, and started west on the somewhat more arduous trip upstream to Mortlak. The waterman, noting his passenger's white velvet cloak and air of gloom, assumed that he was one of Queen Elizabeth's courtiers being sent away in disgrace, as happened now and again. Wishing neither to intrude on the sorrows of such a man nor to become entangled in his follies, the waterman extracted his half-shilling fee and the name "John Rimer" from his passenger, and after that was silent.

The silence suited John. He had had high hopes of his venture into London, for the city had seemed the obvious place to find the wizard he sought, but he had searched the city for a week without success. Now success was no longer possible. Whatever transformation had struck Hugh down, it was complete. John knew it, as he knew that his brother was still alive and no longer within the borders of Faerie, by a kind of sympathy between them that had existed as long as he could remember. He had known, when he was eleven, that Hugh had fallen into the den of one of the giant worms that mortals call dragons; Hugh had known ten years later when John had broken a leg on one of his journeys and found himself unable to return to Faerie without aid.

Now both brothers were barred from their homeland, Hugh by the implacable law that had cast him forth and John by his determined defiance of the Faerie Queen's orders. The bond between them was not likely to do either of them any good. Denied the timelessness of Faerie, they would each live a mortal span of years and die, if they did not first run afoul of hunters, plague, thieves, or human law.

They could, however, live out their lives together, and it was for this reason that John was returning to Mortlak. Whatever shape his brother had taken on, whatever beast Hugh had become, John was determined to find and protect him. Hugh was somewhere near Mortlak. John was certain of it, and equally certain that he would know his brother at once when they met. Finding Hugh would be another matter; the uncommon bond between the brothers was no more than a general guide.

The snow thickened as the day wore on. By the time John reached his destination, it was falling in white swirls and the streets were growing muddy. John thanked the waterman and handed him half a crown, which caused that worthy to comment later to his cronies at the Barking Dog how sad it was that such an open-handed young man had had to bury himself in the country.

John hired a porter to carry the bag he had bought in London, inquired directions to the nearest lodgings, and set off. By the time he reached his destination, agreed on a price for his room and board, and saw his bag carried upstairs to his apartments, it was too dark to think of searching for Hugh.

Morning brought no better prospects. The snow had continued throughout the night, growing thicker and thicker until it made a dense cloud over the entire town. Enough had accumulated in the night to make walking a difficult task, and it showed no signs of stopping. John, staring out the small rectangular panes of the window in the sitting room he had hired, could barely see across the street. Everything was shrouded in white.

"The Queen of Faerie mourns," he murmured, then shook his head and sighed. Natural or not, the snow made it impossible for him to look for Hugh that day.

◆   ◆   ◆

The black bear stumbled through the forest, sliding on icy mats of fallen leaves and lurching over the hidden unevenness of the ground. He was hungry, but the snow covered the late berries and seeds on which he might have fed, and hid the burrows of small animals he might have eaten. The cold wind cut through his fur and swirled the falling snow into dense, confusing whorls that hid his path and stung his eyes. The bear would have known how to find food and where to hide from the weather; the man in the bear's body did not.

Stubbornly, Hugh blundered on. Whether because his human half stayed with him when his Faerie essence was stripped away or because the spell binding him was less effective in the mortal world than in Faerie, Hugh had retained more of himself than those who had cast him out would have believed. He did not understand all that had happened to him, but three things he was sure of. His form was not his own; he had once been in Faerie but was no longer; and somewhere ahead of him was his friend and brother, who would help him. He did not know the reason for his certainty, nor did he recall the bond that linked him with John. He only knew that he had nowhere else to go. Cold, tired, and nearly exhausted, Hugh made his slow, uncertain way through the forest, heading toward Mortlak.

◆　　　◆　　　◆

The Widow Arden had hoped to venture into town, but one look out her door had convinced her that this would be inadvisable, at least until the snowstorm ceased. Instead, she and her daughters spent the day mixing herbs and boiling them down into soothing syrups for coughs or fevers. The Widow was sure that the early snow would bring customers to her door in search of such remedies.

By the time the last of the carefully prepared jars had been sealed with melted beeswax and the clutter of tools and crushed herbs cleared from the table, it was nearly dark. The Widow put a turnip, an onion, and a double handful of well-soaked beans into the copper kettle and set it on the hob to cook, while Rosamund sorted through the mending. Blanche was busy with the lamb, which was doing well enough to have become something of a nuisance indoors. As soon as dinner was on the fire, the Widow went to the chest in the corner, where she kept the four treasured books she had saved from the ruin her late husband had brought down on her.

"Mother," said Rosamund as the Widow bent over the chest.

"What is it?" the Widow said, straightening. Rosamund and Blanche exchanged glances, and the Widow smiled. "Do you want to choose for yourselves what I'll read to you tonight?"

"In a way," Rosamund said cautiously. She looked at her sister again. Blanche nodded. Rosamund swallowed and went on, "Thou hast taught us much, Mother, and of many things that are not common—of herbery, and of Latin, and of Faerie."

The Widow closed the chest and sat down on it. "I have; go on."

"We think, Blanche and I, that thou knowest more of magic than the uses of Faerie herbs and the wearing of hawthorn to turn away harm," Rosamund said.

"An that were true, what would you?"

"We'd have thee teach us all thy knowledge, and not fragments," Rosamund said. She already regretted mentioning the subject, but it was too late to take back her words no matter how much her mother was displeased. "Blanche and I agreed together two days ago, when thou didst spend the day at Mortlak."

"Did you so?" the Widow said angrily. Her irritation was as much at her own carelessness as at Rosamund's temerity in broaching this particular subject. She had never meant for her daughters to guess how great her knowledge was, nor for them to learn anything whatever that could be considered suspect. "And did you not think I might have strong reasons for keeping such instruction from you?"

"I know thou'st feared lest someone call us witches—"

"Yet you dismiss it lightly! You have not seen women hanged for witchcraft, as I have. You do not know—"

"I know enough!" Rosamund broke in. "You fear so much that someone shall miscall us witches that you see no other dangers, though they be thick as flies on spilled honey in June. God will protect us from malice, but we must guard ourselves from carelessness."

There was a pause. "What do you mean?" the Widow said. Her voice was calmer, and Blanche gave a small sigh of relief. Blanche hated quarreling.

"This," said Rosamund. "The air's been thick with spells and strangeness since before All Hallows'. If Blanche and I are not to step amiss, we must know more than how to slip safely in and out of Faerie."

"You need not mix yourselves in these affairs," the Widow said.

"How not?" Blanche said quietly. "We've seen wizards at their work, and one who is of Faerie has watched us across the border. 'Tis tardy, I think, to speak of mixing or not mixing."

"We must know what's best to do and not to do when we meet such things," Rosamund said. "We'll not make use of spells ourselves."

"Nor will we speak of magic where we may be overheard," Blanche added. "Thou shouldst know as much, for thou knowest we speak not of Faerie, nor have ever done."

"'Tis not so simple as thou makest it sound," the Widow said, sighing. "Well, I'll do't, though my heart misgives me. Thou'lt not forget the danger of this learning?"

"We'll not forget," Blanche said soberly, and Rosamund echoed her words.

"And the snow is a blessing today," Rosamund added. "For 'tis unlikely anyone will come to our door, and find us at such studies."

"As thou sayest," the Widow said. She glanced toward the window as if to reassure herself that the snow was still falling heavily. Then she rose and opened the chest. From the very bottom, she removed a thin, dark book, handwritten and showing signs of much use. She closed the chest and seated herself on it once more, then looked at her daughters. "To your work, girls; I'll read slowly, and you may question me as you will."

Blanche and Rosamund nodded as one. Blanche set up the spinning wheel beside the window and sat on the rolled-up straw pallet to work. Rosamund threaded her needle and took up the gown that lay on top of the pile of mending. The Widow eyed them both a moment longer; then she opened the book and began to read.

" 'The forms of magic are many and several, to wit, that which is of Faerie, that which is of scholarship and careful knowledge, that which is of ancient lore and ritual, that which is of wisdom and instinct, and that which is of the devil and to be well avoided. And these are not the sum of magics, for certes there be others that we know not of.

" 'Now, the forms of magic may be distinguished each from the other by certain things . . .' "

The Widow's voice went on, pleasant and even, though raised somewhat to carry over the steady hum of Blanche's spinning wheel. The girls listened intently while their fingers flew. The lamb drowsed by the hearth and the smell of cooking onion crept out of the pot above the fire to permeate the little room.

Finally, the Widow stopped. " 'Tis enough for tonight, I think, and dinner's ready," she said. "Blanche, hast thou—"

A heavy knock interrupted her. All three of the women started, and their heads turned to stare guiltily at the cottage door. The Widow jumped up, raised the lid of the chest, and shoved the dark book inside. She let the lid fall and sat down again just as the knock was repeated.

"Open the door, Rosamund," the Widow said with creditable composure. "It must be some poor man caught unawares by the storm, and now half frozen."

Rosamund set her mending down and went to the door. She put back the latch and opened it, leaning forward to peer into the darkness outside. A swirl of snow and cold air came in, and then Hugh shouldered the door wide and thrust his black bear's head into the room.

CHAPTER · NINE

•

"Rose Red opened the door, thinking it was a poor man. Instead, a bear stretched his broad, black head into the room. Rose Red screamed and sprang back, and Snow White hid herself behind the bed while the lamb bleated in fright. But the bear spoke to them and said, 'Do not be frightened! I won't hurt you. I only want to warm myself a little at your fire.'

" 'Very well,' said the mother. 'You may lie by the hearth, but be careful that your coat does not catch fire.' Then she called to her daughters, 'Snow White, Rose Red, you may come out, for the bear will not harm you.' So the two girls came out, and after a time the lamb, too, came nearer and was not afraid."

•

ROSAMUND GASPED AS THE DOOR WAS WRENCHED from her hands, then let the extra breath out in a scream when she saw the broad, furry bear's head with its pointed yellow teeth. She sprang backward, and Hugh took another step inside. Blanche's eyes grew huge. She rolled off the pallet she had been sitting on and crouched in its inadequate shelter. The lamb scrambled to its feet and bleated a complaint at the uncomfortable cold that was entering along with the unexpected visitor.

The Widow rose and reached for the eating knife she carried at her belt, though it was far too small to be of much use against so large an animal. Rosamund took two more hasty steps backward and snatched up the long, heavy branch they had been using to poke up the logs in the fire. Pale and frightened, she stood brandishing her makeshift weapon like a club, while the bear shed snow onto the rush mats and peered shortsightedly around the room.

The Widow cleared her throat, and the bear's head swung in her direction. She froze, while the bear squinted intently at her. Then it began to growl, its upper lip curling back to show sharp teeth. Rosamund clenched her hands around the branch until her knuckles showed white. She was about to force herself to step forward, when the bear sat back on its haunches, raised its muzzle to the ceiling, and gave a long howl of agony and despair.

Until that moment, Hugh had not realized that he would be unable to communicate with people once he found them. He had seen the light shining from the windows of the Widow's cottage and gone toward it, half out of instinct, half from a reasoned desire for warmth and shelter. He had not stopped to consider how the inhabitants might react to the appearance of a large black bear at their door.

The fear on the faces of the three women confronting him, and the complete failure of his attempt to speak to them, brought home to Hugh the full extent of the trap he was in. He howled his despair in the only way he had left to express it, then shook himself and began backing out of the cottage. He would not terrify these people further to no purpose.

The Widow Arden had not moved since the first wave of her astonishment and fear had driven her to her feet. She stared at the bear, remembering the vision she had had while scrying for Rosamund and Blanche, but one bear is very like another and the light near the door was poor. Only when the bear began to back away in such an unbearlike fashion did the Widow summon her courage to say tentatively, "Bear?"

Hugh paused and swung his head to look at the Widow, and she was shocked at the tortured bewilderment in his eyes. Rosamund raised her branch threateningly, and the Widow caught her arm. "Peace, Rosamund. This creature's done no harm."

"But it's a *bear!*" Rosamund said, bewildered by her mother's strange response.

"Belike," the Widow said. "And belike not. Canst thou understand me, bear?"

Hugh swung his great head up and down in an exaggerated nod. Rosamund stepped backward involuntarily, and her eyes widened. Blanche stared from behind her meager cover. Even the Widow was momentarily startled into silence. Hugh looked at her with an air of patient expectation, and she hastily collected her thoughts.

"Then in the name of Jesus I adjure thee, bear, to answer truly: mean'st thou aught that's ill for any of us here?" said the Widow.

Hugh shook his head with even more energy than he had nodded earlier. Blanche jerked back behind the straw-stuffed pallet, and Rosamund shifted her grip on the branch she held.

"Art thou in need, then?" the Widow went on. The bear nodded, and shook himself. Great, slushy drops of half-melted snow flew in all directions, and the smell of wet fur rose to fill the cottage. The Widow flinched, then almost smiled. "Is't the cold that's thy first difficulty? Dost thou seek shelter from this most untimely storm?"

Hugh nodded again. The Widow hesitated, then said, "Rosamund, lay down thy club and shut the door, ere the cold doth freeze us all."

"Thou'lt never let this creature stay!" Rosamund said, astonished.

"How not?" the Widow said. "The bear hath promised to do no ill. Wouldst thou take the promise and turn him out to freeze? Do as I bid thee!"

Muttering under her breath, Rosamund set her branch down beside the fire and edged around the bear to the door. The noise of the storm lessened as the door swung shut. Rosamund glanced at her mother, then dropped the latch into place. The musky odor of bear intensified. Rosamund turned, shivering, and stared at their visitor.

There was a long silence. Hugh could smell the fear permeating the room, and he stood still as a post, afraid to move lest he make matters even worse. The Widow bit her lip, already regretting her impulsive generosity and wishing the bear had not had the haunted eyes of the young man she had seen in her vision three weeks before. Blanche crept slowly out of her hiding place, hoping the bear would continue to overlook her presence, and Rosamund leaned against the door and looked longingly at the branch her mother had made her leave beside the hearth.

The impasse might have gone on much longer if the lamb had not chosen that moment to investigate the new arrival. It tottered forward, its hooves making soft crunching noises against the rush mats that covered the floor. Blanche gasped. Forgetting her own fear, she ran to the lamb's side and pulled it back toward the hearth, away from the bear.

"Thou foolish creature!" Blanche scolded the lamb. "Stay where thou'rt meant to. Or dost thou desire to be eaten?"

Blanche settled the lamb in its place and turned, to find the bear's eyes fixed reproachfully on her. She caught her breath, then said as steadily as she could, "I apologize if my words offended thee, bear. Yet I pray thee, remember that not all thy kind have thy restraint. I'd not have this lamb grow too familiar with thee, lest it come to grief with some other of thy fellows."

The bear nodded awkwardly and looked away, and Blanche thought it seemed ashamed. Much of her fear vanished in concern. Impulsively, she reached out and laid a hand on the bear's shoulder, where the fur was matted and still damp from the snow.

Rosamund's gasp of horror mingled with the Widow's dismayed cry of "Blanche!" The bear flinched, and Blanche pulled back as if she had been stung. Blanche and the bear stared at each other. Then, slowly, Blanche put out her hand once more.

"Blanche, do not!" the Widow said sharply.

"Nay, Mother, thou hast said there's no harm here," Blanche replied, but she drew away. "And I think he was as startled as I. Wast not, bear?"

Hugh gave a careful nod. Blanche smiled at her mother. "Seest thou? 'Tis no common bear, Mother; thou hast said as much thyself."

"Of a certainty, 'tis most uncommon large," Rosamund said tartly. She was surprised by, and a little jealous of, Blanche's unaccustomed bravery, and so she spoke more sharply than she intended.

"Rosamund." The Widow gave Rosamund a warning look, and Rosamund flushed. Satisfied that Rosamund would say nothing else that might irritate their alarming guest, the Widow turned back to the bear. It was, as Rosamund had pointed out, very large; it was also very black and bearish. If only its eyes were not so strange and human . . . "Bear," said the Widow, "art thou of Faerie?"

Hugh hesitated, knowing that he could no longer truthfully make such a claim yet unsure whether the Widow cared for such nice distinctions. He shook his head, then nodded and looked up at the Widow, hoping for understanding.

The Widow stared in complete incomprehension. Blanche looked at her mother, then back to Hugh and said gently, "Wast thou once of Faerie, but art no more?"

Gratefully, Hugh nodded. Blanche looked at her mother again, and the Widow nodded encouragingly. "Hast thou abandoned thy former home, then?" Blanche asked. Hugh shook his head in the negative. "Wast thou cast out?"

Again, Hugh nodded. Blanche hesitated. "Was it thine own faults which brought this banishment upon thee?"

Hugh shook his head emphatically. There was a moment's silence. Then the Widow said, "Bear, is this thy true form?"

Hugh shut his eyes, wishing that bears could weep as men did, and shook his head again.

"Mother!" said Rosamund. "Meanest thou he is enchanted?"

"'Tis likely," the Widow replied, while the bear nodded again. Blanche reached out to touch Hugh's shoulder briefly. "Poor bear," she murmured.

Rosamund studied the bear with considerably less fear and more interest. "What wast thou, ere thou wast made a bear?" she asked. "Wast thou some strange creature of Faerie, or wast thou human-shaped?"

Since this question was obviously too complex for a simple yes-or-no response, Hugh did not answer. Realizing her mistake, Rosamund restated it more plainly, and soon determined that the bear's true shape was manlike.

"Mother, thinkest thou that we may find some way to remedy this spell?" Rosamund asked.

"Perhaps," the Widow answered cautiously. "But thou wilt recall that thou and thy sister did promise just this evening to forego the working of spells if I would tell you more of them."

"Mother!" Blanche said. "How canst thou compare that to the breaking of such a horrible enchantment as is this? And how can we refuse to do all in our power to correct this evil?"

The Widow hesitated, but she knew her daughter was right. "We cannot refuse," she replied with a smothered sigh. "But 'twill be neither easy nor safe even to try, and success is most uncertain. My small store of knowledge may not be enough for this task."

"Doubt not that thou'lt do it, Mother," Rosamund assured her with the buoyant confidence of youth. "And we'll take whatever measures thou thinkst necessary for our safety, and observe them to the smallest detail."

"'Tis not enough," the Widow said. Rosamund and Blanche looked at her in surprise, and she smiled through her apprehension. "Nay, look not so grim; I cannot deny you parts in this whate'er my wishes, for I'll need your help. But 'twill not be sufficient for you two to follow all my strictures. You must both be wary of yourselves, and careful beyond what I tell you. This matter is of Faerie, and will require all your caution and good sense."

Rosamund looked sober, and Blanche solemn. "We understand, Mother," Blanche said.

Rosamund nodded agreement. "What must we do?" she asked.

The Widow smiled. "Little enough, for tonight. Settle thyself beside the fire, sir bear, where thou'lt be warmer and less a hindrance to my daughters and me. Rosamund, Blanche, go back to your places, and we'll question this bear further while we work. We must know more of this spell ere we attempt to counter it."

Rosamund and Blanche were a little disappointed by this prosaic answer, but they did as they were told. In contrast, Hugh, settling himself carefully on the hearth, felt a faint stirring of hope. He quashed it firmly. He had no doubt that his mother had used every power at her disposal to counteract the spell that bound him, and where the Queen of Faerie herself had failed, what could a mere mortal accomplish?

Questioning the bear became a game for Rosamund and Blanche, and the evening passed quickly. When the time came to put out the rushlight and go to sleep, they had established that the bear did not know who had enchanted him or why, that he had no friends in Faerie on whom to call, and that the spell had struck him on the afternoon of All Hallows' Eve. This last information made Blanche and Rosamund exchange speculative glances, but a warning look from their mother made them keep silent about the two sorcerers they had seen at the edge of Faerie that day.

Early next morning, the bear left the cottage with stern instructions from the Widow to return in the evening, and not before. As soon as he was gone, Rosamund and Blanche began a lively discussion about their strange guest and the likelihood of successfully disenchanting him. The Widow listened with familiar feelings of misgiving. She had no reason to mistrust the bear, but neither did she have reason to accept his story without question, and creatures out of Faerie were notoriously chancy to deal with.

She let Rosamund and Blanche talk until breakfast was over, then sent them to begin their daily chores.

◆　　　◆　　　◆

In the lodging house in Mortlak, John, too, rose early. Impatient and eager to begin his search for Hugh, he dressed swiftly and swallowed his breakfast in almost a single gulp. Then he bundled his cloak around him and went out into the streets of the town.

The snow had nearly stopped; only a light dusting of flakes still sifted down from the dark grey sky. John looked around, then shrugged and started walking away from the river, toward the edge of the town. The passage of wagons and foot traffic had churned the fallen snow into a slippery, ash-colored slush in most places, and he had to go carefully. He was picking his way past a large stone house when Joan Bowes, hurrying in the opposite direction with her head down, ran into him.

They teetered for a moment, their feet sliding on the slush in an attempt to regain balance. John recovered first, but kept a grip on his companion's arms until he was sure she, too, was firm on her feet once more. Then he released her and bowed. "I beg your pardon, Mistress," he said.

"The fault was mine, sir," Joan answered in a breathless voice. "And I do thank you for your timely rescue."

"'Twas but a trifle," John said, wincing slightly, for he shared the Faerie distaste for being thanked. He stepped aside to let her pass, but Joan reached out and caught his arm.

"It was no trifle to me! I'd show thee now what I mean, but I've an errand for my mistress that may not wait. Come to Master William Rundel's house this evening, and ask for Joan Bowes, and I'll repay thy kindness well."

"I see. Good day to you, Mistress Bowes." John bowed again, forcing Joan to release his arm. Two quick steps took him out of her reach, and then he turned and continued on his way. Joan stared after him, her lower lip caught between her teeth and her eyes narrowed in vexation. She was not accustomed to being dismissed in such firm fashion, and dismissal it had been, for all the polite formality of the words. She glared at John's retreating back, then tucked her anger and the imagined injury away in the special corner of her mind she kept for grudges. Smoothing out her expression, she resumed her careful progress down the snowy street.

John had already forgotten her in his absorption with the search to which he had committed himself. He slogged determinedly through the slush to the edge of Mortlak, then paused to survey the fields and the forest beyond. After some thought, he decided to begin with the area farthest from the Faerie border, on the assumption that Hugh would keep as much distance as he could between himself and the home that had rejected him. Whistling softly between his teeth, John set off across the snowy fields.

CHAPTER · TEN

"After a time, the bear said, 'Girls, come and brush some of the snow out of my coat.' So the two girls took the broom and brushed at the bear's coat, and he stretched out by the hearth growling contentedly. They soon became accustomed to their visitor, and even began to play roughly with him. They tried to pull him this way or that, they rode on his back, and even took a thin branch of hazel and pretended to beat him with it. The bear took it all very well, but when they grew too rough he would cry, 'Leave me alive, children! Snow White, Rose Red, will you beat your suitor dead?'"

JOHN'S SEARCH FOR HIS BROTHER BORE NO FRUIT that day, nor in the weeks that followed. His magic was no help at all. Outside the borders of Faerie, John's abilities were limited, or so it seemed to him, who all his life had seen what the lords of Faerie could accomplish. He could pluck a blooming rose from a dead bush, turn dogs away, and mislead pursuit, but skills such as those were not what he needed now. The ring of invisibility was the only thing of power he had been able to bring with him, and it was of no use whatever in locating Hugh.

Stubbornly, he continued to tramp through the fields and forest south of Mortlak whenever the weather permitted, and to follow the tracks of every deer, bear, hound, and ox whose traces he saw in the forest snow. More often than not, he failed to find them, but he clung grimly to his purpose despite his growing discouragement. In December, John hired a house in Mortlak, for he was convinced that Hugh was still somewhere nearby. A few of the townsfolk wondered at the strange, solitary man in their midst, but most were too busy with preparations for Christmas and the Twelve Days of celebration that followed to pay much attention to John and his wanderings.

Joan Bowes was one of the exceptions. She made it her business to learn all she could about the man who called himself John Rimer, and she was irked by how little there was to learn. He ate little and talked less; he went walking nearly every day; and he paid promptly for his few purchases with a seemingly inexhaustible supply of gold nobles, ryals, and sovereigns. He also seemed to have no interest whatever in women, particularly Joan. Joan bit her lips, stored up her growing resentment, and continued to watch.

In the Widow's cottage, the days passed in a flurry of activity, much of it centered on the bear. At first he visited irregularly, staying away for days at a time and then reappearing suddenly just after nightfall. As the weather grew colder, he came more frequently, until by Christmas he was a nightly guest. The Widow fretted about possible consequences, should any of the townsfolk learn of the bear's presence at the cottage, but she could not bring herself to turn him away. So each morning she sent Blanche and Rosamund to sweep away the bear's tracks, and prayed that no one would accidentally stumble over traces of his visits.

The Widow and her daughters worked hard to find a means of breaking the spell holding the bear, but they did not find it an easy job. Questioning Hugh was a long process that yielded little information. He was unable to tell them outright the few details of his transformation that he remembered, and the Widow, Blanche, and Rosamund did not know what questions would produce useful answers. After several evenings spent in this frustrating work, Rosamund and the Widow abandoned it entirely, and turned instead to perusing the Widow's slender volume of magic in hopes of finding a counterspell. Blanche alone continued patiently questioning the bear, trying to piece together exactly what had happened to him and when.

The efforts of the three women were of necessity irregular, despite their good will. The early winter brought with it a steady stream of customers for the Widow's cough remedies, fever cures, fleabane, and warming possets. A few experienced women from the wealthier houses purchased stomach cures in preparation for the Christmas feasting, while their younger counterparts sought rinses to brighten their hair. Rosamund and Blanche were frequently kept too busy grinding and mixing herbs to think much about ways of helping the bear. In addition, they had preparations of their own to make for Christmas, as well as their studies and their chores. As a result, their quest for a means of disenchanting Hugh made little progress.

The fact that she still did not know the identities of the two wizards her daughters had seen on All Hallows' continued to trouble the Widow, but as time passed without incident she began to hope that the wizards, whoever they were, were not aware that they had been observed. Then, on Christmas Day, while the Widow and her daughters were tightening their mufflers in preparation for the long, cold walk home from the village church, Mary Hudson appeared at the Widow's elbow.

"Mary!" the Widow cried joyfully. "Where hast thou been, that I've not seen thee in so long a time?"

"That's no matter," Mistress Hudson replied. "Blanche, Rosamund, look there. See you those men with Master Bettgran, the justice? Do you know them?"

The two girls turned their heads, and simultaneously recognized the men as the two wizards they had seen at the border of Faerie. Blanche paled; Rosamund, seeing this, returned a cautious answer for them both. "We've seen them before."

"Where?" the Widow said sharply.

Rosamund hesitated again, then said, "In the forest, while we were gathering herbs last All Hallows'."

"There!" Mistress Hudson said to the Widow. "I told thee 'twas like to be those two." Without waiting for a response, she turned to the girls and said, "The elder man is the Queen's Astrologer, Master John Dee; the younger is his friend, Ned Kelly. An that one chance to cross your paths, be wary. He is a smiling lecher."

"Mary!" the Widow said reprovingly. "Thou shouldst not speak so, and on Christmas Day!"

"Thy daughters have years enough to be warned in plain words," Mistress Hudson said unrepentantly. "And if 'tis wrong to speak the truth, whate'er the day, then I've been most sorely misinformed."

The Widow shook her head, but smiled. "Thou'rt near as headstrong as my Rosamund."

"'Tis counted a virtue in a woman of my years," Mistress Hudson retorted.

"I pray you, Mistress Hudson, tell us more of Master Dee," Rosamund broke in.

"Rose! Where are thy manners?" the Widow said quickly.

"Well, but I want to know," Rosamund persisted. "And 'twas plain that thou wast not prepared to ask. Wilt thou tell us, Mistress Hudson?"

"Not now," her mother said firmly. "Thou'lt grow chilled with standing in this cold, and we should not keep Mistress Hudson from her family. My thanks, Mary; I'll visit thee as soon as I may."

"I'll hold thee to that promise," Mistress Hudson replied.

◆　　　◆　　　◆

When they left the village and were in no danger of being overheard, Blanche and Rosamund began questioning their mother about Dee and Kelly. The Widow was not surprised by their interest, for though they had not learned much from the bear, they had learned enough to make it seem entirely possible that the two wizards were responsible for his enchantment. Nonetheless, the girls' curiosity troubled her.

"Master Dee is a great wizard, so 'tis said," the Widow warned. "If 'tis truly he whose spell doth hold the bear, it may be dangerous indeed for us to meddle with it."

"'Tis no less dangerous to mix with Faerie," Rosamund pointed out.

"And how should we let such concerns keep us from work we know is right?" Blanche said. "And whoever cast the spell, 'tis plainly right for us to break it if we can."

"True," the Widow said. "But keep in mind that Master Dee's charms are not easily broken, and if we err we may make things worse than ever for the poor bear."

"That's not why thou dost frown," Rosamund said shrewdly. "Thou'rt troubled because we question thee so closely. But Mother, is it not wise for us to know all that we can about these wizards? What we know of Faerie has often kept us from falling into trouble there; may this not be the same?"

The Widow had to admit the force of this argument, but she extracted a promise that the girls would not speak of Dee or Kelly to anyone but her without permission. The girls were quite willing to promise what she asked, and the conversation turned to more innocuous topics for the remainder of the walk to the cottage.

◆　　　◆　　　◆

By mid-January it was obvious that the Widow's book contained no useful counterspell. Rosamund's exasperation was boundless, and she began dropping dark hints about invading Dee's house itself in search of a remedy. This seriously alarmed the Widow, but before matters went too far Blanche made a suggestion that put an end, for the time being, to Rosamund's imprudent proposals.

"An there's no spell in Mother's book, we must make one ourselves," Blanche said in a calm voice. "It cannot be an impossible task, or how were the ones we've read created?"

"Make one?" the Widow repeated blankly.

"Of course!" Rosamund cried, clapping her hands. "We'll take a bit from this spell, and another from that, and make a new one that will do what we wish!"

"'Tis not so easy, Rose," the Widow said, furrowing her brow. "And there are far more pitfalls in this course. An untried spell's a chancy thing."

"We must attempt it, Mother," Blanche said.

The Widow saw the quiet resolution on her daughter's face. Her gaze slid to the black mound of the bear, lying in front of the fire and looking at her with his uncanny, human eyes. The Widow sighed, foreseeing a time-consuming period of dangerous activity ahead, and nodded. "I suppose we must," she said reluctantly. "But keep in mind, girls, that what you've proposed will be neither quick nor easy."

The accuracy of this prediction soon became apparent. Promising bits of one spell proved incompatible with those from another, or worse yet, contradicted them completely. Incomprehensible ingredients were called for, and comprehensible ones were far more expensive than the Widow's meager means could afford. Nearly everything had to be memorized; the girls made occasional notes on horn slates, but they were careful to wipe them clean after each session. The Widow's single spellbook and her jars of Faerie herbs would be damaging evidence enough at a witchcraft trial without adding proof of more recent activities.

Progress was therefore slow, and the winter dragged on without a sign that success was near. This left the Widow in a private quandary. On the one hand, the longer they waited to make their attempt to disenchant the bear, the greater grew the likelihood that someone would notice his visits to the cottage or see some sign of the questionable research in which the Widow and her daughters were engaged. On the other hand, the Widow was well aware of the dangers inherent in casting an improperly constructed or too-hasty spell; too, the thought of crossing Dee and Kelly continued to make her nervous. The only solution to the dilemma was to abandon the bear to his unpleasant fate, and this her conscience would not allow. As January gave way to February, and February to March, the Widow's anxiety increased, though she drew no nearer to a decision than the work appeared to be to a conclusion.

◆   ◆   ◆

The arrival of Mistress Townsend at the Widow's cottage in the first week of March finally put an end to this state of affairs. Mistress Townsend appeared in mid-afternoon, wearing a look of determination and a bulging hamper strapped to her back. Blanche let her into the cottage, and the Widow took one look and burst into greetings before her visitor could open her mouth.

"Why, Mistress Townsend, 'tis good to see you," the Widow said mendaciously. "But I wish you had told me at church last Sunday if you needed cough remedies and fleabane for your charity basket! I might have brought them into town tomorrow, and saved you walking all this way with such a heavy load. Help Mistress Townsend with her hamper, Blanche; Rosamund, fetch her some camomile tea, while I search out those crocks we sealed up yesterday."

The girls did as they were bid, suppressing smiles. By the time they finished fussing over Mistress Townsend, she had accepted the fact that she had been outmaneuvered once again, and the Widow Arden would not accept the charity she had brought. Not only had her walk from the village been in vain, but she would have to carry the full load back with her. The thought did not improve her temper. "Thank you for all your bounty," she said sourly.

"'Tis the least we can do," the Widow answered, setting another crock on the table.

Mistress Townsend watched the line of jars grow, and the lines at the corners of her mouth deepened. "I haven't room for so many," she said. "I'll take one or two, no more, and then be off."

"You'll not stay and eat with us?" the Widow said solicitously.

The lines around Mistress Townsend's mouth deepened further. "Nay, I must be home by dark."

"Why's that?" Rosamund asked politely as she poured camomile tea into a handleless mug.

"I think it unsafe to wander so close to the woods after nightfall," Mistress Townsend answered. She sniffed, and added, "And so you all should think as well, had you more sense."

Rosamund stiffened with indignation and opened her mouth. The Widow glanced at her and said hastily, "We've become accustomed to the forest and its ways."

"'Tis not its ways that are a danger to you, but its beasts," Mistress Townsend snapped. She saw their blank expressions and said less sharply, "You cannot mean you've not heard about the bear!"

Blanche paled. Rosamund jerked and nearly burned her hand on the kettle she was still holding. "Bear?" said the Widow in a strained voice. "What bear?"

Gratified by these reactions, Mistress Townsend unbent a little. "I thought surely that you would have heard. There is a bear about the forest, and near to Mortlak; Master Milling saw its tracks i'the snow on Thursday last, as he was coming back from Richmond. An the beast stay nigh, you should have a care where your wanderings take you." She looked pointedly at Rosamund as she spoke.

"My girls have no need to wander in the woods at this time of year," The Widow said with a touch of sharpness. "'Tis not the season for gathering herbs."

"That's as may be," Mistress Townsend said. "But all the same, I tell you, have a care. There's no fence about the forest, to keep creatures in or out." She saw how white Blanche's face had become, and said in a kinder tone, "There, child, I did not mean to fret thee. Belike you'll not have need to watch your steps for long. Master Kirton speaks of a hunting party, and if that fails, no doubt a bear-catcher will come down from London."

Blanche grew, if possible, paler than before. "'Tis kind of you to tell us, Mistress Townsend," the Widow said quickly. "Now we may take precautions, until the hunt is done."

"'Twould certainly be wise," Mistress Townsend said, pleased that for once her warnings seemed to be accepted. She made several more suggestions, then departed with a warm glow of self-satisfaction.

◆　　　◆　　　◆

The moment the door closed behind Mistress Townsend, Blanche and Rosamund both began trying to talk at once, and the Widow had some trouble making herself heard above the din.

"One at a time," she said. "Else I can make no sense of what you tell me. Blanche, thou'rt eldest; begin."

"Mother, what can we do?" Blanche cried. "They'll kill the poor bear, or use him for a bear-baiting!"

"Belike, and belike not," the Widow said. "'Tis no ordinary bear they go a-hunting. An he be warned, they'll likely find no trace of him."

"And that's the sum of thy council?" Rosamund said indignantly. "To warn the bear, and do no more?"

"What more can we do?" Blanche said in despairing tones. "Master Kirton will not set aside his hunting for our asking, and our spell to free the bear is not yet ready."

"Thou'rt right, Blanche," the Widow said with a sigh. "Yet I think we must make our attempt to break this spell soon. It may be our only chance to try."

"Thinkest thou we may succeed, then?" Blanche asked eagerly.

"I've small hope of it," the Widow admitted. "But small hope is better than none, and we've no other choice. Bar the door, Rose, and both of you come sit with me. We've much to plan."

◆　　　◆　　　◆

The three women spent the remainder of the day bent over the table, arguing over each detail and scribbling the agreed-upon results on the girls' horn slates. Gradually, the design of the spell took shape. They were still hard at work when Hugh arrived that evening. Blanche's face lit with relief when she saw the bear, and she set her slate aside at once.

"Come in, bear," she urged. "Quickly, before thou'rt seen. We've much to tell thee."

Hugh's surprise at this unusual greeting changed quickly to alarm as Blanche recounted, in considerable detail, Mistress Townsend's unexpected visit that afternoon. Something in the way she sat and the tone of her voice made Hugh think, for the first time, of what the consequences might be if he were found at the Widow's home. Muddled as his mind was, it had never occurred to him that his visits might bring trouble to the Widow and her daughters, but it was clear, now that he thought of it, that this was the case. That consideration loomed far larger than his own danger; as soon as he understood, he got to his feet and lumbered toward the door, his paws knocking the rush mats askew as he shuffled across them.

Rosamund jumped up and ran in front of him. "Thou'lt not leave before we've even told thee of our plans," she declared firmly.

Hugh studied her for an instant, then growled, deep in his throat.

"Bear!" Blanche said in a horror-stricken tone. "Thou dost not mean it!"

Hugh winced inwardly, but he growled again, and this time he showed his teeth. He had had all winter to become familiar with Rosamund's stubborn streak, and without a voice he had no other way to make her move aside.

"Stop that, thou ungracious lump!" Rosamund said, unimpressed. She set her back firmly against the door and went on, "We've spent this day devising a way to break thy bonds, and

Mother thinks it may succeed. An it does, the hunters are no danger to thee, and thou'lt have no reason for this hasty flight."

Hugh looked at her, then turned his black, beady eyes toward the Widow, and his ears twitched.

"Rosamund speaks true," the Widow told him. "Wilt thou listen?"

After a moment's hesitation, Hugh nodded. The Widow gave a relieved sigh and began outlining the proposed spell they hoped would disenchant him. "There's no certainty 'twill work," she cautioned when she finished, "nor even that 'twill do thee no more harm. 'Tis thy part to agree to this attempt, or not. Dost thou understand me, bear?"

Hugh nodded again. He sat on his haunches and cocked his head to one side, considering. The spell described by the Widow was like none he had ever heard of before, but he knew little of mortal magic. He looked at the Widow again and whined, deep in his throat.

The Widow stared, completely at a loss. Blanche leaned forward. "Wouldst thou know more, bear?" she asked, and Hugh nodded emphatically.

The lopsided explanation went on well into the night. Hugh tried hard to understand, to decide whether the spell would have a chance of succeeding or would only make matters worse, but he was defeated by the complexity of the arrangements. His frustration was even greater because he knew that once he would have had no trouble whatever comprehending what Blanche and Rosamund were telling him.

After a time, it occurred to Hugh that being entirely a bear would be better than this half-and-half state. He stopped trying to understand, and when the Widow asked anxiously if he would chance the spell, he nodded at once. If the attempt made matters worse, it would not matter, because he would not know. In a way, even that would be a relief, and if nothing else it would eliminate the danger his continued visits posed to the Widow and her daughters. Hugh sighed and settled by the fireplace to sleep while the Widow and Rosamund went back to their notes. Only Blanche cast a look of concern in his direction, and she did not voice her disquiet.

CHAPTER · ELEVEN

◆

"When it was time to go to bed, the mother told the bear, 'Stay there by the fire, where you will be safe from the storm.' So the bear slept all night by the fire, and in the morning the two girls opened the door and let him go back out into the forest.

"After that, the bear came back every evening to sleep by the hearth. The girls liked his company, and they became so accustomed to his visits that they always left the door unfastened until their black friend had arrived."

◆

IN SPITE OF THE URGENCY FELT BY ROSAMUND AND Blanche, it was nearly a week before all the preparations for the bear's disenchantment were complete. Some of the ingredients the Widow had chosen were not easily come by or required painstaking grinding, measuring, and mixing. Blanche took these tasks on herself, while Rosamund and her mother searched the woods and garden for the first swelling hawthorn buds and the early shoots of violets and wormwood. Their everyday chores were neglected while they gathered dry branches of oak and ash and rowan wood, or searched their mending piles for red-dyed thread to knot into an intricate web. Each evening, they went over the day's work with the bear, anxiously asking his opinions and advice.

The most time-consuming task was the preparation of a special ink to be used in the early part of the spell. Blanche spent half a day boiling dried rosemary leaves and rue in the copper kettle, hovering constantly nearby to make sure the brew neither stopped boiling nor boiled dry. When the fragrant mixture had cooled, she poured it into a new crock and added three juniper berries. Then the crock had to stand untouched in a cool corner for four days, after which the liquid inside was pressed through a linen cloth and sweetened with a drop of rosewater. Only then could it be used to draw a circle, a square, and a cross on one side of a dried oak leaf, and the word "return" on the other.

At last everything was finished. Blanche and Rosamund packed two willow baskets with the tools, ingredients, rushlights, and cloths, while the Widow tied their carefully chosen firewood into faggots. Then they waited with considerable impatience for nightfall, and the bear's arrival.

It was full dark when Hugh came at last. Rosamund was inclined to scold him for his tardiness, but the Widow and Blanche refused to let her waste more time in this pursuit. The three women took up their faggots and baskets, and the Widow led the way out into the fields between Mortlak and the woods. The Widow had chosen the time and location of the spell herself. She claimed to base her choices on the theory that the spell Blanche and Rosamund had watched on All Hallows' Eve day was indeed the one which had stricken the bear, and that their counterspell should therefore be in some ways opposite to the one Dee and Kelly had worked. So the Widow proposed that they work their magic at night instead of at midday, and in the open fields instead of in the forest, and Rosamund and Blanche agreed.

The Widow's argument owed as much to her misgivings about the whole enterprise as to her thoughtful consideration of ways to insure its success. No travelers would interrupt them after dark, nor was it likely that their strange antics would be observed. The little hollow the Widow had picked as a location was protected by a screen of bushes, which further reduced their chances of being seen. Even if someone noticed their fire, it would almost certainly be put down to charcoal burners or traveling tinkers. Furthermore, the shifting border of Faerie was somewhere in the woods; it never approached the fields and commons of the village. Thus the Widow was reasonably sure their activities would not attract unwelcomed attention from her unearthly neighbors either.

When they reached the hollow, Rosamund and Blanche untied the three faggots of oak, ash, and rowan branches and laid the wood in alternating layers to make a bonfire, while their mother drew a large circle on the ground with a pointed stick. When she finished, the Widow helped the girls lay out the other ingredients on the ground, then checked everything while Rosamund fidgeted impatiently. The bear hovered in the background, trying to watch and stay out of the way at the same time.

"'Tis ready," the Widow said at last. "To your places, girls. Bear, thou'lt stand beside the fire, and for all our sakes I pray thee not to move before this work is finished."

Hugh nodded and walked clumsily over to the heap of wood. He studied it for a moment, then backed away a little and looked inquiringly at the Widow.

"Come this way a little," the Widow commanded. "There! 'Twill do. Art ready, Blanche? Begin!"

Blanche bent and picked up a tin pannikin, half full of clear water. Carefully, she lifted it above her head, and said in a voice that shook only slightly, "Lord God, Thou rulest all; we pray that Thou wouldst bless our work this night."

"Be with us, Lord," the Widow and Rosamund echoed.

Again, Blanche bent, lowering the pannikin to the ground. From a small linen bag at her feet she took four whole, dried leaves. One by one, she dropped them into the water, saying as she did, "As these dead leaves soften and return to a semblance of themselves, so let our living friend return to his true form. Fiat."

As Blanche picked up the pannikin and rose, the Widow began to speak. "Lord God, Thou rulest all; we pray that Thou wouldst bless our work this night."

"Be with us, Lord," said Rosamund and Blanche.

The Widow picked up a small linen bag, very similar to the one Blanche had used. She poured its powdery, sweet-scented contents into her left hand and dropped the bag, then flung the powder into the air with a wide, sweeping motion. "As the winds of spring return to this cold land, so let this bear return to his true form. Fiat." She drew her arms into her chest in a swift, complex gesture, then let them fall to her sides as Rosamund in turn began to repeat the blessing prayer.

Again the Widow and Blanche responded. Rosamund stooped and picked up a clod of dirt and a third linen bag. From the bag, she poured the freshly gathered tokens of returning life: the curling green shoots of new violets; the silvery, feather-edged knots of the first wormwood leaves; the swollen, reddish leaf-buds of hawthorn and apple, just beginning to break. She crumbled the dirt in her hand and mixed it with the greens, saying as she did, "As these plants return from their winter sleep i'the earth, so let our friend return to his true form. Fiat."

"So have we said; so let it be," the three women said together. Rosamund scattered her dirt and herbs over the unlit pile of wood, while Blanche lifted her pannikin of water over her head. The Widow spread her arms once more and began a long recitation in a singsong voice. A puff of air swept over the hollow, ruffling the bear's fur and bringing with it the damp, cold smells of late winter or very early spring. Blanche shivered very slightly, and a drop of water fell from the upraised pannikin onto her cheek.

The Widow finished, and Blanche lowered her arms. Rosamund knelt beside the pile of wood and carefully tipped four glowing coals out of the small stone crock in which they had been carried to the hollow. The coals fell among the smallest twigs, which caught quickly. Rosamund rose and backed away, and for a moment there was no sound or movement but the crackling of the growing fire and the hungry flicker of the flames. Then the Widow crossed her arms against her chest and began to chant again.

Hugh stood like a statue through the first half of the spell-casting. He felt nothing, no hint of change nor pull of magic, and his last faint hope began to die. His head drooped, and if it had not been for the Widow's warning he would have walked away in the middle of the spell. But that warning, and some lingering memory of courtesy, held him where he was through the whole long process in spite of his despair.

Sparks rose snapping on the heat of the bonfire, making a scintillating column against the dark. The Widow raised her arms for the final invocation. Blanche, still holding the pannikin of water, stepped closer to the fire. On the other side of the fire, Rosamund picked up the oak leaf inscribed with the laboriously made ink. As the Widow began the final line, Rosamund dropped the leaf into the fire. For the barest instant, the leaf lay among the flames; then it curled and charred and vanished. Hugh felt a stab of pain like the cut of a sword, and Blanche flung the pannikin of water onto the blaze.

With a fierce hiss, a cloud of smoky, herb-scented steam billowed out of the fire. There was far more of it than could be accounted for by the amount of water Blanche had flung. The cloud spread quickly in all directions, hiding Hugh and the three women completely from each other's sight. Only the light from the fire was visible, a dim, reddish glow at the center of the mist.

The Widow's voice rang through the hollow in the final "Fiat!" The fire flared once and died. The scented cloud hung a moment longer, then broke apart and vanished, leaving the Widow and her daughters blinking at the silent darkness. A shadow moved among the other shadows in the center of the circle, and Blanche said uncertainly, "Bear?"

Hugh shook himself to rid his fur of the bits of ash and leaves that had settled on him during the spell, and without thinking said, "My name's Hugh." He blinked at the ragged sound of his own voice, and realized that the spell had been at least partially successful. His mind was clear, and he could talk again.

"We've done the thing!" Rosamund cried triumphantly.

Blanche stepped forward eagerly, then stopped short. "Nay," she said in a flat voice. "He's still a bear."

"But a most uncommon bear, I do assure you," Hugh said. His voice rasped in his bear's throat, but the discomfort was nothing compared to the pleasure of being able to speak.

"The bear speaks?" the Widow said incredulously, coming around the remains of the bonfire.

"Aye, and you have my gratitude for't," Hugh answered. "If there's a service I may do you, you have but to ask."

"This is a hopeful sign, though all unlooked for," the Widow said.

"Then dost thou think we should make another attempt?" Blanche asked quickly.

"Nay, Blanche, only a fool repeats a spell that's partly failed. We must consider what this means before we try again."

"But not here," Rosamund said pointedly. The Widow laughed and agreed, and the women began gathering up their belongings to carry back to the cottage, where they could discuss the effects of their spell in relative comfort.

◆   ◆   ◆

At the instant Blanche began the spell, Hugh's brother John sat bolt upright in bed. It took him an instant to realize what had awakened him; then he threw on his clothes and pulled on his boots as fast as he could move his hands to do so. He was out the door and halfway down the street, heading for the forest, before his conscious mind fully grasped that finally and with certainty he knew where Hugh was. As soon as he realized it, he broke into a run.

◆   ◆   ◆

In the house of Master John Dee, the quartz globe flared redly in the empty study. It rocked slightly, then rolled across the table and dropped off the edge. The thump it made as it hit the floor echoed through the house with unnatural loudness, and summoned Dee and Kelly to the study in time to be half blinded by a second, more brilliant flash of light. When their eyes cleared the globe lay beneath the front window, quiescent once more.

The two men looked at each other in horrified speculation. Kelly had just time to scoop the crystal up and restore it to its accustomed place before one of the housemaids arrived, half dressed and frantic with fear of fire (that being the first explanation she thought of for the queer red light that had awakened her). It took considerable time and all Dee's diplomacy to soothe the girl, and by that time half of the other servants and most of the family were also awake and demanding explanations. Neither Dee nor Kelly got much sleep during the remainder of the night.

◆   ◆   ◆

Mistress Rundel's servant girl, Joan Bowes, was also awake, though not for any arcane reason. Earlier in the day, she had complained of a putrid sore throat coming on, and been convincing enough to be excused from her duties to the relative comfort of her narrow bed in the attic at the top of the house. The mid-afternoon nap, though pleasant, had made her unusually restless that night, and she had slipped out of bed to kneel by the window and watch for the fall of a wishing star.

So it was that Joan was looking out over the dark fields and roads when Rosamund lit the bonfire for the spell. The flare of light was clearly visible from the attic window, and Joan at once lost interest in gazing at the stars. She dismissed the impulse to assign responsibility for the fire to tinkers or peddlers, and seized at once on the far more interesting idea of witches or fairies. But though she leaned forward over the sill and squinted with all her might, the distance was much too great for her to make out any figures around the fire. She was still watching when the fire went out, even more abruptly than it had begun. Joan blinked, and her lips curved in a small, satisfied smile as she stored her observations carefully in her memory against the time when they might become useful.

♦   ♦   ♦

And in the realm of Faerie, a tremor passed through the crystalline night air, like a shimmer on a soap bubble, and was gone.

Brief though it was, it did not go unnoticed. Throughout Faerie, strange night creatures paused to raise their heads and peer about with wide, dark eyes, or sniff the air questioningly for an instant before returning to their occupations. Only two in all that unnatural realm, however, had more response than that. Madini stiffened as the invisible ripple passed her, and her dark eyes flamed. She waited, and when the strange phenomenon was not repeated she frowned, and went to call her fellow conspirators to see if she could discover what had happened and how it might affect their plans.

On the opposite side of the palace, the sleepless Faerie Queen walked through a garden made for night, where ghost-white blossoms reflected moonlight and dark leaves shed a subtle scent into the air. Like her subjects, the Queen lifted her head as the tremor in the air went past, but when she lowered it there was an infinitesimal line between her perfect eyebrows. She stood motionless for a long time amid the flowers, breathing in their perfume. Then she turned and went back to her rooms without finishing her walk.

CHAPTER · TWELVE

"When spring came and the trees began to turn green, the bear said to the girls, 'The time has come for me to leave, and I will not come back again until the end of summer.' 'Where are you going, bear?' asked Snow White. 'Back to the forest, where I can guard my treasure from the wicked dwarfs. In winter they cannot come up through the frozen ground, but as soon as the earth has warmed a little they come out to pry and steal. Once they have laid their hands on something and hidden it in their caves, it seldom sees daylight again.'"

DESPITE HIS RESTORED CLARITY OF MIND, HUGH WAS not immediately aware of his brother's approach. Unlike Rosamund and Blanche, who considered their partial success to be little better than an outright failure, Hugh was pleased indeed. The restoration of his mind and voice was far more than he had expected, and the relief he felt left him no room to notice more subtle tugs at his emotions. It was not until he was back in the Widow Arden's cottage, lying before the hearth to watch the Widow and her daughters unload their baskets, that he felt the stirring at the back of his mind that told him John was somewhere near.

Hugh stretched lazily, reveling in the knowledge that now he could *tell* the Widow what he knew. He searched his mind for an elegant phrase or two to convey his meaning. Before he found them, there was a knock at the door.

The stricken expressions on the faces of the Widow and her daughters brought Hugh to his feet with a low growl. Blanche turned frightened eyes to him and whispered, "Hush! They must not find thee here, dear bear."

"The blanket!" Rose said in an equally low voice. "Lie down, bear, and we'll drape it over thee."

"Hurry, girls," the Widow said. She whisked the baskets out of sight behind the table and cast a quick eye around the room in search of other signs of their unorthodox excursion. Finding none, she started toward the door, just as the knock was repeated with polite insistence.

♦   ♦   ♦

John had run nearly all the way from Mortlak, and he was still panting when the Widow opened her door. "Good evening, Mistress," he said between puffs. He paused, unsure of how to phrase his questions. "May I come in?"

"No," the Widow said firmly. "If you have business with me, tell it to me here; if not, be off with you. The hour's a late one for an honest man to call."

"True," John said. "But my need's urgent." Over the Widow's shoulder he caught a glimpse of the white faces of the girls, standing in front of the hearth, and he gave them his most charming smile. "I'm no rogue, I do assure you."

His voice carried clearly into the room, and Hugh recognized it at once. He surged to his feet and shook off the blanket Rosamund and Blanche had hidden him under. "John!" he shouted, and was immediately stricken with a fit of coughing.

Afraid that Hugh was somehow being held prisoner, John shoved hard at the door. The frightened Widow tried to shut it in his face; Rosamund ran to help her mother, and Blanche stood in front of the bear and spread her skirts in a futile attempt to hide him.

"'Tis my brother John!" Hugh said hastily. "Let him in, I pray you."

As soon as she understood, the Widow stepped back and let John enter, though not without misgivings. John went straight across the room and knelt at the bear's side. "Hugh?" he said uncertainly, and then, "Oh, Hugh!"

"'Tis not so bad as it seems," the bear told him. "Though that's ill enough, I warrant thee."

"I've been seeking thee these three months past," John said, his voice muffled against the thick fur of the bear's neck. "Where hast thou been?"

"Here," Hugh replied. "And in the forest. No more than that, I think, though before tonight my memory's less than clear."

John raised his head and eyed the bear narrowly. "How's that?"

"The tale's a long one, and talking irks my throat," Hugh said. "Sit down and speak with these my benefactors, and I'll add what things I must."

Reminded of his audience, John rose and turned. "Forgive my lack of courtesy, Mistresses," he said, bowing extravagantly. The joy of having found Hugh at last, and the relief of finding him unharmed, was making John feel as light-headed as if he'd been drinking Faerie wine.

"'Tis excusable, I think," the Widow said. "It seems we were at cross-purposes when you arrived; for that, I beg your pardon."

"'Tis freely given," John replied. "But will you tell your story? I would know how it happens that my brother's welcomed here in such unlikely guise."

"We'll tell you, an you'll do the same," Rosamund said, coming forward to stand beside her mother.

"Why, Rosamund, well met!" John said, recognizing her at once. "I'll tell you whate'er you will."

"Knowest thou this man, Rose?" the Widow said in surprise.

"I do not think so," Rosamund said doubtfully.

"I well believe you have forgot a common peddler," John said, "but how has Rose forgot my most uncommon rose?"

Rosamund stared for a moment, then blushed a fiery red. Blanche looked from her sister to John and asked, "Then 'twas you who plucked a rose for her in late October?"

"It was," John said. "And were a rosebush near, I'd give you one as well, though I know not your name."

"My daughter's name is Blanche," the Widow said in a tone of mild censure. "And I am Widow Arden. I can see that we have much to talk on; sit down, and let's begin."

This was easier to say than do; the Widow's tiny cottage had been overcrowded even before John's arrival. Eventually they all found places: Rosamund and Blanche on the straw-stuffed sleeping pallet, the bear on the floor before the hearth, and the Widow on the single storage chest beside the table. John, though offered his choice of more comfortable places, preferred to sit on the rush-covered floor beside his brother, an act of affection that did him no disservice in the eyes of his hostesses.

The Widow and her daughters told their tales first, guessing that it would be easier for John to answer their questions once his own had been answered. Both John and Hugh listened without interrupting, but as soon as the Widow finished John said, "And are you certain Dee and Kelly are the two you saw in the forest?"

"We're certain," Rosamund said. She put up her chin and went on with a trace of belligerence, "And you should not question us further till your own tale's told."

"Rose, mind thy manners!" the Widow said.

"Well, but I can see that he'd not think to tell us anything if no one reminded him," Rosamund said unrepentantly. "And our curiosity's as great as his."

John laughed despite himself. "I stand corrected. What would you know?"

"Who are you, you and your brother bear?" Rosamund asked promptly.

"I'm called John Rimer, and this bear's my brother Hugh," John replied with equal promptness. "What more?"

Rosamund's eyes flashed angrily. "That's no answer!"

"If you prefer not to tell us, we'll not compel you," Blanche said in a quiet voice. "You have no need to mock at us."

"She's right," Hugh said, startling them all with the deep, rumbling rasp of his voice. "And they've the right to know, John."

John hesitated. "I beg your pardons all," he said finally. "My intent was not to mock you; 'twas but habit. I have long been used to avoiding all such questions."

"Our pardon waits upon your answer," Rosamund said.

"Hugh and I are the sons of the Queen of Faerie by a mortal lover," John said with quiet simplicity.

The Widow's eyebrows rose. "If that be so, how is it that you two have come to such a pass as this? I'd think the Faerie Queen could do somewhat to guard her sons."

"What she could do, she did; 'twas precious little," John said, and his voice was bitter. "There was no remedy for my brother's transformation. Faerie learning doth not encompass much of mortal magic, and she would not give me leave to search outside her lands, because she said the blame was mine."

"What?" Hugh's voice was a muffled roar that made everyone else jump.

"Softly, softly," John said. "I did not mean she thought the spell was mine. She said only that 'twas my wanderings that drew it to thee, and would not lift her ban."

"What ban is that?" Rosamund demanded.

Briefly, John described his most recent return to Faerie and the Queen's unexpected refusal to let him leave again. "Then when Hugh began to be . . . affected, she would not heed me, nor let me go to seek a remedy. She said that 'twas some carelessness of mine that drew the eyes of mortal wizards to Faerie, and to Hugh, and she forbade me once again to leave her lands."

"And yet you left?" Blanche said. Her eyes were wide with wonder and sympathy.

John shrugged. "What choice had I? There was no help for Hugh in Faerie."

Rosamund's head moved unconsciously in the smallest of approving nods, but the Widow Arden frowned. "So you're here in defiance of your mother and your Queen. And in another month the border of Faerie will be open and unlocked."

"Do not trouble yourself with thinking that she'll look for me or torment you for standing as my friends," John said. "'Tis not her way. Faerie's done with both of us, unless I try to return."

Blanche, who had been studying John with care throughout his narrative, leaned forward. "How is it that you have such a taste for mortal lands, and your brother has it not? Or have I mistaken the matter entirely?"

"'Twas a difference in our raising," John said. "I've told you that our father was a mortal man, and that's the root of it. He was a poet from the north, near Ercildoune; his name was Thomas Learmont, sometimes called the Rhymer. He was up in the hills, alone, when he saw our mother riding by and called to her. She tricked a promise from him: seven years of service to her. Though I doubt that there was great need for trickery on either side of that bargain; he was as eager to go as she to have him. So she brought him back to Faerie, and to keep him true she laid it on him not to speak until his time of service was done.

"When the seven years were up, the Queen had one son by Thomas and was carrying another. She did not want him to leave, I'm told, but the laws of Faerie have a certain . . . implacability about them." John glanced at Hugh, then looked away. "Seven years he'd promised, and seven years she'd had, and she could not hold him longer. Nor could he stay, though he'd leave his sons behind.

"Our father could not be content with that decree. The child in the Queen's womb he could not touch, but me he stole away the night he left."

"You?" Rosamund said.

"Aye, I'm the elder by two years," John replied, and his lips twisted in a wry smile. "For all the good it's been to me."

He shook himself, and continued, "The Queen gave chase as soon as she discovered what her lover had done, but she could not ride as headlong as she wished for fear of harming the child within her. So when she came up with my father at last, she was too late to take me back. For Father'd learned more than a little in his time in Faerie; he'd gone straight to a priest and had me baptized."

"I remember," Rosamund said. "When you gave me the rose, you said that you were baptized Thomas."

"'Twas true," John said. "And after that, the Faerie Queen could not touch me 'gainst my father's will. 'Tis why I'm now called John; my mother took a dislike to the name my father gave me, and will not suffer it to be used in Faerie."

"I am much amazed, if that was all she did," the Widow commented.

"Oh, she was greatly angered, of course, yet Faerie folk admire such cleverness, even when 'tis they that lose by it. So the Queen gave her lover one last gift before she returned to her own land. She said that, since in Faerie she'd silenced his tongue to keep him true, his tongue would speak the truth and truth alone now that 'twas no more silent. Then she left."

"So you were raised a mortal?" the Widow said.

"In the main," John replied. "Yet Faerie kept close watch on me, and I learned as much from them as from my teachers. Then, too, my father could not lie when I grew old enough to question him about my mother." He smiled slightly. "I think 'twas half the reason she bestowed on him his truthful tongue."

"It seems a most uncomfortable present," Rosamund said, frowning.

John shrugged. "'Twas double-edged, as are most Faerie gifts. My father learned to use it well; his prophecies are famous still."

"How did you come to know your brother?" Blanche asked, nodding at Hugh.

"When I was old enough to understand, my mother came for

me," John said. "Twice each year, at May Eve and Midsummer, she took me to join the Faerie revels. And when I turned fifteen, I chose to stay in Faerie. Yet I never lost my fondness for travel in the mortal world, and that, it seems, has been my bane and Hugh's together."

"Belike you're wrong to say so," the Widow said thoughtfully. "If 'twas Dee and Kelly's work that changed your brother thus, I do not think 'twas done apurpose."

"Why not?" Hugh growled.

"My daughters watched the greater part of that spell-casting, yet they heard no mention of thy name. Nor did the wizards speak of bears, nor transformations, nor fay with mortal blood."

"I fear I do not apprehend your meaning," John said, frowning.

The Widow looked at him in surprise. "Spells need such clear direction, if they're to work specific tasks. Know you so little of magic?"

"Of Faerie magic I doubt not I know more than you," John answered. "But I've never learned much of mortal spells. It seems they differ more than I'd supposed."

"The intention of those wizards doth not matter, but only that we break their spell," Rosamund said impatiently.

"'Tis not so simple, Rose," the Widow said, shaking her head.

"Your spells have done much good already," Hugh said with some anxiety. "And now you know still more."

"Our chances would be better now, 'tis true, an this were but a change of shape," the Widow said reluctantly. "But I think the spell is more than that. I think it's torn some part of thee away, and little more can I or anyone do for thee unless it be returned."

"Then we must study how to fetch it back," John said. The Widow looked at him with a kind of surprised horror, and he smiled. "Nay, Mistress Arden, I'll ask no more of you. This work's for me, and Hugh."

"For you and Hugh?" Rosamund said in an indignant tone. "Would you have us wash our hands of him?"

"You've done enough," John answered. "You've given Hugh

himself again, which all of Faerie could not do. And you have given me hope, which of late I've not had in great quantity. The coming tasks will be a danger I've no wish to lead you into."

"'Twas dangerous to watch the wizards at their work," Blanche pointed out. "And also to give aid and shelter to a bear. An untried spell's a danger; so, too, is a walk in Faerie. We're not afraid of danger."

"Aye," Hugh rumbled. "'Tis why I'll not come again."

Blanche and Rosamund stared in shock, then broke into a volley of protests. "Girls!" the Widow said sharply, and they subsided.

"What dost thou mean by this, sir bear?" Blanche said more calmly.

"As I said. If my presence here was known, you'd be hanged for witches. I did not realize it till tonight, but now I know, and I'll not risk it even if you're willing."

"What of thine own risk?" Blanche cried. "Tomorrow's Master Kirton's hunt!"

Hugh chuckled, and his furred back shook. "Master Kirton is small danger to me now."

John's expression, which had been first surprised and then thoughtful, slowly changed to devilish glee. "Small danger, indeed! This hunt will not soon be forgotten, I warrant you!"

Rosamund immediately began trying to pry some further explanation out of the brothers. She was not successful, though her efforts distracted Blanche and the Widow from Hugh's expressed determination not to return to the cottage. By the evening's end, they were on familiar terms with John as well as Hugh, and Rosamund had wormed a promise out of the two brothers to come back after the hunt and tell them what had happened.

Once this was settled, the Widow, who had been keeping a careful eye on the dwindling rushlight, pointed out that the hour was late indeed. John and Hugh courteously rose to leave at once. Blanche was only just able to swallow a protest at the bear's departure by reminding herself that John was, after all, Hugh's brother, and that they had been separated for three months. She watched with quiet resentment as the bear followed John out the door, then silently chided herself for her unwarranted pique.

Outside, John and Hugh walked a short way down the road and stopped. They waited there, talking in low voices, until the lights from the Widow's cottage had been out some time. Then John walked back to the Widow's gate. He picked up a nearby twig and scratched a symbol on the ground, then pulled up a tuft of dried grass and shredded it over the drawing until the marks were completely hidden. He went back to Hugh and nodded. The two brothers, man and bear, turned together and disappeared among the forest shadows.

CHAPTER · THIRTEEN

◆

"Snow White was sorry to see the bear leave, but she held the door open for him as he asked. As the bear went out, he brushed against the latch and tore away some of his fur. Snow White thought for a moment that she saw a gleam of gold underneath, but she could not be sure. The bear ran on into the forest, and was soon out of sight."

◆

THE MORNING OF MASTER KIRTON'S BEAR HUNT dawned grey and cool, but the weather did not dampen the enthusiasm of the people who had come to join in the sport. The unusual entertainment drew a large crowd of onlookers in addition to the participants; half the village of Mortlak lined the streets from dawn onward, hoping to see the hunt ride out. Sawyers and shopkeepers, charcoal burners and weavers, wine merchants and watermen, all found some errand or excuse to take them out into the streets. Kitchen maids slipped away while carrying in the wash water, and those whose work kept them indoors found reasons to linger near windows.

The hounds, unused to such confusion at the beginning of a

hunt, milled about uneasily as the men and women mounted their horses. Master Kirton had brought a bear ward down from London, so that at least one member of the hunt would be used to handling bears. The bear ward's mastiffs had come with him; they stood behind the horses, growling ferociously at Master Kirton's hounds and shaking their iron-spiked collars.

The hunt left Mortlak at around ten in the morning, and shortly afterward it passed the Widow Arden's cottage. A few of the hounds lowered their heads to sniff the path that led to the Widow's door, but the symbol John had scratched beside the gate was a strong one, and the dogs continued on without giving their masters a hint that they had smelled the musky odor of a bear. Inside the cottage, the women watched with deep misgivings as the cavalcade went by, but there was nothing they could do but pray that Hugh had been right to be so unafraid of this gay, deadly company. Shortly after, they heard the belling of the hounds in the forest, and knew the bear hunt had begun in earnest.

◆　　　◆　　　◆

In a small, brushy hollow behind the half-rotted trunk of a fallen beech, John and Hugh heard the first of the hounds give tongue. At first, the cry was uncertain; Master Kirton's dogs had been trained to the scent of hares and deer, not bears. Then a second dog joined in, and the cry firmed and deepened as the rest of the pack took it up. Bear and man exchanged looks as the sound grew louder. Then John nodded, and the two slipped out of the concealing bushes and headed deeper into the forest.

The hounds found the hollow soon after John and Hugh left it, and the fresh scent made them wild. The mastiffs, too, recognized the smell, and the bear ward had difficulty restraining them. The huntsmen pressed forward eagerly as the hounds leapt over the hollow, each man hoping to be the first to catch sight of the quarry. The trail twisted among the trees and ended abruptly at the edge of a clearing packed with shrubs and brambles that showed no sign of the passage of any large animal.

The master of the hounds was furious, convinced that his dogs had "hunted counter" by following the traces of a hare, and his temper was not improved by the pithy comments of the London bear ward. He tried to call the pack together, to return to the hollow and try to pick up the correct trail, but less than half of the hounds came back at the call of his horn. The others scattered among the trees on either side of the clearing and were soon lost to sight.

The remaining hounds cast about for a new scent, and soon the hunt was off once more. The dogs ran as if they were possessed of demons, and the hunt strung out behind them. The hounds' excitement made the hunters certain that the bear was near, and they urged their horses on, each anxious to be the first to spy it. The route wound through the darkest parts of the forest, along the boggy banks of streams, up and down steep hills. Low branches whipped the riders' faces constantly, but when they tried to pull their horses up, they discovered that they could not do so. They could only ride on and on, like the Wild Hunt itself, following the hounds deeper into the shadowy forest on the track of a quarry they never saw.

The men and women who had been left behind by the hurtling rush of the foremost riders had no better luck in remaining together. Here and there, a rider caught sight of a broad, furred back disappearing among the trees. With a shout of triumph, the hunter would spur his horse onward, only to have the creature vanish without leaving so much as a footprint. The hunt became more and more scattered, and the riders began to lose sight of each other. At first, few of them were concerned, for each could plainly hear the crashing and hallooing of his companions up ahead. Each followed the noise, plunging onward until the calls ceased abruptly, and he found himself alone and lost in the heart of the forest.

A mist began to rise, thick and cold, hiding the traces of the horses' passage and turning the forest into an eerie, shifting maze.

It writhed in and out among the long, bare tree trunks like a living thing, and through occasional, unexpected gaps the lost and frightened hunters glimpsed impossible things. In one part of the forest, a bear three times the size of a man roared once at a huntsman and then vanished, leaving claw marks deep in the bark of an oak, while elsewhere men swore they'd seen their quarry holding converse with the hunt master. Here a man heard roaring all around him but never saw the smallest sign of the bear's presence; there two women all but fainted at the sight of not one but three bears, ghostly white and silent, rising out of the mist on either side of them. One horse, maddened by the heavy scent of bear, threw his rider and ran into the trees, leaving the man lying paralyzed with the fear that in another moment the bear would appear to maul him.

It was nearly sunset when exhausted horses with their weary riders began to emerge, in ones and twos, from the edge of the forest. The horses were flecked with foam and muddy to the croup; their riders' clothes were torn and dirty and their faces showed the marks of branches and tall brush. The hounds were next, panting and footsore. Last of all came the cowering, whimpering mastiffs, none of whom could ever after be made to take part in a bear-baiting.

❖　　❖　　❖

Rosamund and Blanche had strained their ears all day, listening fearfully for the blowing of the morte that would tell them Hugh had been taken. They rejoiced when they saw the first of the hunters riding slowly back toward Mortlak, and they grew happier with every tired man and animal that passed the cottage. By the time the last of them had gone by, it was fully dark, and the girls were impatiently awaiting the arrival of Hugh and John, to tell them what had happened.

They had almost given up when they heard the familiar knocking at the door. The Widow opened it at once, and exclaimed when she saw them. John was leaning heavily against Hugh's side, and he looked very little better than the hunters the girls had watched with such glee. His doublet was muddy and full of leaves, his face was tired and pale, and there were dark circles under his eyes.

The Widow gave a tiny gasp and hurried to help John inside. "A cup of water, Rosamund, and quickly. Blanche, see to the bear."

"Naught's amiss with me," Hugh said.

"Then how has John come to such a sorry state?" Rosamund snapped as she hastened to do her mother's bidding.

"Nay, 'tis no great matter," John said. "I'm tired, that's all."

Rosamund sniffed scornfully. "You look worse than Mother's herbs when all the virtue's been boiled out of them." She pushed him to a seat with one hand and held out the cup of water with the other.

"Thy description's amazingly apt," John replied, taking the cup from her and draining it at a gulp.

"Not so fast; thou'lt do thyself an injury," the Widow said. "How came thee to this pass, Master Rimer? Was it the hunt?"

"In a way." John looked up and smiled suddenly. "'Twas a greater crowd than I'd expected, and 'tis no easy thing to pixy-lead so many. Still, I think 'twill do."

Hugh snorted loudly. "'Twill more than do, brother mine. Robin Goodfellow will envy thee this day's work, if he hears of it."

"You've pixy-led the whole of Master Kirton's hunt?" Blanche said, wide-eyed.

"I thought it would discourage them," John explained in an apologetic tone. "I wanted no more bear hunts."

Rosamund choked on a laugh. "From the look on them as they came homeward, I think you'll get your wish. I doubt there's man or hound among them who'll hunt so much as a rabbit through that forest again."

"Aye. The beasts will bless your day's work," Blanche said.

"An the hunters stay away, I'll be content," John said, and smothered a yawn.

"Cease thy chatter and rest a little," the Widow said in a scolding tone. She set a tin dish half-filled with lentil stew on the table before him. "And eat. Thou'rt all but spent."

"Oh, surely not so bad as that," John said, but he took his eating knife out of his pouch and set to work on the stew with an alacrity that gave the lie to his words.

The Widow watched him for a moment, then nodded in satisfaction and turned to Hugh. "'Twill be a day or two before we know how sure thy brother's work has been. I think thou shouldst keep from sight a while."

"Aye," Rosamund said sagely. "It will be better far if thou'rt not seen. Meantime, we'll study how to steal thy true shape back for thee."

John's head came up quickly, and he spilled stew across his knees. He muttered a curse and brushed at it, which only served to mix the warm stew more thoroughly in with the mud and twigs that already covered his hose. Rosamund laughed. Blanche shot her a reproving look, but John did not seem disturbed.

"Plainly, I'm more tired than I had thought," he said, abandoning his brief effort to improve his appearance. "But I cannot let thee do this, Rosamund. Thy family's done enough already."

"You cannot stop us," Rosamund said, lifting her chin. "And we want to help."

"I think thou'lt need what we can offer," Blanche said quietly but with determination. "Thou'st said already that thou knowest little of mortal magic."

"And you, Mistress Arden?" John said to the Widow. "What say you to this idea?"

The Widow bit her lip. "I like it not," she admitted. "'Tis dangerous to think of crossing Master Dee and Master Kelly, and there's always the chance that the work will be discovered and we'll all be taken up for witches. But I have never liked it, and what

Blanche says is true; thou'lt need our knowledge, an thou hope to restore thy brother." She looked up and smiled wryly. "And will I, nil I, Rosamund at least has set her mind to this. 'Twill be far better an I'm there to aid her."

"No," Hugh rumbled, getting to his feet. "You've done enough, and more."

"If we'd done enough, thou'dst have thy proper form," Blanche said with unusual acerbity; then she bit her lip and dropped her eyes to avoid Hugh's surprised look.

"Mother's right; we'll do this whether you wish or not," Rosamund declared, glaring impartially at both the brothers. "So sit down, and do not trouble us with these foolish arguments."

"'Tis you who're foolish," John said. "Your danger's double: once from these wizards and again from those who'd hang you all as witches if they knew what you're about."

"Our danger's no greater than thine," Rosamund shot back hotly. "Or dost thou think the witch-hunters will pass thee by because thou were of Faerie once?"

"Rosamund, control thy temper." The Widow's voice was cool and disapproving. Rosamund flushed and fell silent. The Widow waited a moment, then added, "I agree with what thou'st said, but I like not the manner of your saying it."

Rosamund smiled triumphantly at John, who said to the Widow in a tone of exasperation, "Thou'rt as foolish as thy daughters!"

"And both of you are near as stubborn," the Widow retorted, looking from Hugh to John. "Blanche spoke true: you know little of mortal magic, and less of hiding from the eyes of those who look for witches beneath each stick and stone. I know somewhat of both, and I know, too, that 'twould be wrong to let you go without our aid because it seems a danger. John cannot keep a bear in Mortlak, but he must live there if he hopes to watch Master Dee. What will you do, if you reject our help?"

"It may be that thou'rt right," John said in a thoughtful tone.

"No!" Hugh said.

"Or it may be that I am but too tired to think," John went on as if Hugh had not spoken. "Perhaps we could continue in the morning?"

The Widow and her daughters agreed at once, the Widow reproaching herself for allowing the argument to go on so long when John was clearly exhausted. John made a token attempt to leave, and was immediately and unanimously stopped. It was clear to all of them, even Hugh, that John was in no condition to make the long walk back to Mortlak. The Widow unrolled the straw pallet and made him lie down while Blanche and Rosamund cleared off the trestle table. Then they took the table down and stacked the pieces on top of the chest, giving them enough room for everyone to sleep on the floor. By the time they finished, John was asleep.

◆   ◆   ◆

John Dee and Edward Kelly were among the few residents of Mortlak who did not crowd the streets to see the bear hunt off. They were busy in the study, checking the symbols they had chalked on the windowsills and lintels of the study as a protection against Faerie, for the unaccountable behavior of the crystal globe troubled them greatly. Knowing nothing of the Faerie Queen's half-mortal sons, nor of the Widow's attempt to free Hugh from the effects of their spell, the wizards had concluded that the midnight flashes they had observed were the result of Faerie meddling.

But the seals were intact and the symbols clear and unblurred, and the men turned to their books in search of some explanation. They found nothing to help them.

"'Tis some flaw in the spell itself," Dee said at last, rubbing his eyes as he straightened up from the volume he had been reading. "We must refrain from working with the crystal till we learn how we have erred."

"Impossible," Kelly said flatly. He had, after much experimentation, discovered that base metal, if treated with certain powders and then exposed to the light of the crystal for a full day, would turn to gold, and to say that he was unwilling to give up this new source of prosperity was a grave understatement.

"You know as well as I the dangers of employing such a tool without full knowledge of its lacks," Dee responded in a tired voice. "Would you see the house burn down around us, or be driven into madness, and all for want of caution?"

"An I agreed with your conjecture, I'd be the first to cover the globe and make use of it no more," Kelly said mendaciously. "But I do not think it is the crystal that's at fault."

"What else could it be, Ned? I can think of no other reason for such misbehavior."

"There are an hundred things more likely than that we've erred! That spell was finely crafted as the Queen's jewels."

"You should be more wary of your pride, Ned," Dee said, shaking his head. "I'll admit I cannot see where we have gone amiss, but there's much in this we do not know."

"Aye," Kelly said swiftly, "and till we've learned some of it you should not lay the blame on our work."

John Dee laughed. "You've a ready tongue, my friend, but you have not yet told me what else may be to blame besides ourselves."

"It may have been some humor of the night," Kelly said airily. "Or wait—the crystal draws its power out of Faerie; how if there's some disturbance there?"

"'Tis possible," Dee said with a troubled frown.

"'Tis more than that; 'tis likely! Or why have we seen no sign of defect in our work ere now? Be sure that 'twas some resonance of Faerie, and now 'tis past. I'll wager that we have no further difficulty."

"I hope you have the right of it, Ned," Dee said, but his expression did not lighten. "I hope, but hope's not certain. Wait a little ere you try the globe again."

"I will not wait," Kelly said, his lips tightening into a thin line.

"Why should I? Faerie has no power to harm us while our protections stand. Now tell me that you'll seek another ally in your work."

Dee sighed. "Nay, Ned, you know that I cannot. There's none who has your gifts and knowledge both."

"You do not need me," Kelly persisted, watching Dee narrowly. "You have the crystal."

"But I cannot see the spirits in it," Dee said. "No, no; I will not have you leave. Do as you will; I'll say no more against it."

Kelly nodded and stroked his beard and went away to prepare a particularly large quantity of base metal for transmutation into gold. If Dee proved right and they were forced to suspend their experiments, he would at least have gained enough to pay his debts.

♦   ♦   ♦

The strange vibration in the air, which was the sign in Faerie of the Widow's spell, troubled Madini greatly, though she would have admitted this to no one save the Faerie Queen herself. For some three weeks she observed each quiver of the leaves and turned to catch each half-seen movement at the edges of her vision. When the Faerie border opened in mid-March, she crossed it twice, performing certain spells on either side; then she called her fellow conspirators together once again.

"Our work's been all for nothing!" she told them in tones of icy rage. "Hugh's gone; John's gone; their mortal taint's purged out of Faerie—and yet they bind us still!" Her voice rose as she spoke and echoed through the oak glen, startling a crested blue bird into flight.

"Softly," Furgen said. "Or the whole forest will hear."

Bochad-Bec snorted. "'Twill not be the first time."

"Thou overgrown toadstool!" Madini sneered. "My anger's justified; I marvel that thou'rt so calm."

"If we knew all thy reasoning, perhaps we would be angry too,"

Furgen said. It looked at Madini from under half-lowered eyelids. "Pray, tell us thy news."

"I've told it, an you had the sense to hear. Do you recall that shiver i'the air some three weeks past?"

Furgen inclined its head. Bochad-Bec snorted again. "Some foolishness or other," the oakman said. "I did not heed it."

"Thou shouldst have done so!" Madini's tone was vicious. "Till then, all had gone as we'd planned. Without John's presence or Hugh's to hold it, Faerie was withdrawing from the mortal world. That shiver was a check on that withdrawal, and now we're bound again, as surely as we were before!"

"It's not the best news," Furgen admitted. "Dost thou know why?"

"An I did, I'd also know what we should do!" Madini snapped.

"That's clear enough," Bochad-Bec said. "We start again."

"Where, and with what?" Madini snarled, rounding on him. "Or didst thou not hear me say that we know not the cause of this?"

"Then we start by looking for it," the dwarf said stolidly. "There's no need to make such a piece of work of it."

"Madini likes to be dramatic in all things," Furgen said absently. "But thy thought's a good one, Bochad-Bec. And here's another: if none of Faerie made this magic, then it came from mortal lands. And who's more likely than the human sorcerers to be at the bottom of it?"

"They're mortals," Bochad-Bec said dismissively. "They have not the power."

"I think they have," Furgen said gently. "Remember, they hold that part of Hugh which is of Faerie. That's enough to tie our realm to earth, if they've learned how to use it."

"'Tis possible," Madini said. Her eyes narrowed. "Canst thou discover how or where Dee and Kelly keep their stolen power?"

Furgen hesitated. "I do not know. They are not fools; they've warded all their doors and windows against Faerie. I can listen, but I dare not look."

"Listen then," Madini said sweetly. "And be back within the week with what thou'st learned."

"I serve thee most obediently," Furgen said in a tone of humble mockery. "Our purposes are much the same."

Madini gave him a thin smile and made a regal departure. The water fay looked after her with cold, unfathomable eyes.

CHAPTER · FOURTEEN

◆

"Soon after, the mother sent the girls into the forest to gather wood for the fire. As they walked along, they came across a large tree which had fallen to the ground. When they came closer, they saw a dwarf with a sour, wrinkled face and a long white beard jumping back and forth beside the tree trunk. The end of his beard was caught in a crack in the tree, and the dwarf was trying to pull it free, but all his twisting and tugging was in vain."

◆

IN THE DAYS THAT FOLLOWED THE BEAR HUNT, JOHN Rimer became a frequent visitor to the Widow's cottage. His presence was necessary as well as welcome, for the Widow Arden knew little of the strange and twisted spells of Faerie. To steal back Hugh's Faerie magic required Faerie lore that only John or Hugh could provide, and Hugh refused to leave the forest lest he be seen and bring the witch-hunters down on his mortal friends. It fell to John to help the Widow and her daughters devise a new enchantment to reverse the spell on Hugh.

John was, however, handsome, young, and well-to-do. Moreover, he was unmarried, and the Widow knew what scandal the gossiping tongues of Mortlak could fabricate from his regular attendance on her daughters. She spent some time considering how best to deal with the potential problem, and then, on the third day following the bear hunt, she made her way to Mortlak to call on Mary Hudson.

Mary greeted the Widow with joy and whisked her up the stairs to her antechamber at once, sending her maids flying to bring hot wine and pillows for her guest. When they were settled in comfort before the fire, the Widow sighed in contentment and said, "Thou art kind, Mary, and good to me, indeed. An thou continue in this fashion, thou'rt like to ne'er be rid of me."

"'Twould be no hardship, I do swear," Mistress Hudson answered. "How dost thou all this winter?"

"Well enough," the Widow replied evasively, thinking of the Faerie bear and the questionable activities that had followed his arrival. "But I did not come to talk of my affairs. What's toward in town?"

Mistress Hudson gave her a sharp look, but only said, "The talk is all of Master Kirton's hunt; hast ever seen such disarray as they returned in? 'Tis said a spirit or a devil haunts the forest in the outward shape of a bear, and that is why it came to such confusion. Hast heard the tales?"

"A handful," the Widow replied. "And to me they sound unlikely."

"I see thou hast no fear of phantom bears," Mistress Hudson said, chuckling. "Well, I've none, neither, but not many are of our mind. There's few who'll brave the woods at night, and some who'll not go nigh it even when the sun is high. The curate speaks of sending off to London for someone to free the forest of the apparition."

"He means to bring an exorcist to Mortlak?" the Widow asked in some alarm.

"He does, but 'tis no matter," Mistress Hudson said. "Such men have much to do; no one will come unless more bears are seen. And even if one came," she added pointedly, "'twould be John Dee he would remark, not thee."

"What meanest thou by that?"

"Dost think that I am blind to the trouble that haunts thy face whene'er someone doth mention magic?" Mary demanded. "Thou dost fret overmuch, I think, but, an thou dost not tell me all, I cannot know how great's thy cause for care."

"I have some little skill, 'tis true, though I have seldom used it," the Widow said, sighing. "The rest I'd tell thee gladly, save that it runs further than what touches me and mine. There's nothing evil in't, I do promise thee, but more I may not say."

"An that's all thou wilt tell, 'twill have to be enough," Mistress Hudson said. "But remember thou must count me as thy friend, whate'er betide, and let me help thee as I may."

"I'll not forget, be sure," the Widow said, and her eyes were very bright. "And thou mayest help me first by telling me what's said of Masters Dee and Kelly in the town."

"So 'tis they who worry thee so much? Nay, I'll not press thee for an answer. Master Dee hath been made much of these past months; 'tis rumored that he's found some new and potent marvel. There's many from the Queen's court who've come to see him, Lord Grey, and Mr. Edmunds of the Privie Chamber, and Sir Francis Walsingham and his lady wife among them, and I know not who else. And, scarce two weeks since, Queen Elizabeth herself rode by Dee's door and called him out to her, and he walked beside her stirrup for the length of the town."

"The Queen herself," the Widow murmured, impressed. "And what of Master Kelly?"

"He hovers near, when he may, and tries to please whome'er might be of use to him," Mistress Hudson said with a derisive snort. "Though of late he hath had gold aplenty for his needs; 'twas much remarked on before the strangeness of the bear hunt drove all else from people's lips."

The Widow frowned. "I see. This likes me not, though Heaven knows 'tis not so bad as it might be."

"Then Heaven knoweth more than I," Mistress Hudson said, somewhat exasperated. "What is it that thou fearest?"

"I hardly know," the Widow answered in a low voice.

Mary rolled her eyes. "An that's the way of it, belike thou shouldst take thyself to Bedlam straight, and save thy time and trouble."

"My thanks for thy advice," the Widow said, smiling slightly. "I'll think on't."

"Do thou so, but later, for I think thou'st not yet come to the end of what thou wouldst learn of me. What more?"

"Knowest thou the man John Rimer?"

"Very little; he's but newly come to Mortlak. An thou hast an interest in him, I'll discover what I can. Come see me in a week."

"Nay, thou dost mistake my meaning," the Widow said quickly. "I know somewhat of him already, and 'tis mostly good."

"Then why ask me of him, thou muddlehead?"

"Because he will be often at my house these next few months, and I would give out some reason ere idle tongues devise their own," the Widow retorted. "Thou'rt known to be my gossip; an thou dost mention that Master Rimer suffers from a failure of the blood, and seeks my tonics to relieve it, thou wilt be believed."

"So?" Mistress Hudson gave her friend a penetrating look. "And why does he visit thee? Or are thy daughters the magnet that draws him thither?"

"'Tis just such speculation that I would avoid! Wilt thou do it or no?"

"I'll do't. Will it seem likelier, thinkest thou, if I let slip that he was known to thy late husband?"

The Widow smiled in relief. "'Tis well thought on, and again, my thanks. Thou art a true friend, Mary."

"Tcha! Did I not say as much within these last five minutes? Thou shouldst attend with greater care to my speeches."

The two women chatted amiably for another hour before the Widow left to complete her errands and start home. Mistress Hudson was as good as her word; by the time talk of the bear hunt gave way to less unusual topics, word had spread that John was an old friend and customer of the Widow Arden's, and there was little consideration of his merits as a suitor to one of the girls.

•   •   •

Relieved of her vexation over possible gossip, at least, the Widow was able to turn more of her attention to developing a spell to set Hugh free. This was no simple task. "A complex spell requires a complex remedy," the Widow warned John and her daughters. "And this spell's both complex and powerful."

"Where should we begin?" John asked.

"With Hugh," Blanche said firmly. "Begin with Hugh." The others looked at her in surprise and she flushed a little. "If Masters Dee and Kelly began with their desire, which was of Faerie power alone, or so we think, then is't not fitting that we should start with Hugh?"

"We'll go by opposites!" Rosamund said, her eyes lighting with quick excitement. "Master Dee worked his enchantment on All Hallows'; let us work ours on May Eve, at the contrary time of the year."

"'Tis well thought of," the Widow said approvingly. Her expression changed, and she glanced at John. "Unless thy Faerie lore gives thee a reason why 'twould be unwise."

"The power of Faerie's great on both those nights," John said. "Yet they are a time for dancing and for revels, not for spells. I think that's nothing that would hinder us."

"Then tell us of thy brother," the Widow commanded. "For Blanche is right, and Hugh must be the beginning and the basis of our spell. We've known him only as a bear; tell us of Hugh, the man."

"He's tall," John said after a moment. "As tall as I, and somewhat like to look at, but more polished in his manner. Swift to laugh, and proud, and gentle . . ."

His voice trailed off and he looked down at the rough planks of the Widow's trestle table. Blanche turned her head away from the expression on his face, her own eyes thoughtful, but Rosamund was unable to do the same. Her hand moved forward half an inch, as if in an uncertain offer of comfort or reassurance; then John took a deep, shaky breath and went on with his description.

The work continued on the next day, and the next. Progress was slow but steady, despite John's impatient urgings, for the Widow and her girls had other things to do as well. The lamb had grown into a young sheep and arrangements had to be made to pasture it with Master Hardy flock; there was spinning and mending and cooking to be done, and portions of the garden had to be dug over in preparation for the coming year.

Despite all these delays, the pattern of the spell began to grow, and with it grew John's respect for the mortal magic that was so despised in Faerie. Part herbery, part ritual, part prayer and poetry, the Widow's spell was as strange and wonderful to John as Faerie itself was to Rosamund and her sister. Slowly, almost without his conscious knowledge, he allowed himself to hope.

Several times Blanche and Rosamund took John and Hugh to the place where they had watched the wizards at work, to study the ground and to see whether there were any lingering traces of the spell. They found none; too much time had passed since All Hallows'. They were, however, able to decide in advance where and how to arrange the tools they would use in their own spell. Their excitement grew as the end of April neared, and with it the chance to put their plans into action.

◆   ◆   ◆

Kelly's confidence in the performance of the crystal seemed at first to be well justified; the coins and lead rods that he had laid beside it had turned heavy and golden by the following night. His jubilation over the success of the alchemical transformation was short-lived; a day later they were all base metal once more.

"Faerie gold," Kelly said with disgust. "And we were so close!"

"'Tis as well we spent so little of it," Dee said.

"As well? I'd rather we'd sold it all! Then we'd at least have some profit for our pains."

"More likely we'd have constables at the door, to take us up for witches," Dee said. "Have done, Ned!"

"Have done?" Kelly swung angrily around to face the older man. "I'll have done when that curst globe is mended, not before!"

"Perhaps we should abandon this entirely," Dee said, shaking his head. "'Tis longer work with the other sphere, but 'tis sure, at least."

"The older globe doth not make gold," Kelly said. "Nor will it ever, for it has not the power. An we want gold, 'tis *this* that must be cured!"

"Why does it make you so distraught?" Dee asked slowly. "The spirit's knowledge is a greater loss than gold, to my mind. What have you done, that it means so much to you?"

Kelly hesitated, eyeing his colleague carefully as though assessing his temper. "I've told some few of the court what we could do," he said at last. "They'll come to us for proof, no doubt, and soon."

"'Twas not wisely done."

"How should I guess that our crystal'd fail? Now, an we can find no remedy, we needs must use some trick to make gold for those who look for proof."

"I do not like this talk of trickery, Ned," Dee said, frowning deeply.

"What other choice have we, an we're not to look like fools?" Kelly demanded.

"We can do several things, I think. May Eve's six weeks from now; an all else fail, we may repeat our spell then. Meanwhile, I've found descriptions of a powder which may help to strengthen our first spell. It may be, too, that the charms we've set about this room to hinder Faerie entrance have in some way harmed the crystal." Dee turned away from Kelly to pick up a book from the carved oak desk behind him as he said mildly, "There's no need yet to talk of deceit."

Kelly grimaced at Dee's back and said smoothly, "Aye, John, you're right. I had not thought."

"We will succeed, Ned, never fear. Now let's to work. Who knows but we may have the answer by tomorrow morning?"

But as the days went by it became more and more evident that the magicians' efforts were having no effect. Kelly's temper grew shorter and shorter, though he tried not to show it in Dee's presence. The pressures on the two men were increased by the news, brought by a traveler, that Prince Albert Laski of Poland had expressed great interest in meeting them on his forthcoming visit to England, and in learning more about their wondrous process of making gold.

It was the chance that Kelly, at least, had been waiting for, and both men considered it a cruel trick of fate that it should come just as something had gone wrong with the best example of their craft. They worked in a kind of frenzy, trying to restore the crystal's powers before the Prince's arrival, but without success. Finally they had to admit that they could think of nothing more to try except to duplicate their original spell on May Eve.

With grim concentration, they set about their preparations. Every part of the spell was examined and argued over, for John Dee still felt sure that the fault in the crystal was due to some flaw in the original ritual. Kelly made the beeswax tablets himself, melting down the wax in a long-handled dipper and straining it twice before he let it harden. Dee went through jars of dried herbs, choosing whole, unbroken leaves and seedheads. Together, the two men performed the careful cleaning and purification of the dagger and the brazier.

◆　　　◆　　　◆

All this activity was watched with sly interest by the water creature, Furgen. A week to the day after Madini set it to the task, it returned to the oak, bringing the news that Dee and Kelly had determined to repeat the spell they'd first cast on All Hallows' Eve.

"And when will they attempt it next?" Madini demanded.

"May Eve," Furgen said, giving her a sideways look. "Or rather, May Eve Day. They seem to think the sunlight benefits the spell."

"May Eve," Madini said, narrowing her eyes. "They could have picked a more convenient time."

"I doubt they chose it for our benefit," Furgen said politely.

"Peace, fool! Thou'st done well, but do not try my temper. What's next to do?"

"Steal back whatever thing they keep their part of Hugh in," Bochad-Bec replied promptly. "A purblind cow could see as much."

Madini pressed her lips together angrily; then, slowly, she smiled. "Indeed thou'rt right, goblin," she purred. "And thou wilt be the one to steal it."

"Why me?" Bochad-Bec demanded. "Thy skill's greater."

"Because thou'st done the least of us thus far," Madini snapped. "And I must be with the Queen all day, in preparation for the evening revels. Is it agreed?"

"Agreed," Bochad-Bec said sourly. "An thou'lt tell me what I am to steal."

"Hast thou no ears, or has some wight filled them up with lead? Thou'st heard what Furgen said: the mortals' spell hath trapped Hugh's essence in a lamp. That's the thing we want. And when thou hast it, do naught with it thyself, but bring it to me straight. I'll not have our hopes brought to ruin by thy clumsy-fingered magics."

Bochad-Bec snorted derisively. Madini ignored him and turned to Furgen. "And do thou still keep thy watch on the humans and bring me news of all their doings. We needs must know more than the paltry scraps thou'st told us thus far. Until tomorrow, fare you well."

Madini nodded to her companions and swept out of the clearing. Bochad-Bec spat in the general direction of the ground where she had been standing. "Why dost thou bear with her?" he asked Furgen.

"I've reasons," Furgen replied. It smiled suddenly, showing all its pointed teeth in a humorless grimace. "Even as I've reason to bear with thee. Canst thou perform her bidding?"

"Oh, aye; I'll steal whate'er those men bring. Mortals are blind and deaf in the woods."

"I trust thou'rt right to think so," Furgen said dryly. "I do trust thou'rt right."

With that, the Faerie conspirators parted, Furgen to its continuing vigil outside John Dee's study window and Bochad-Bec to his preparations for the theft of the lamp. Among other things, these included a visit to the place at the edge of Faerie where Dee and Kelly planned to work their magic. Fortunately, he chose a day when Rosamund, Blanche, and John were scouring the commons outside Mortlak in search of the small, pendulous flowers of wild daffodils. Thus, Madini and her compatriots remained ignorant of the existence and the plans of this second group of human magicians. Likewise, John and his friends knew nothing of either the Faerie plots and plans, or those of Masters Dee and Kelly. Dee and Kelly, in turn, did not suspect that there were others who knew of their business in the forest, or who would have business of their own on May Eve. So, in whole or partial ignorance, the three groups prepared to converge on the glen at the edge of the Faerie border.

CHAPTER · FIFTEEN

♦

"The dwarf glared at the girls and cried angrily, 'Why are you just standing there? Come here and help me!' 'What are you doing?' asked Rose Red. 'You stupid goose!' the dwarf answered. 'If you must know, I was trying to split this tree for firewood. But the cursed wedge was too smooth, and when I drove it in it popped right out again and the tree closed on the end of my beautiful beard. So now I am caught tight and must stand here while you silly, stupid girls laugh.'

"The girls tried hard to free the dwarf, but his beard was caught too firmly. 'I'll go and bring someone to help,' said Rose Red. 'Fool!' snarled the dwarf. 'There are already two too many of you to suit me. Think of something else.' 'I know,' said Snow White, and she took her scissors out of her pocket and cut off the end of the dwarf's beard."

♦

THE LAST DAY OF APRIL DAWNED CLEAR AND COOL. Well before the sun was up, John Dee and Edward Kelly were out of Mortlak and heading for the forest, their bags and bundles swinging awkwardly about them. Their departure was noticed only by Furgen, comfortably ensconced in a stand of reeds beside the water stairs. The water creature watched through slitted eyes as the two men left; then it slipped away to warn Bochad-Bec of their coming.

John and the Widow's daughters set out somewhat later in the day, but the Widow did not accompany them. At the last minute, while the girls were packing their supplies in baskets, Mistress

Townsend appeared unexpectedly at the cottage door. Fortunately, the Widow's inquisitive neighbor took Rosamund and Blanche's preparations for the beginning of an ordinary herb-gathering.

"I marvel that you let your daughters roam the woods so freely still," Mistress Townsend told the Widow disapprovingly.

"'Tis kind of you to think of them," the Widow answered.

Something in her tone reminded Mistress Townsend of the tongue-lashing she had gotten the last time she broached this subject, and she said hastily, "'Tis because of that strange bear that haunts the forest. You've heard the tale of Master Kirton's hunt, have you not?"

"As many versions as there were men," the Widow said calmly. "I see no reason to be troubled by such wild stories. But what brings you here, Mistress Townsend?"

Mistress Townsend was, it developed, in search of a poultice for her husband's strained shoulder. She was also in a mood for talking, and it was soon plain that she would not easily be detached from the Widow's side. Blanche and Rosamund finished their packing quickly and quietly, then stood uncertainly beside the door. The Widow, turning from her shelves of herbs, saw Mistress Townsend looking curiously in their direction, and realized that if her unwelcome visitor were not to suspect that this was an unusual venture, the girls would have to leave without her.

"What, still here?" the Widow said. "Off with you, now, and have a care to the chicory, if you find any."

"I thought thou wert to join us," Rosamund said.

"Your mother's busy, girl," Mistress Townsend answered. "Surely that can wait for another day!"

"I'll show you the shoots I spoke of on the morrow," the Widow said. "This day's task you must accomplish without me."

"But, Mother—" Blanche began.

"Go on! Needs must, and there's an end on it." She turned firmly away as her daughters reluctantly complied with her command.

◆   ◆   ◆

Rosamund and Blanche were still unsettled when they met John at the edge of the forest. He noticed their disquiet at once, and the Widow's absence, and immediately asked the cause.

"Mistress Townsend came to visit," Blanche explained, "and Mother had to stay behind with her. 'Twas plain that she was uneasy."

"She was the same the first time we went berrying without her," Rosamund said. "Remember, Blanche? And when we returned, she sorted through our baskets twice, to see that we'd brought no harmful herbs in error."

"Our errand's somewhat more serious today," Blanche said gently.

"Must we abandon our task, then?" John said, frowning.

"I do not think so," Rosamund replied. "Mother said that we could accomplish this without her, and I think that 'twill make small difference to the spell if her part's split twixt Blanche and me."

"She did not say we could," Blanche corrected. "She said we must; 'tis not the same. What if we do some harm to Hugh without her?"

"We've practiced our parts till we could do them half-asleep," Rosamund retorted. "Neither thou nor Mother need fear we'll get them wrong, and if it is the spell itself that's faulty, there's naught that she could do in the midst of it. Nor need Mother think we'll change the spell without her counsel; she's taught us both too well for that."

"That's not her true concern, and thou knowest it. Mother frets lest someone see and call us witches, and she frets the more because she cannot come with us."

"Her presence would not lessen such a charge," Rosamund said practically. "And there's no advantage in all three of us being imprisoned. Belike we should have thought of it sooner, and planned all along for her to stay behind."

John laughed, and Blanche frowned at him. "'Tis no matter for laughter, sir," she said. "Do you not know what becomes of witches, if they're caught?"

"They're hanged," John said promptly.

Rosamund frowned at his tone. "You should not take it lightly, Master Rimer."

"Nor do I," John said more seriously. "But I assure you none of us will face that fate for this day's work."

"How can you be so certain?" Rosamund asked. Her tone was skeptical, but her eyes betrayed curiosity, and perhaps something stronger.

"My skill in magic's small, yet I think I can weave a barrier to keep unwanted folk from intruding on us," John answered.

"I do not doubt it," Rosamund said, widening her eyes in mock sincerity. "For I remember that 'twas your 'small' skill that pixy-led all Master Kirton's hunt." She spoiled her pretense of innocence with a sudden impish smile.

John could not help but smile in return, but he shook his head. "And you've seen what it led me to. The Great Ones of Faerie could have performed the task with a nod and an eyeblink, and danced the night through after. Do not mispraise my skills because they're more than yours."

"Then thou must not miscall them 'poor' because thy Faerie friends have different ones," Rosamund shot back, a hint of real anger in her voice. "Nor mayest thou claim thy power is less because it is unlike; thou art as able as the best of them, I'll warrant!"

"You know but little of the Faerie folk," John said, astonished by her vehemence.

"I know they could do naught to help thy brother," Rosamund retorted fiercely. "Thou wilt try, at least."

"That may be credit to my care for Hugh, but it means nothing where my skill's concerned. In Faerie—"

"Thou'rt not in Faerie now!" Rosamund interrupted.

"She has the right of it," rumbled a voice from a clump of

bushes, and an instant later Hugh shouldered his way through them. "And thou shouldst pay more heed to thy surroundings. A pack of townsfolk singing could have come upon you all without your noticing."

"Nay, I was watching," Blanche said, smiling warmly at the bear. "But I see thy shape affects thy temperament; 'tis as well we go to change it now."

"Oh, Hugh's temper has always been thus," John said, looking slyly at his brother.

This prompted a denial from Hugh and an indignant and somewhat muddled defense from Blanche. The mock quarrel continued until they had almost reached their destination, when Hugh, who had taken the lead, suddenly sat back on his haunches and raised his nose to sniff the air.

"What art thou about, bear?" Rosamund said irritably, as she barely stopped in time to avoid running into his broad, furry back.

"Quiet," Hugh growled. "Someone is before us." In the course of the winter, he had of necessity learned to understand and use the abilities of his bear's body. The strong scent of humans had been one of the first and easiest to identify, and he smelled it on the eddying air ahead. "Two men." Hugh hesitated, and his snout wrinkled, pulling the edges of his mouth back in a grimace that showed his pointed yellow teeth. "Two men, and something else."

"Fay?" John said sharply.

"Possibly," Hugh replied. "'Tis no scent I know."

"Wait here, while I go and look," John said, stepping forward.

As John disappeared among the bushes, Rosamund frowned and started to follow. Hugh growled warningly, and at the same time Blanche said urgently, "Rosamund, do not!"

Rosamund stopped and looked uncertainly from Blanche to the woods. "But—"

"'Twill be a moment's wait, no more," Blanche coaxed.

"Oh, very well," Rosamund said ungraciously. "But I do not like his high-handed ways."

Hugh snorted but would not comment further, and they waited

in silence for John's return. He reappeared sooner than Rosamund had expected, and his expression was disturbed. "There are two men ahead, and in the very spot we looked to work," he told them. "Worse still, they've the appearance of the sorcerers you saw at All Hallows'."

The fur on Hugh's back twitched all over, and a low growl rumbled through his chest. Blanche's eyes widened, and she turned very pale. Rosamund said sharply, "The sorcerers? Thou'rt sure?"

"They look uncommon like to thy description," John said.

"What were they about?" Rosamund demanded.

John shrugged. "They drew a circle on the ground; I did not see clearly, though I tried."

"We must stop them!" Blanche said with sudden passion. Rosamund looked at her with surprise and Blanche said impatiently, "They must seek to do Hugh some further mischief; how else would they be here? Oh come; hurry; we may have little time."

Hugh made an uncertain noise, half growl of assent, half whine of warning. His fur prickled at the very thought of the half-remembered agony of his slow transformation, but he was equally disturbed by the thought of Blanche facing dangerous sorcerers. John glanced at him, then said to Blanche, "Softly. I do agree with thy purpose, but 'twill do no good to run our heads into a snare. We must plan what's best to do, ere we approach these men."

Reluctantly, Blanche admitted the good sense of this argument, and several minutes more were spent in discussion before they finally set out again, moving as noiselessly as possible in the direction of the clearing at the edge of Faerie.

◆　　　◆　　　◆

John's brief inspection of the area had gone unobserved. Dee and Kelly had little attention to spare for anything besides their preparations. Similarly, Bochad-Bec, watching avidly from the huge oak that spread its branches above the sorcerer's working area, had eyes only for Dee and Kelly. None of them noticed John.

Dee and Kelly had completed their circle as John left. The two men then set about carefully removing every twig and rock from the ground within it. Kelly removed a folded square of red silk from one of the packs, and he and Dee spread it on the ground they had just cleared. Dee remained to smooth out the wrinkles, while Kelly went back to the packs and began unloading the smaller items that would be required for the spell.

"You're certain we've no need to make all these afresh?" Kelly asked, holding up a knife.

"Nay, Ned, the tablets and the herbs will suffice," Dee said absently. "They must; 'twould take a year or more to reforge the lamp alone."

"I hope you're right," Kelly muttered. He pulled the lamp out of the bundle, inspected it for scratches, and set it down beside the knife. Bochad-Bec, peering down through the oak leaves, tensed as the lamp came into view. His eyes darted from Kelly to Dee and back, as if judging the distance between them. The dwarf's habitual frown grew deeper, and he muttered a curse under his breath.

"There," Dee said, straightening. "'Tis done. Shall I set out the brazier, or would you have help?"

"I'll take your assistance here, and gladly," Kelly replied. "'Tis too much for one pair of hands."

Dee nodded and walked toward him. In the tree above, Bochad-Bec took one final measuring look at the two wizards, then closed his eyes. He pressed his hands against the bark of the tree, his gnarled fingers outspread in a near caress. Softly, he began murmuring.

"The wind is rising," Kelly commented as Dee approached. "We'll have no easy time of this."

The branches of the oak swayed and creaked as if in agreement; then, with a loud grinding noise, one of them tore free and hurtled down upon the two men. Kelly tried to dodge, but was beaten down and trapped in the tangled side branches, while Dee was thrown to the ground under a part of the main section. The tools and ingredients of their spell were scattered and hidden under the spreading leaves. In the instant of calm that followed the crash, while the leaves were still trembling with the shock of the fall, Bochad-Bec leapt down from the oak.

The dwarf landed on his flat, splayed feet and bounced into the air like a ball. He caught one of the projections from the fallen limb and swung himself along it, peering down among the leaves. A gleam of light on polished metal caught his eye and he pounced. Triumphantly, he tucked the lamp under his arm and turned to leave. As he did, his eyes fell on the horrified, half-stunned face of Edward Kelly.

Bochad-Bec gave the sorcerer a grin of fiendish glee and ran along the fallen branch. A moment later he had vanished through the barely visible shimmer of the Faerie border beyond. Kelly blinked and shook his head; then, after briefly inspecting his extremities to make sure everything was still in working order, he began struggling to free himself.

Kelly's efforts sent a ripple of movement through the leaves and outer branches of the fallen limb. Immediately a somewhat shaky voice called anxiously, "Ned? Is't you? Are you badly injured?"

"Nay, John, I am but scratched and bruised," Kelly called. Feeling that this belated reassurance might well be considered inadequate, he added, "'Twill take me but a moment to get free; then I'll come to you."

"Praise Heaven," Dee said with fervent sincerity. "I, too, am little injured, but I doubt I can get free without help."

Kelly's attempts to wriggle out from beneath the branches were more than noisy enough to cover the sounds of a hasty, whispered conference beneath a tall holly bush nearby. Rosamund, Blanche, and their two half-Faerie companions had heard the crash of the falling branch and arrived just in time to see Bochad-Bec abscond with the lamp. Rosamund at once proposed that they follow the dwarf, but John and Hugh instantly rejected that idea.

"Oakmen are surly and dangerous to cross," John said. "And he's in Faerie now, where neither Hugh nor I can go."

"Then let's accost these others," Rosamund whispered back. "Belike we can discover more of their plans and purposes."

"And how wouldst thou explain how it is that two girls are found in company with a man and bear?" John said sarcastically. "No, we'll learn enough by watching."

"Blanche and I can go alone, and you shall stay here and watch," Rosamund said persuasively.

"Look!" Blanche broke in, her tone horrified. "His ears have been cropped!"

All eyes turned toward the clearing. Kelly had succeeded in freeing himself at last, but in the process he had lost the black skullcap he always wore, and the truth of Blanche's surprised exclamation was clear to them all. "So he's been taken for wizardry before," John said in a speculative tone.

"Nay, cutting off the ears is too mild a punishment for witchcraft," Rosamund said. "He must have been convicted of some lesser crime—theft, perhaps, or forgery."

"Are you there, Ned?" Dee's voice, coming from the other side of the fallen branch, had a touch of querulousness. "Are you free?"

Kelly glanced swiftly toward the sound and saw that the swelling curve of the branch screened him from his companion's view. He gave a sigh of obvious relief and called back, "A moment only, and I'll be there." He snatched his skullcap from the ground where it had fallen and shook it to dislodge the twigs and bark, then crammed it on his head. He felt the edges with his fingers to make certain it was properly positioned to hide his deformity; only then did he go to help his fallen friend.

His efforts were unsuccessful. The heaviest part of the branch lay across the small of John Dee's back; a slight unevenness in the ground was all that had kept him from being crushed. Kelly's strength was enough to shift the branch, but not quite enough to raise it, and Dee's agility was not sufficient to enable him to wriggle out from under.

"'Tis no good, Ned," Dee said at last. "You needs must fetch help."

"And what am I to tell them?" Kelly said angrily. "That we brought red silk and an iron brazier into the forest to gather firewood in? Nay, I've no desire to hang for witchcraft."

"Nor have I," Dee replied. "But my desire to die of thirst and hunger beneath this branch is equally small." He sighed and suddenly looked older than his fifty-seven years. "This is what comes of greed; it is the judgment of Heaven on our presumption."

"'Twas no angel stole away our lamp," Kelly retorted. "That I'll swear to."

"I did not see the apparition of which you speak," Dee said. "Yet if it was some demon it but proves my point."

"Have done, John!" Kelly said in exasperation. "'Twas neither devil nor angel, but some wight out of Faerie, and what its presence proves is that our spell's had more effect than we knew."

Within the holly bush, John snorted softly. "He's right on that account," he said under his breath to Hugh. "But I'm puzzled what interest an oakman would take in these two."

"For now 'tis more important that they leave, else our own work will ne'er begin," Rosamund said impatiently. "Turn thy mind to that, and save the dwarf for later."

"We must help them," Blanche said. "They'll not think it strange to see Rose and me, and I think we two can add enough to Master Kelly's efforts to set Master Dee at liberty. "But you"—she looked at John and Hugh—"you must stay well hid, or they'll know we're more than what we seem."

"No," John said, and Hugh nodded his agreement.

"We've no choice," Blanche insisted. "Rose—"

"No," John repeated, and caught hold of her wrist. "There's no need."

"But there is!" Blanche whispered urgently, pulling against his grasp. "Dost thou not see it?"

"Thou dost misunderstand," Hugh rasped. "He'd have thee wait on his attempt ere thou makest thine own."

Blanche looked from Hugh to John, and nodded uncertainly. John released her wrist and turned. He studied the scene before him. Kelly was preparing to make another assault on the branch that pinned his companion. As the wizard set his shoulder against the bark, John's eyes narrowed to slits and he stretched out his left hand.

The heavy oak branch shifted. "Once more, Ned!" Dee cried. Kelly's face turned purple with effort. Beads of sweat formed on John's forehead, and his outstretched hand trembled. The branch shifted a little farther and rose slightly as it rolled onto a projecting limb. John Dee made a strangled noise and scrabbled his way to safety; an instant later Kelly sprang away, panting, and the branch fell back to its original position.

"Well done, Ned!" Dee said as he climbed to his feet. "I owe you much."

"Well done?" Kelly kicked viciously at the fallen branch. "We're ruined!"

"Perhaps," Dee said gently. "But we're alive, not crushed to death, and that's worth more than gold, or even knowledge. Thank Heaven for your life, my friend, and let the rest go."

"Let it go?" Kelly said, his voice rising. "The crystal's failed and we've no hope of remedying it now; by tomorrow eve we'll look like fools in motley before Lord Laski and the court—and you say, let it go?"

"'Tis Heaven's judgment, Ned."

"'Tis rather Faerie's malice! And that I'll not accept, for all your pious mouthings!"

"What mean you?" Dee said, taken aback by Kelly's fierceness. Kelly, still scowling heavily, described the dwarf and the stealing of the lamp. When he finished, Dee, too, was frowning.

"This puts a different face on things," the elder wizard said. "An't be Faerie that we war with, we may not be altogether lost."

"How so? Without the lamp—"

"The lamp's no matter. Think, Ned! An we'd failed as completely as we thought, there'd be no reason for this mischief."

"Faerie needs no reason save spite," Kelly said, but the bitter edge was gone from his voice and a sly, considering expression had appeared at the back of his eyes.

"We've still some time for study," Dee said. Kelly rolled his eyes; Dee, preoccupied, did not notice. "Prince Laski will not expect great works all at once; 'twill be enough to show ourselves men of learning. We need not demonstrate the crystal yet."

"Now or later, what matters it? The crystal's dead."

"I think not, but 'tis a matter we cannot solve here. Come, Ned!"

Kelly shrugged, and the two men gathered up their scattered implements, brushed the leaves and twigs from their robes, and left. As he passed the shimmering curtain of the Faerie border, Kelly bit his thumb at it; behind the screen of holly, John choked on a laugh. In another moment, the sorcerers were gone and the glen was empty.

CHAPTER · SIXTEEN

•

"When the dwarf was free, he shook himself. Then he picked up a bag of gold which was lying at the foot of the tree and set off into the woods muttering, 'Stupid, inconsiderate girls! How dare they cut off a piece of my beard? Bad luck to you both!' "

•

ROSAMUND WAS THE FIRST TO LEAVE THE SHELTERing screen of holly. John followed, frowning, and Hugh and Blanche brought up the rear. Rosamund went straight to the oak branch and gave it a tentative shove.

"I think together we can move it," she said doubtfully, "but it weighs more than I had thought."

"Not there, Hugh!" Blanche said. "Thou'lt wipe out all their drawings, and we'll learn nothing."

"We've learned enough already, and 'twill be good luck indeed if we've not learned it too late," John said. "Did none of you recognize that dwarf for what he was?"

Hugh sat down very suddenly. "An oakman, of course," he growled. "But I had not seen the implications."

John nodded. "We must leave at once."

"Leave!" Blanche protested. "But we've not even tried—"

A roar from Hugh cut her off in mid-sentence. She and Rosamund both jumped and stared at the bear, wide-eyed.

"Come," John said, and they followed him out into the forest once more.

John led them well away from the glen and the Faerie border, to a small clearing surrounded by beech trees. He studied them for a full minute before he turned to the girls and apologized for his hurry. "An oakman can, if he chooses, know all that passes beneath his trees," he explained. "Had we stayed to talk, we'd have had no secrets from him, and I doubt that he's a friend."

"Thy doubt's well justified," Hugh said. "I know him, and he's no friend to aught that has the smallest smell of humankind. 'Twas Bochad-Bec."

John scowled. "I've heard of him, and nothing good. I wish I'd not cast that spell to lift the branch; he cannot help but notice, even if he misses all the rest."

"But surely he'll think 'twas Master Kelly's work," Rosamund said.

"I doubt it," John replied, and his lips twisted in a bitter smile. "No denizen of Faerie could help but recognize so odd a mix of human and Faerie magic as I must use."

"I see why thou didst stop my tongue," Blanche said to Hugh. "Though even if he'd heard us, 'twould surely not surprise him that thy brother aids thee."

"True enough," John said in a more cheerful tone, though the glance he shot at Hugh belied his voice. "And if that's all he learns, we've lost little." He did not add that it was the presence of Rosamund and Blanche that he wished had been kept from the oakman's knowledge. The human girls were far more vulnerable to the dwarf's malice than either he or Hugh.

"Little or much, 'tis too late now to remedy," Rosamund said practically. "What of the work we came to do? We've still the afternoon and evening to try the spell, can we but find a safe and proper place for it."

"Yes, we must attempt it," Blanche agreed. "Why, 'twould be Midsummer ere we could try again, if we let this chance slip. 'Tis far too long to wait."

"'Tis not the wait that troubles me," John began, but Hugh broke in with a growl.

"Before you two take chances with my hide, I'll thank you to consult Mistress Arden. Or do you think that what we've learned has naught to do with the shaping of that spell you intend to use on me?"

Rosamund and Blanche at once begged the bear's pardon and agreed to return home immediately to ask their mother's advice. Hugh left them well before they came near the edge of the forest, where they might meet other travelers. John continued on with them, but he was so preoccupied that even Rosamund failed to elicit more than a grunt in response to her remarks and speculations. Finally, just as they were leaving the woods, she taxed him with the flaws in his behavior.

"I crave your pardon, Mistresses," John said, shaking himself out of his daze and bowing extravagantly. "I am indeed remiss."

Blanche smiled, but Rosamund was not so easily satisfied. "If you'd have our pardon, tell us what your mind's so busy with," she commanded.

John's brief good humor vanished, and he hesitated. "'Tis but a question that worries me."

"Indeed," Rosamund replied. "And you worry at it like a dog gnawing at a bone. Tell us what it is; maybe we can enlighten thee."

"Not this time, I think," John muttered; then he shrugged and capitulated. "My question's this: how was it that the oakman interfered in such a timely fashion with Masters Dee and Kelly? Has he some use, perhaps for the lamp he stole? For it seems to me unlikely that 'twas chance alone that brought him to that spot on this day."

"Belike he had some spell of his own to try, as we did," Rosamund said after a moment.

"Belike," John said in a dry tone that expressed his doubt, and then they reached the Widow's gate.

"Wait!" Rosamund said as John put his hand on the post. "We'll go ahead, and see if Mistress Townsend's gone. We're back early as it is; 'twould not be wise to add to her questions by returning in thy company."

◆   ◆   ◆

Fortunately, Mistress Townsend had indeed departed, though they had only missed her by a few minutes. The Widow was both reassured and disquieted by their quick return, and demanded a complete explanation. Rosamund made sure to mention John's suspicions of the oakman when she told their story, and the dwarf's possible purposes were the subject of considerable speculation in the Widow's cottage. The Widow Arden was inclined to agree with John that the oakman's presence was no coincidence, but she was at a loss for any other explanation. The discussion stopped only when Blanche reminded everyone once again that May Eve Day was passing, and they would soon lose their chance to help Hugh. This prompted an abrupt change in subject, followed by a hasty search for various new materials, before the little group left the cottage once more, with the Widow accompanying them.

Hugh rejoined them at the edge of the woods. "I see from all your faces that you still intend to work this spell," he said when they came close enough to hear.

"I thought you would be pleased," Blanche said, frowning slightly. "Dost wish to stay a bear?"

"No," Hugh said, and turned his head away from her. Blanche stared at him, her brows knit as if she were deep in the study of some idea of vast importance and great difficulty.

"Then we must not tarry here," the Widow said briskly. "'Tis too close to the road; if thou'rt seen—"

She was interrupted by a howl of agony from Hugh.

◆　　◆　　◆

The argument between John Dee and Ned Kelly continued all through their walk back to Mortlak, in spite of Dee's attempts to turn the conversation. Kelly returned again and again to the dwarf and his possible reasons for stealing the lamp; he paused only when they passed someone who might overhear. Even after they reached the study on the second floor of the riverside house, Kelly continued his diatribe, pacing around and around the inscribed table where the crystal lay, while Dee sat wearily at the small desk where he took notes during their work with the eerie gem.

Without warning, the crystal flared into life. Kelly stopped in mid-sentence and whirled to face it as the flare died back to a warm, steady glow. Dee's head jerked up from the hand he had been resting it on, and without thought he reached for a pen. "Look into it, Ned, quickly, and tell me what you see! Belike 'tis some message that will solve our dilemma."

The words prodded Kelly into action; he stepped forward and sat down in the gazer's chair, his eyes fixed on the crystal. "Light," he said after a moment. "Only light . . . no, wait! I saw a woman's face, and now there is a curtain, a gold curtain, hiding the center of the crystal!"

"Calm yourself, Ned," Dee said, though his own voice was shaking with excitement. "'Tis likely you'll see no more if you're too eager."

But though Kelly tried to follow these instructions, and though he sat staring into the globe until his eyes watered, he could not make the curtain part. This put him out of temper for a while, but both he and John Dee were greatly encouraged by the resumption of activity within the crystal. Dee took it as a sign from Heaven that their work would be rewarded. Kelly was inclined to give the credit more to their own efforts than to Heaven, but he kept this opinion to himself.

◆　　　◆　　　◆

Madini was waiting beneath the oak when Bochad-Bec came bounding through the Faerie woods, Dee's lamp held high in one broad hand. "There," the dwarf said ungraciously, handing her his trophy. "My part's done; now 'tis thy turn to work."

"Peace, prattler!" Madini snapped. "I must have silence, to see how best Hugh's Faerie power may be unraveled from this mortal foolery."

The oakman snorted. "I thought you'd not be so quick as your talk made it seem."

"Hold thy tongue!" Madini commanded, and turned her attention to the lamp. A moment later her eyes narrowed and her lips drew back from her teeth in an involuntary hiss. "Thou fool!"

"Now what's toward?" Bochad-Bec said.

"Thou'st stolen the wrong object," Madini said with quiet venom. "*This* bears no Faerie power, if it ever did."

"Thou toldest me to bring thee the lamp," Bochad-Bec said stolidly. "There it is. An it's not what you wanted, 'tis thy fault, not mine."

"Who speaks of fault?" Furgen said, stepping out of the shadows. Its cold eyes flickered from Madini to the lamp and back. "'Twas good of thee to wait on my arrival," it said pointedly.

"The thing this dullard stole is useless," Madini said with great disdain, ignoring Furgen's second comment. "Hugh's essence is not in't."

"'Tis the lamp the wizards used," Bochad-Bec insisted. "I heard them say so."

"Then even if 'tis empty now, it has not always been," Furgen said. "If that be true, can we not use it as a link, to reach whatever thing we truly want?"

Madini looked startled; then a slow smile spread across her face.

"'Tis possible; give me a moment." Again she raised the lamp and studied it, then closed her eyes and concentrated. The lamp began to glow. In John Dee's study the crystal flared into life, and in the forest outside Mortlak Hugh sat back and howled in pain before the startled eyes of his brother and his friends.

On the polished surface of the lamp's side, a picture of Dee's study formed. Madini studied it with care, noting the glowing crystal and the surprise of the two men as they hurried toward it. She smiled and murmured a spell to bring the crystal to her.

Nothing happened. Madini's smile faded. Kelly bent over the crystal and for an instant his eyes looked out of the side of the lamp, directly into hers. Then Madini drew her sleeve across the surface of the lamp and muttered yet again. After a moment, she drew her sleeve away. Kelly's eyes still stared intently out of the side of the lamp, but they saw nothing now.

"What happened?" Bochad-Bec asked.

"The mortals have wrought better than I guessed," Madini said. "They've prisoned what they took from Hugh inside a crystal, and tied it somehow in the mortal lands. It will take time and study to learn how to bring it to us. Meantime, we must discourage them from further foolishness. Go and see that any tools they've left behind will be no further good to them."

"We have the lamp. Is't not enough?" Bochad-Bec said, not moving.

"No, 'tis not!" Madini snapped. "Do as I bid thee!"

Muttering balefully, Bochad-Bec departed.

◆   ◆   ◆

The bear reared back on his hind legs and clawed blindly at the air in front of him; one huge paw missed John's shoulder by less than an inch. "Hugh!" John protested.

The bear did not seem to hear. He had stopped howling, but he was making a high-pitched whining noise that hurt to hear. Then, without warning, he collapsed into a panting heap.

Blanche started forward, but Rosamund caught her arm and held her back. "Let me go!" Blanche cried.

"And how if Hugh's taken with another such fit, and knocks thy head from thy shoulders in the midst of it?" Rosamund answered.

"Aye, stay back a bit," John said. "Hugh, what happened?"

"No," Hugh growled. He heaved his forequarters up and shook his coat, then with visible effort said, "Don't know."

His companions looked at him with dawning horror. "Hugh, thy voice . . ." Blanche said pleadingly.

"Hard to talk," Hugh said, and the words were almost drowned in a deep, bearish rumble.

"He's slipping back," John said. His voice was full of pain. "The spell that gave him back his voice comes undone."

"I think not," the Widow said, studying the bear with a small frown. "Look you, 'twas not the kind of spell that lingers; when we cast it, it served its purpose and was gone. This must be the work of those magicians."

"Or of the dwarf," Blanche said.

John's face went white with anger. "Bochad-Bec," he said. "Oh, indeed, that's likely."

"Like enough, I warrant you," Rosamund said. "But what are we to do about it?"

Blanche looked at her sister as if she were an idiot. "We must do what we came to do! Cast the spell again, and give Hugh back his voice, if not his form."

"And make Hugh the rope for a pulling-contest?" Rosamund shot back. "We do not know why this has happened, nor whether it may be done again. What good is it to Hugh if we restore him now and then tomorrow the wizards or the dwarf make him a bear again?"

"We have to try," said Blanche.

"We must do something, true," the Widow broke in, halting the incipient argument, "but I think we must consider better what it should be. And in the end, the choice belongs neither to thee nor to thy sister. What say you, Hugh? Shall we postpone this spell-casting?"

"Aye," Hugh rumbled, and that put an end to the argument. Blanche was somewhat put out by this decision, but having seen Hugh's pain she was willing to go to considerable lengths to avoid bringing it on again. So, once more, the little group trudged back to the Widow Arden's cottage to plan.

◆　　　◆　　　◆

Bochad-Bec was not absent from the glen in Faerie long. He returned with half a wax tablet and the news that he'd found traces of John's magic all around the fallen oak branch.

Madini's eyes blazed with rage at this news. "John! An he choose to interfere, I'll see he rues it."

"He may already," Furgen said. "Is it not likely that his purpose was the same as ours? And 'tis we who have Dee's lamp."

"True." Madini's eyes narrowed, and she smiled coldly. "And he'll have more regrets ere I've done with him. He no longer has the Queen's protection."

"The human sorcerers are more important to our plans," Furgen pointed out.

"And wouldst thou have those plans overset because of John? He knows too much of Faerie for my comfort."

"Aye, he should be watched," Bochad-Bec said.

"Then find him for me, dwarf, and his wretched brother as well. They'll not be far, I think."

"And what of the humans?" Furgen said.

Madini looked at him. "I cannot bring the crystal here, as yet, but I have barred it from their use. They'll get no good of it till I've had time to learn what we need to know."

"And if there *is* no spell to gain the crystal?"

"Then I'll find some way to bend these humans to my will so we may take it," Madini said impatiently. "Go back to your work, mud-dweller, and leave me to mine!"

Furgen held Madini's gaze with his flat, expressionless eyes for an instant; then he nodded and slipped into the shadows. Before Madini could transfer her irritation to Bochad-Bec, the oakman had also vanished. Madini grimaced, then hid the still faintly glowing lamp behind a fold of her cloak and departed, leaving the meeting place empty.

CHAPTER · SEVENTEEN

♦

"Some time later, the mother sent Snow White and Rose Red to catch some fish. As they neared the brook, they saw something jumping like a giant grasshopper on the bank. When they ran up, they found it was the dwarf. 'What are you doing?' said Rose Red. 'Be careful, or you'll fall into the water!' 'Don't be a fool!' said the dwarf. 'Can't you see that that fish is trying to pull me in?' The little man's long beard had gotten tangled in the fishing line; before he could get it free a big fish took the bait on the other end, and the dwarf was not strong enough to haul it in."

♦

HUGH SUFFERED NO MORE VIOLENT ATTACKS OF PAIN in the days that followed, but this was little comfort to his brother or his friends. Something seemed to be eroding all the good the Widow and her daughters had accomplished with the first of their attempted disenchantments; the bear was slowly losing both his voice and his ability to think clearly. Horrified by this development, John and the girls tried everything they could think of to reverse the decline. They prayed over the bear and over the site of John Dee's ritual; they fed Hugh Faerie herbs mixed with wine and honey; they hung cold iron about his neck and draped him in garlands of rowan berries; they rubbed his coat with earth and pine tar, then washed it with clear water that had been left three nights in moonlight, three in firelight, and three in darkness.

Nothing did any good. The bear continued to grow more and more like a real bear as May blossomed into June. His voice became more guttural, and his temper shorter. Sometimes, with John, the cloud appeared to lift for a moment from his mind, but it never lasted. The slow decline was not as distressing as a swifter setback might have been; nonetheless, when he returned to Mortlak after some ten days spent scouring the back streets of London for new spells and exotic ingredients that might help his brother, John was shocked by the way Hugh's humanity had faded.

"I think that soon 'twill be unsafe for you to come here," he told the girls in a heavy tone.

"Mother thinks so already; do not you start as well," Rosamund said crossly. She was seated on a rock, plaiting willow withes into a bear-sized halter, to be used in their next attempt to assist Hugh. Flecks of sunlight danced across her dark brown hair as the breeze ruffled the new leaves overhead; a few feet away, Blanche was arranging bits of colored rock in a complex pattern on the ground, while the bear lay stretched in a patch of sun beside her, his head sunk on his great paws, his eyes following the motions of her hands.

John's expression grew more somber as he studied Rosamund's bent head, but his voice was steady as he said, "An your mother thinks that Hugh becomes a danger to you, you should listen and stay home."

"Hugh?" Blanche said, looking up so quickly that she knocked three dull blue pebbles out of line. "What's Hugh to do with Mother's fears?"

At the sound of his name, the bear raised his head and snorted. He shook his coat, then looked toward John and whined deep in his throat. When John did not respond, the bear gave a gusty sigh and stretched his head onto his paws once more, his mournful gaze fixed on Blanche.

"If it is not Hugh's . . . decline that troubles your mother, why do you say she thinks this work unsafe?" John asked with a comprehensive wave that included Rosamund, Blanche, the oaks and beeches, and the bear lying stretched in the sun.

"'Tis talk that Mother fears, not Hugh," Rosamund replied absently, picking up another withe.

"What talk?" John said, and when Rosamund looked up in evident surprise he added apologetically, "Remember that I've been in London near a fortnight."

Rosamund shrugged. "There's rumor of black magic in the town, and foul witchcraft, and of devils in the forest, and whenever such things are talked of, Mother starts to fret."

"Belike she hath good reason," John said, frowning.

"Belike the fault is yours she hath," Rosamund snapped back. "'Twas you who misled Master Kirton's hunt, and that's the root of all this gossip."

"That is but part," Blanche corrected gently. "There would be talk of Dee and Kelly no matter what the tales were of the hunt."

"An there be talk of Dee—" John began, but Rosamund interrupted him.

"There!" she said, holding up the willow halter. "'Tis done. Art ready, Blanche?"

"A moment only," Blanche replied, carefully placing the last pebble. "Hugh! Come hither, and let us make trial of this latest charm."

But when the halter had been placed about the bear's neck, and John had led him across Blanche's pebbles and back, there was no visible improvement in Hugh's condition. Blanche turned her head away, hiding her face from the other three while Rosamund and John scattered the pebbles and destroyed the halter, and she was even quieter than usual on the walk back to the cottage.

The repeated failures finally convinced John that the key to Hugh's release lay somewhere in the Dee household. He began watching it, and tried several times to gain entry to the house in hopes of finding the solution he sought so desperately. He was not successful, but on his third attempt (posing as a rag-and-bone picker) he noticed recent traces of Faerie visitors in the kitchen garden.

⋄   ⋄   ⋄

The resumption of activity within the crystal, however obscure, gave John Dee the confidence to meet his distinguished foreign visitors without trepidation. Ned Kelly, however, was not so sanguine, particularly since they were unable to coax any further response whatever from the glowing ball. In the weeks that followed May Eve the two men tried everything they could think of, to no avail. Kelly even made a ten-day trip to London, ostensibly on business but in reality to search for some obscure ingredients for use in one of their spells. Nothing did any good.

Madini's efforts to obtain the crystal were likewise frustrated. Through the lamp she could watch what passed inside the study, but the wards Dee and Kelly had placed around it blocked her every attempt to steal the crystal. She could not free the power trapped within it, nor even use Hugh's purloined magic for herself. Dee and Kelly controlled the crystal, and it would obey no other master.

Direct action having proven useless, Madini turned to roundabout methods. She discovered that she could use the link between the lamp and the crystal to project a simulacrum of herself into Dee's study. Through this image, she began methodically searching the room whenever Dee and Kelly were absent, noting the location and manner of each of the protections the wizards had placed around the study and looking for a crack in their defenses. The servants could not see her, whatever form she wore, so for her own amusement, Madini took to varying the shape of her projection, one day doing her work as a crone and the next as a young man or perhaps a beggar or a child.

One evening in late May, some three weeks after the theft of the lamp, Madini uncovered the lamp to find Dee and Kelly pictured on its side. The two men were seated in a corner of the study, to one side of the inscribed table where the crystal lay.

"I am beholden to God for the good will of the Polish Prince," Dee said. "I would you had been here, Ned, to see the honor that he did me!"

"You've spoken of little else for this whole week past," Kelly replied irritably. "Can you not look ahead a little? He honors you now for your learning—"

"He favors me greatly," Dee said. "He hath asked me to provide him a book, like unto that which I made for the Queen her gracious majesty these two years past, to show the argument for his title."

"Histories and generations are very well, but what will this Prince Laski say when he asks you to make gold for him and you cannot do so?"

"He is a great man, Ned, and he hath striven to confound the malice of the court toward me. 'Tis not possible that such a man would value gold over knowledge."

Madini chuckled contemptuously as she watched Kelly roll his eyes, and she decided that this foolish conversation was no reason to delay the continuation of her search. She pondered a moment, considering what shape to send out, then bent over the lamp.

Ned Kelly broke off in mid-sentence as Madini's projection appeared in the room. "John! Do you see her?"

"What is it, Ned?" Dee said, straightening up.

"A child, a girl of seven or nine, with dark hair rolled up in front and hanging very long behind," Kelly answered in a low voice. "Her gown changeth color, now red, now green, and she doth move among your books and they give way around her."

Madini turned. Kelly's eyes were wide and fixed on her, and she suffered an unpleasant shock. She had become accustomed to working freely in the study, invisible to all the mortals; to find someone who could see her was a jolt.

"Whose maiden are you?" Dee demanded, reaching for the quill pen with which he took notes on the work he and Kelly did.

"Whose man are you?" Madini retorted.

Dee looked in Kelly's direction. Kelly, his eyes still fixed on

Madini's insubstantial presence, said, "She answers, whose man are you."

Dee nodded and noted it on a sheet of paper. Then he responded, "I am a servant of God, both by my bound duty and also, I hope, by his adoption."

Madini stared at him for a long moment. By now she knew the location of every protective symbol and spell with which Dee and Kelly guarded their workroom, but the knowledge did her little good without the ability to erase them. It had not previously occurred to her that she might influence the men themselves directly. She half lowered her eyelids and smiled at Kelly. "Am I not a fine maiden?" she said, and then, remembering that she had given her projection the form of a child, she added, "Give me leave to play in your house."

Kelly repeated her words to Dee, who wrote rapidly. "My mother told me she would come and dwell here," Madini went on, paving the way for another appearance in a more mature guise.

Neither of the men responded. Madini resumed walking up and down the room, and Kelly's eyes never left her. "She goes up and down, with the most lively gestures of a young girl playing by herself," he said, and Dee copied assiduously.

Hiding a derisive smile, Madini turned to a perspective glass in the corner of the study and pretended to listen intently. "One speaks to her from the corner of the study there," Kelly reported, "but I see none besides herself."

Madini, sneering inwardly at the mortals' gullibility, began a one-sided conversation with the glass, which Kelly reported in the same detached tone.

At last Dee grew tired of waiting for his unexpected, unseen guest to say or do something of substance. "Tell me who you are," he demanded, and he would not be put off by her evasions.

"I am a poor little maiden," Madini responded, and then, despite her best efforts to give a false reply, ". . . Madini."

Greatly taken aback, Madini turned the interview into other channels. She pretended to read off lists of kings of England and related nobility from a book her image took from a pocket, and so succeeded in avoiding Dee's further questions about her home. The tactic had an unforeseen consequence; after listening to twenty minutes of Plantagenets, Mortimers, and Lacys, Dee asked her to declare the pedigree of the Polish Prince.

By this time Madini had had enough of the game, so she once more returned an evasive answer. She was careful, however, to leave Dee with some hope of success at a later time before she covered the lamp so that her childish image vanished from the study. She was well pleased with the reactions of the two humans to her manipulations, but she was furiously angry that Dee, through the power of the crystal, had forced her to give her real name. The mortal wizard's presumption alone was enough to enrage her; that he had been successful added fuel to the fire and gave her one more reason to hate the lands outside of Faerie.

Nonetheless, she decided, after much thought, to continue as she had begun. The possibilities were great, and Madini was supremely confident that she would be more than a match for any merely human magic, now that she was prepared for it. For a brief time, she considered laying the problem before the Queen, but in the end dismissed the idea. The Queen's sympathies lay with the mortal world; it was all too likely that she would remain blind to the pitfalls of continued commerce between the realms. It would be better, Madini decided, for her to handle the matter herself.

For the next month, Madini appeared in Dee's study at irregular intervals and under various names. At each appearance she coaxed, commanded, or dropped broad but casual hints regarding the removal or replacement of the spells that guarded the study from Faerie interference. To her chagrin, she found the men less easily manipulated than she had expected. They were perfectly willing to add whatever strange and outlandish symbols she could devise, but her best efforts could not persuade them to remove even one of the charms that kept her from the crystal.

◆　　　◆　　　◆

Joan Bowes became aware of the late-night lights at the Dee house almost as soon as they appeared. It was not long before it occurred to her that Masters Dee and Kelly might be more willing to deal in questionable magic than the Widow Arden had been. Her employer, Master Rundel, no longer interested her, but the newcomer called John Rimer was another matter. Joan would have given a great deal to attract his attention. It would be pleasant to score a triumph over the Widow and her daughters.

Joan had, however, learned a lesson from her unpleasant encounter with the Widow the previous fall. This time, she approached the matter circumspectly. After some consideration, she decided to apply to Ned Kelly, who was, in her opinion, more likely to listen sympathetically to her fabricated tale.

She accosted Kelly in the street near the market one damp grey afternoon in June, having decided (after much thought) that an apparently accidental meeting would attract less attention than would a visit to the sorcerer's house. Joan stepped in front of Kelly as he hurried along the muddy street and said, "Your pardon, Master, but are you not that Edward Kelly who lives by the river?"

"I am." Kelly stopped and studied Joan with far from academic care. Apparently he liked what he saw, for he smiled warmly at her. "Why do you look for me?"

"I've heard that you can do great things," Joan answered with simulated diffidence. "I thought perhaps you'd lend me your aid."

The warmth left Kelly's expression. "Knowledge and secret lore are not for casual use. They require great effort and dedication, even in the least of their practices." He paused. "Nor is the cost of studying them small."

"I am only a poor maid-servant," Joan said, "and I have but little money. Yet perhaps I could pay you in some other fashion." She tilted her head as if to examine Kelly's face and ran the palm of her left hand slowly down the side of her waist and hip.

"'Tis possible," Kelly said. "Oh, 'tis quite possible. What would you?"

Joan licked lips which had gone dry, and glanced quickly around to make certain no one was within hearing. This was the tricky part; until now the conversation had been overtly innocent, without mention of spells or magic. "There is a man," she said carefully.

"Ah." Kelly studied her, his eyes bright and calculating below his black skullcap. "And do you want his name, his fortune, his liver, or his bed?"

Somewhat taken aback by Kelly's bluntness, and by his willingness to be so open in the middle of the street even if no one was near enough to overhear, Joan could at first do no more than stare. Then her imagination formed a picture of John helpless to deny her anything while the Widow and her daughters, equally helpless, looked on. "All that, and more," she said recklessly.

"It can be done," Kelly said, stroking his beard. "But 'twould be best if 'twere not done in Mortlak."

"An you'll grant me this, I'll meet you when and where you will," Joan promised. "A message to Joan Bowes at Master Rundel's house will find me."

"I'll send it in a day or two, when I've had time to prepare the means of achieving thy desire," Kelly said, and with that they parted.

◆ ◆ ◆

Three days later, Joan met Kelly in a small copse of trees on the far side of the Thames, well hidden from the gossiping tongues of the townsfolk and the eyes of passersby. There she rendered Kelly the payment she had promised, and received in return a vial of dark liquid and a white cloth. "Add three of the man's hairs to the vial and leave it in the light of the moon for three nights," Kelly told her. "Then take a quill made from the feather of a swan's wing, and write his name and yours together on this cloth three times with this liquid as the ink. Fold the cloth and put it between two flat stones beneath your bed, and leave it there two nights. On the third night at midnight, take the cloth out and hold it above your head while you say his name and yours three times. Do this for two more nights, then burn the cloth. Can you remember all of it?"

"Aye, and do it, too," Joan said, and hesitated. "But 'twould be best, I think, an you'd show me how to shape the letters for the names."

Kelly showed her. "An you do as I've said, this man will be your slave, unless he is himself a great magician."

"'Tis not possible," Joan said, laughing. A few moments later, they left the copse in opposite directions. Joan headed for Chipping Norton just downriver, her mind occupied with strategies for obtaining three of John's hairs. Kelly returned to Mortlak, to make another trial of the crystal. His interlude with Joan Bowes had given him an idea, and he planned to see whether certain letters written with ink aged in moonlight would persuade the spirits of the crystal to make real gold for him once more.

◆   ◆   ◆

The rumors of devils and black magic in the forest outside Mortlak were not confined to the town. Word of the strange events of Master Kirton's hunt had come to London almost before the hunt itself was over, but a single incident, however sinister, was not sufficient to draw more than a thoughtful nod from those whose business it was to investigate such things. But when stories continued to circulate throughout the spring, the witch-hunters began to take notice.

"The town of Mortlak's uneasy," a slender man in a black scholar's robe said to the heavyset man seated across the table from him. "Would it bear looking into, do you think?"

"An I were certain what 'uneasy' meant, I could perhaps make some answer," the second man replied smoothly.

"There was some talk of phantoms in the woods nearby, and a most unnatural bear, but that was in the winter, and there's been no report since," the slender man said, tapping a folded sheet of paper that lay on top of the pile in front of him. "I am inclined to think no more of the phantoms. But these persistent rumors of sorcery—"

"In the town itself?" the heavyset man interrupted. His companion nodded, and the heavy man shook his head. "Doctor Dee lives in Mortlak; I'll wager he's the root of all this talk."

"The Queen's Astrologer," the slender man said in a thoughtful tone. "He hath powerful friends at court."

"Exactly."

"But he's been accused before."

"He has," the heavy man replied with visible reluctance. "'Twas claimed that he did murder a young boy by sorcery, but 'twas not proven."

The first man frowned at the paper-covered table. "This talk's gone on too long to be ignored," he said at last. "We must proceed, but not with haste. Send someone to speak with Doctor Dee; if more than that's required, we'll decide it later."

"As you wish," the heavy man answered. "Now, as to the woman in Kent who hath bewitched her neighbor's cow . . ."

◆　　　◆　　　◆

Bochad-Bec and Furgen had found Madini's arrogance irritating from the very beginning of their association, and they were nearing the end of their patience. Inevitably, once it became clear that Madini's efforts to obtain the crystal were showing no results, each of them asked to be included in her spell-casting. Equally inevitably, Madini refused.

This slight brought Furgen and Bochad-Bec to their usual meeting place under the oak by the border of Faerie, but this time they did not mention the meeting to their contemptuous partner. They began by comparing the responses they had each received from Madini when they offered to assist her.

"She called me a bumbler because I brought her the lamp and not this crystal that she claims holds Hugh's power," Bochad-Bec told Furgen, all but beside himself with rage. "She said she did not want a bumbler by while she worked!" The oakman spat violently, nearly dislodging his red cap, and looked suspiciously at his companion. "Hadst thou better luck?"

"No," Furgen answered. The water creature's face, usually so impassive, betrayed traces of a cold anger that was no less strong than Bochad-Bec's. "She told me the spells she wove to link the lamp and crystal were too delicate to trust to a lesser magician than herself."

The oakman snorted, but his shoulders relaxed slightly. "Madini insulted us both, then. We should stop her, I think."

"'Tis time for that, and past time," Furgen agreed. It stroked one long, grey finger across the points of its teeth. "And I know how to do it, if I can come at the lamp when she's not near."

"In three days she'll be at court, serving the Queen," Bochad-Bec said. "She cannot take the lamp with her."

"That will do very well."

"What wouldst thou do?" Bochad-Bec said. A breeze rustled the leaves of the oak above him, sending dappled shadows dancing across the ground below.

"Succeed where she's failed," Furgen answered shortly. "She's tried to make the humans let us in; I'll work otherwise, and draw them out to us. And we'll see how Madini talks then."

"It's not the humans we want," the dwarf pointed out.

"They'll bring the crystal with them," Furgen said. "I'll see to that, never fear."

"And what's my part in this?" Bochad-Bec said truculently.

"Why, to be by John Dee's house to snatch the crystal once I've made him bring it forth," Furgen answered.

"Ah." The oakman considered this proposal for a moment, then waggled his beard in agreement. "I'll do it."

"I'm grateful," Furgen said with a touch of sarcasm that passed completely by the dwarf. "Now come, and I'll show thee how to come at the house unseen. The river's best, and thou mayest hide in the kitchen garden." The fay departed to inspect the exterior of John Dee's house in Mortlak.

◆   ◆   ◆

While the Faerie folk were at their work, Dee and Kelly were in the throes of yet another argument. Their money was running short, and the crystal still refused to make anything but Faerie gold, despite Madini's comforting appearances. The proposed genealogy had satisfied Prince Laski for the moment, but it was clear to both the wizards that sooner or later the Polish envoy would request a demonstration of more immediately useful magic. Dee, to his partner's annoyance, refused to consider any of Kelly's suggestions, and instead expressed with some frequency his willingness to leave the matter in the hands of God. This stubbornness at last drove Kelly from the house, to pace the flat bank above the water stairs, while from the shadows by the wall Furgen and Bochad-Bec watched with glittering eyes, then slipped away.

CHAPTER · EIGHTEEN

◆

"The fish was stronger than the dwarf, and though the little man tried to catch hold of the reeds to pull himself back, it did him little good. The reeds bent and the rushes broke, and the dwarf was in great danger of being dragged into the water.

"The two girls arrived just in time. They caught hold of him and pulled him back, but though they tried their best to untangle his beard from the fishing line, they could not do it. In the end, Snow White had to bring out her scissors once again and cut off another piece of the dwarf's beard."

◆

THE EVIDENCE OF FAERIE INTEREST IN DEE'S HOUSEhold increased John's certainty that it held the solution to Hugh's enchantment, and he redoubled his efforts to slip inside. He was unsuccessful, and in desperation he decided to use the only piece of powerful magic he had been able to bring with him out of Faerie.

Late one afternoon, early in July, he visited the Widow's cottage to explain his reasons and his strategy to her and her daughters, and to enlist their help. He had not previously told them of his attempts to search Dee's house, and the girls listened with absorption to his account.

"And you will try again?" Rosamund said. "But how can you now succeed, having failed so often?"

"I have a ring, which three times confers invisibility," John said. "I've used it twice: once long ago in a Faerie war, and once to follow you out of Faerie when the border was closed to me. I am determined to use it for the third and last time in this endeavor."

"'Tis good of thee, to use thy ring in thy brother's behalf," Blanche said softly.

John shrugged. "As may be. I'll have but one chance, and then the ring is useless. I've come to you for help, that we may wring the most advantage from this effort."

"What is it that thou wantest of us?" the Widow asked cautiously.

"'Tis completely safe, I warrant you," John said reassuringly. "I've found a spell that will allow your daughters to see me from afar, and I would have them sit with Hugh and watch me as I search."

"What, and you invisible?" Rosamund said.

"An the scrying spell doth not show me, 'twill show at least the rooms I pass through and what occurs around me," John said. "And if you're with Hugh, you may see some change in him that doth correspond to something where I am, which I could never tell. So we may learn something of use even if I fail."

"'Tis a good idea," the Widow said, much relieved to learn that this half-Faerie man did not intend to take her daughters with him to the sorcerer's home. "When wilt thou make this attempt?"

"Tomorrow," John answered. He frowned. "Hugh's been peevish and unquiet these last few days; I think delay might be unwise."

Rosamund and Blanche exchanged glances. "Then give us your scrying-spell to study," Blanche said for both of them, "and we'll be ready on the morrow."

◆　　　◆　　　◆

Furgen's plans to best Madini had at first gone smoothly. The water creature had had no difficulty in abstracting Dee's lamp from Madini's quarters. It then went swiftly through the streams and rivers to a shadowed, silent pool deep in the Faerie forest. There it stood, waist deep in the mirror-dark water between the shining blooms of the water lilies, waiting for Dee and Kelly to try to use their crystal.

For seven hours Furgen crouched, motionless and silent, while dawn brightened into daylight and minnows nibbled at the webs between its toes. At last Ned Kelly's face appeared in the side of the lamp. Furgen waited a moment longer, hoping Dee would come as well, but he did not, for Kelly's quarrels with his partner had reached the point where Kelly had at last decided to continue his experiments in gold-making alone. Furgen had hoped to snare both the wizards, but it was tired of waiting, so with a flick of its long, grey fingers it set its carefully crafted enchantment in motion.

The faint glow of the lamp dimmed and turned from gold to tarnished silver. Kelly's eyes, staring from the side of the lamp, went wide, and he tried to draw away. The picture on the lamp followed him, and Furgen smiled with all its pointed teeth. The link was now established, from Furgen through the lamp and crystal straight to Kelly. "Come," the water creature whispered. "Come to me, and bring the crystal."

"Be gone, foul spirit!" Kelly said hoarsely, his words echoing along the intangible link.

Furgen chuckled. So long as Kelly bent his mind to dismissing it, the water creature was entirely safe, for it was not present. "Come to me," it said again, and in the Mortlak study the words seemed to issue from the air at Kelly's shoulder. "Bring me the crystal; come."

To Furgen's surprise, Kelly did not move. "Come out," Furgen spat. "Come to the river, and bring the globe."

"I adjure thee, in the name of God: be gone, and trouble me no more!" Kelly cried, raising his fists to his temples.

"Come," was Furgen's answer. Its cold hands stroked the lamp gently, and Kelly shuddered convulsively.

"No! Go hence, go away, be gone!" Kelly cried. He pressed his palms over his ears, then suddenly turned and all but ran from the study.

Furgen hissed in annoyance. Kelly was stronger than it had anticipated, and it was plain that the water creature's spell would not quickly force the mortal to bring the crystal out from behind Dee's protective spells. Now that the link was established, however, there was no need for Kelly to be present in the room where the crystal stood; Furgen could reach him anywhere. "Come," the water creature repeated with monotonous insistence. "Come to the river, with the crystal. Come."

◆　　　◆　　　◆

The struggle between Furgen and Kelly was the direct cause of the distress that John had noted in the bear. The power of the crystal was Hugh's, and its every use touched him, no matter where he was or what his condition. The mortal spells of Dee and Kelly had affected him very little, but Madini and Furgen were of Faerie, and each time they used the link between the lamp and the crystal Hugh felt a little more of himself being chipped away. Soon there would be nothing left but the bear.

By the time Rosamund and Blanche arrived, Furgen and Kelly had been locked in a battle of wills for nearly four days, and the bear was whining and pacing constantly back and forth between two trees. The girls soothed him as best they could. When he was calmer, they laid out the tools they had brought for the scrying spell: a flat bowl, a flagon of rosewater, a sachet of violets, and a small, silver mirror. Blanche put the bowl on the ground, wedging it carefully with stones and small twigs so that it would not tip. Rosamund poured the violets into the bottom of the bowl and set the silver mirror on top of them. Then, while Blanche whispered the words of the spell, she let the rosewater run down the side of the bowl until the mirror was just covered.

The mirror dulled, then brightened, and the two girls bent over it eagerly. John stood in the narrow passageway between Dee's house and the next, turning a small ring over in his hand and watching the entrance of the passage. Suddenly he vanished, and the girls gasped, but the vision in the mirror remained otherwise clear. The picture began to shift, as if it followed someone, and Blanche let out the breath she had been holding. The two girls watched in fascination as the miniature scene moved through the kitchen garden to the door above the water stairs.

◆　　　◆　　　◆

John had to wait until someone left the house; the Dee household was far too conscious of spirits for him to risk a cook or manservant sighting a door opening and closing by itself. The wait was not a long one, for Mistress Dee kept an exemplary household and the servants were constantly coming and going, fetching herbs for the cook, dumping buckets of dirty scrubwater into the river, running in and out of the house on a thousand different errands. John slipped inside with one of the kitchen maids and began methodically searching the house.

The kitchen, buttery, and larder were unlikely places to find evidence of spell-working. John gave them each a cursory look and went on toward the front of the house. The great hall was all but empty; a settle with its back to the fireplace, three joint-stools shoved against the wall, and a faded hanging of ancient lineage were the sum of its furnishings. In one corner a heavy wooden staircase led upward. John gave a cursory look behind the hanging, then crossed to the stairs and started up to the second floor.

The gallery above looked as if it would take more time to search. John went to the first of the chests that stood along the walls, but as he opened it, he heard voices from the next room. Carefully, he closed the lid, then walked the length of the gallery to the door at the opposite end. Just before he reached it, the door flew open, and Ned Kelly's voice came clear and loud through the opening.

◆　　　◆　　　◆

Once Furgen's spell was cast, it did not matter whether Kelly was gazing into the crystal or not. Furgen's whispers followed him wherever he went, so long as Furgen continued to focus his attention on the lamp. At first, Kelly had been able to keep Master Dee unaware of his difficulties, but his irritability and unusually preoccupied state of mind finally drove Dee to confront him.

"What ails you, Ned?" Dee demanded with, for him, unusual force. "And say not that 'tis naught; you've been unlike yourself these four days past."

"'Tis more than nothing, true," Kelly answered with a sigh, "but I know not how best to say what 'tis."

"Tell me howe'er you can," Dee said.

"I am . . . most sorely troubled by some spiritual creature," Kelly admitted after a moment's pause. His eyes avoided the gazing table and the crystal resting in its center. "It sitteth on my left shoulder, here, and whispers 'come' and gurgles of the river. Methinks it calls me on to drown myself."

Dee stared at him with an appalled expression. "Nay, Ned! You must not do so! 'Twere deadly sin to kill yourself."

"To kill is deadly? Never say so," Kelly responded sourly. "Be sure that I've no wish to, but this creature's whispering's like to drive me mad."

"Resist it!" Dee said, growing more agitated. "Think of our work!"

"Thinking's been no help to me," Kelly said, irritated. "My need's to rid myself of this tormenter, not to think on't."

"I'll to my books at once," Dee said, brightening a little. "We'll find some way to accomplish this removal. Belike the spirit of the crystal—"

"Enough!" Kelly shouted. "God knows, you're as bad as this spirit that troubles me. Next time I'll heed it when it says, 'Come away and drown!'"

"Nay, Ned, you must not!" Dee said. "'Tis some evil wight that seeks to do you injury."

"'Tis injury enough to stay here!" Kelly snapped. He strode to the door of the study and threw it open with a crash that made Dee wince and gave a moment's pause to the invisible John outside. "I'd rather drown than hear more of this prating."

"I will not let you go," Dee said, grabbing Kelly's arm.

Furgen, who had been watching all this through the lamp, chose this moment to exert its influence. Whether Kelly stayed or went mattered little to the water creature, but it was clear that if Kelly left now he would not take the crystal with him, and Furgen's time was growing short. So, grimacing with effort, Furgen made one final try at getting Kelly to scoop up the crystal and take it with him.

♦   ♦   ♦

John reached the open door and peered through it just as Kelly lurched backward three paces, wrenching his arm from Dee's grasp. Dee went after him, determined to keep him in the room by force, if necessary. On the far side of the room, the crystal sat in the center of the gazing table, light dancing and shifting in its center. The sight attracted John's attention immediately, and he recognized at once the similarity between the glow at the heart of the crystal and the shifting light of the Faerie border. He felt a surge of excitement, and since the doorway was now clear he ignored the scuffle on his left and started forward.

He could not pass the door. John, whose blood was half of Faerie and who wore Faerie magic on his finger, was barred from John Dee's study by the same spells and inscriptions that kept Madini and her friends at bay. Though he fought with all his might, he could not cross the threshold. He stared at the crystal in chagrin, sure that it was what he had come for and unable to reach it.

Furgen's face appeared in the crystal, contorted in agony. John jerked back in surprise. The vision winked out, and the light within the crystal dimmed to a glowing pinpoint. Simultaneously, Kelly ceased his struggle with Dee and said in tones of deep relief, "'Tis gone!"

"Praise Heaven!" Dee replied. He was panting and disheveled, and rather more the worse for wear than his companion. "Now, come away and rest, and tell me your tale in full. We'll work no more until the morrow."

"Nay, I'm fit for it," Kelly said, but he gave the crystal an uneasy look as he spoke, and he did not resist as his companion drew him toward the door.

John recovered from his surprise in time to move out of the way before Dee ran into him. He hesitated briefly, then followed the two men. The object of his search was in the study, where he could not venture, but he might still learn something from the wizards' conversation.

◆   ◆   ◆

Rosamund and Blanche, watching the mirror intently, knew at once when John broke off his hunt to investigate the study. They saw the door fly open as John approached it, though they did not hear Kelly's shouting; their enchanted mirror could not reflect sound. At the sight of the two sorcerers struggling, Blanche started and nearly struck the viewing bowl in her surprise. Rosamund's cry of warning was drowned by a howl from Hugh.

The heads of both girls jerked in the bear's direction. Hugh was rocking back and forth on his haunches, shaking his head as if to dislodge a bee. "Hugh, what is it?" Blanche cried, but all he could do was whine.

Rosamund glanced back at their scrying mirror and clutched Blanche's arm. "Look!"

The mirror, which should have reflected all of John Dee's study, showed only the crystal. Light shifted and flowed in its center, swirling around a central point from which three tendrils reached out. Two of the tendrils were only partially visible; their ends vanished off the edges of the mirror, out of sight. The third seemed to rise impossibly out of the surface of the mirror, connecting the image of the crystal to Hugh with a thin, almost invisible cord of light.

"No!" Blanche cried, and she leaned forward and knocked over the bowl that held the mirror.

The tendril of light that was the link between Hugh and the crystal vanished from sight as the direct connection forged by the scrying spell was broken. The sudden change upset the balance within the crystal, and Kelly, still fighting Furgen's spell with all his will, was able to break free at last. The recoil from the two links, one severely reduced, the other completely shattered, surged down the sole remaining link and overwhelmed Furgen. For a brief instant, the crystal reflected the water creature's agony; then the image vanished, having been seen by John alone, and Furgen slumped lifeless over the melted remains of the lamp he had been working through.

◆   ◆   ◆

In the instant between Blanche's instinctive action and Furgen's death, the air of Faerie trembled with the faint, tingling vibration that heralds the presence of great power. The Queen of Faerie felt it, and her eyes narrowed dangerously, for such strong spells may never be cast in Faerie without the knowledge and permission of the Queen. Madini felt the tremor, too, and, suspecting something of its cause, she impartially cursed John and Hugh, her fellow plotters, and the fate that kept her bound to the court for another day. All she could do was to hide her anger and misgivings, and hope that she could retrieve the situation once her service at the court was done.

CHAPTER · NINETEEN

"When the dwarf saw what they had done, he screamed, 'You toadstool! Wasn't cutting off the end enough for you? No, now you have to slice off the best part! How can I let myself be seen, disfigured this way? I wish you may run the soles off your shoes!' Then he took up a bag of pearls which he had hidden among the rushes and left without saying another word."

WHEN BLANCHE BROKE THE SCRYING SPELL, HUGH'S spasms stopped at once. The girls stayed with him long enough to be certain he had not been harmed, then gathered up their things and left. Much subdued, they headed home to wait for John, hoping his story would explain at least some of what had happened.

They did not have long to wait. John arrived barely an hour later, his expression grim. He and Rosamund disagreed almost at once over who was to tell his story first; each of them wanted to hear the other's tale before telling his own. The Widow intervened when the argument seemed about to deteriorate too far, and decreed that Rosamund and Blanche should begin. Rosamund showed a tendency to pout at this decision, but Blanche accepted it without demur. She gave John a quick summary of the strange behavior of the scrying mirror, its apparent effect on Hugh, and her own instinctive reaction and its result.

"The crystal filled the mirror entirely?" John asked when she had finished.

Blanche and Rosamund nodded.

"And all you saw within was light? Are you certain there was no image?"

Blanche looked doubtful, but Rosamund shook her head positively. "There was no image, only light, until Blanche overset the bowl and broke the scrying spell. I am sure of it."

"This is strange indeed," John murmured. He shook himself, then gave a straightforward account of his own experiences.

"And since I could learn no more where I was, I followed the wizards," he finished.

"And did you learn more?" Rosamund asked pointedly when John showed no sign of continuing.

"'Tis conjecture, in the main, pieced together from their conversation," John said. "The wizards have stolen Hugh's magic, and 'tis prisoned in that crystal that you saw. I think they do not know what they have done, for they spoke only of 'Faerie power' and never of Hugh, and they guard their workroom against all Faerie. 'Tis why I could not enter and take back the crystal while they fought; there is enough of Faerie in me to give their warding spells some purchase."

"Then Blanche or I must find a way," Rosamund said, as if it were the obvious solution. "We're only mortal; spells to frustrate Faerie will not ward us off."

"No," said the Widow with absolute finality. "I forbid it. Neither thou nor thy sister will go near the house of Master Dee, now or in the future, and there's an end on't."

"But, Mother—" Rosamund started.

"No! Thou'st done more than is wise already; this time I'll not be swayed against my better judgment."

"How else may we free Hugh?" Blanche asked with a calm and overly reasonable air that betrayed her inner tension. "We cannot abandon him now, and I see no other way to help him."

"Aye, and 'twill be the end of all this business," Rosamund added swiftly. "Will it not, John?"

"Nay, ask me not to add my voice to yours," John said. "In this, I agree with your mother. And I think there is one other path still left to try, ere we are driven to such desperate measures as you propose."

"What path is that?" Blanche asked warily.

"One that's mine to deal with," John answered. "Nay, hear me out! I fear we've learned all that we can from Masters Dee and Kelly, and I doubt that we can steal the crystal from them. Their skill's not small, and they are well protected. But the wizards are not our only rivals in this matter."

"The oakman, who stole the lamp!" Rosamund interrupted in sudden enlightenment.

John nodded. "And the water fay whose image I saw in the crystal. There's more here than we know, and till we learn it we may do Hugh more hurt than help by descending on the wizards alone."

Rosamund was disposed to argue this conclusion, but her efforts were foredoomed to failure. The Widow supported John, for while she was not pleased by the thought of still more Faerie involvement in their affairs, she was far more unhappy with Rosamund's proposed invasion of Dee's house. Blanche, too, took John's side; the hint of harm to Hugh had been all that was needed to set her firmly against any precipitate action.

The talk soon turned to ways of discovering what they wanted to know. It was quickly obvious that none of them had any promising ideas, and eventually they agreed to let the matter rest for a day or two. John departed for Mortlak, and the Widow Arden and her daughters returned to their work.

❖   ❖   ❖

The question of Faerie involvement in the spell that affected Hugh preoccupied John throughout his walk back to the house he had rented in Mortlak. Until very recently, he had assumed (as he had told the Widow on the night they met) that Faerie had no further interest in himself or Hugh. Bochad-Bec's theft of the lamp had cast some doubt on this assumption, but John had been inclined to believe that the oakman's interest was in Dee and Kelly rather than himself. The appearance of a water fay in the crystal, and the description Rosamund and Blanche had given of the simultaneous effects on Hugh, severely shook John's certainty in that regard. He still saw no sign of active Faerie interest in Hugh, but it was beginning to appear that indirect curiosity might well be even worse.

Deep in thought, John followed his usual route through the town, half unconscious of his surroundings, until a low, startled exclamation behind him made him turn, just as hands clutched at the back of his neck and his right shoulder.

Joan Bowes had been trying for over a month to obtain the three hairs Kelly had told her were necessary to the love spell he had given her. It was not, she found, an easy task. John Rimer was not a regular visitor at any household other than the Widow Arden's, and there was no easy way for Joan to gain access to his home. She had tried delivering an invented message, but she had not been allowed past the entry hall, much less had any opportunity to search for John's comb.

Having failed with indirect methods, Joan had determined to try a direct one. She lay in wait for John as he returned from the Widow's cottage, then deliberately stumbled as he passed her. Her outstretched hands clutched at his back: one on his shoulder, the other in the hair at the nape of his neck.

"Oh, pray pardon me, sir," she said with wide-eyed innocence as John turned, wincing. "I tripped and lost my balance."

"'Tis no great matter, Mistress," John answered. "You are not hurt, I trust?"

"Nay, I'm a little shaken, that is all."

"Then I am glad to have been of service to you," John said. He bowed, and smiled formally, and left, while behind him Joan carefully opened her left hand and counted the strands of fine, dark hair that twined around her fingers, then tucked them carefully into the band of her kirtle.

◆　　　◆　　　◆

The stirring events of the morning precipitated yet another argument in the half-timbered house by the river. John Dee had hovered over his friend Kelly until he began to recover somewhat, then proposed once more, and with considerable force, that they cease all experiments with the Faerie crystal.

"What! When we're so near success?" Kelly exclaimed, sitting bolt upright on his stool beside the dining table.

Dee stared into space, stroking his beard. "Are we?" he said at last.

"We must be," Kelly said firmly. "How can you doubt it? The renewal of the crystal's fire—"

"—need not portend success," Dee said. "It meaneth activity only, and we know not what manner of activity it may be. Indeed, to my mind it seemeth more likely to mean obstruction than success."

"Who could oppose us?" Kelly said in tones of dismissal.

"I know not, but someone doth," Dee answered seriously. "Since the end of winter, when first the light in the crystal failed, we've had naught but ill luck in all our doings with it. That spirit which so lately did torment you is but the freshest of these malicious interventions."

"I do not think . . . No, you may be right in this." Kelly frowned. "But, look you, to cease our work is to retire from the battlefield before the fight's engaged. We cannot do it."

"Yet to continue doth endanger all within these walls," Dee said. He looked exceedingly unhappy. "How long will these evil spirits be satisfied with tormenting you and me alone? No, Ned, I do not see how we can go on in conscience."

"A pox on these interfering wights, whate'er they be!" Kelly said passionately. He slammed his fist down on the oak boards of the tabletop. "Curse them! Curse—" Suddenly his eyes widened and he stared at Dee as if thunderstruck. "That's it, John!"

"What?" Dee said cautiously, bewildered by his companion's sudden shift of mood.

"We'll curse them!" Kelly said triumphantly. "We'll set a snare upon the crystal, and when they meddle with it again, we'll catch them and destroy them."

"Have we the power for that?" Dee asked, his expression troubled.

"Our spells have kept these meddlesome beings from active deeds, have they not?" Kelly said. "These creatures have worked only through the crystal. I think that answers your misgiving."

"In part. 'Tis very well to say 'we can,' but we'll not have certain knowledge of it till we put our plans to the test, and then 'twill be too late an we're mistaken."

"You fear to take the risk?"

Dee considered. "For myself, no," he said at last. "The benefit far outweighs the danger, in my mind. But I'll not risk my books and family, nor my servants and this house, and I fear that's what this ultimately means."

"Then we'll lay our snare so that we'll not confront the wicked spirits here," Kelly said dismissively. "We'll trace them to their lairs, and face them there; an we're well prepared, it will not matter much. Then if things go awry, your house is safe."

"Evil spirits have no lairs, Ned," Dee said.

"But wights of Faerie do, and I am much mistaken if 'tis not Faerie meddling that we face," Kelly retorted. "What say you, John?"

"I must think on it," Dee responded, and that was all the answer Kelly could get from him that day. The following morning, Dee agreed to Kelly's proposal, but with enough conditions and caveats to make Kelly lose his temper all over again.

In the end, Kelly acceded to Dee's demand that further experimentation with the crystal should cease, but he was far from happy about it. He had been counting on crystal-made gold to relieve him of some of his more pressing financial embarrassments, and the loss of this potential revenue was hard for him to bear. Dee, who was not insensitive to his friend's difficulties, did what he could, giving Kelly a small sum of money and a promise of fifty pounds a year (which he could ill afford). With this, Kelly had to be content, and the two wizards began the work of designing spells to trace and trap the beings who had been disrupting their labors.

◆   ◆   ◆

No outside force interrupted them, and for this there was good reason. The Queen of Faerie had sensed the recoil of power from the breaking of Furgen's spell of influence, and the Queen was not pleased. She sent some of her most powerful servants to find the source of the disturbance. They returned very quickly with Furgen's body and the melted remains of the lamp, but they had no way of telling what the water creature had attempted to do. The lump of metal that had been Dee's lamp was too changed to hold more than the barest hint of magic, and that hint was human, not of Faerie. Further than that, no one would speculate.

In cold anger, the Queen dismissed her ladies and her court and retired to her chambers, and all of Faerie walked very softly for some time thereafter.

Among those who exerted the greatest care to go unremarked were Madini and Bochad-Bec. The oakman had learned of Furgen's death almost immediately upon his return to Faerie, and had prudently gone into hiding at once, as much from fear of Madini's reaction as from dread that the Queen would learn of his part in the matter. Then, too, dealing with mortal magic had proven unexpectedly hazardous. Bochad-Bec had no desire to share

Furgen's fate, and in any case he was tired of plots, tired of mortals, and tired to death of Madini's arrogance. It was only just, he felt, that she should have to do some of the real work—and take some of the risks—herself.

Madini was furiously angry. The primary object of her rage was Furgen, who had dared to steal the lamp and use it, and then escaped into death before she could properly punish it. She was furious, too, with the mortal sorcerers. Not for an instant did she believe that their magic was the cause of Furgen's death; in her opinion, the water fay had simply overreached itself, and paid the price of its presumption. The sorcerers were, however, the fundamental reason for the whole sorry state of affairs: it was their last-minute change in the timing of their spell that had kept her from guiding it toward John instead of Hugh, their wards that made retrieval of Hugh's stolen power so difficult, and their stupid, stubborn refusal to cooperate that had made Madini look bad to her fellow conspirators.

Without the lamp, Madini could no longer reach and use the power of the crystal, nor influence Dee and Kelly as she had previously tried to do. Her fellow conspirators were dead or vanished, which limited her access to information about the mortal world. Worst of all, the Queen was angry and suspicious, and would be watching with great care for hints of Furgen's purpose, and for other, similar spells. It would be some time before Madini could risk making another move against the mortal magicians and their crystal. Fuming inwardly, Madini settled down to wait, and plan.

◆　　　◆　　　◆

By mid-July, the slow mill wheels of authority had begun to move. A small, sly man was summoned to a long, bare room on the third floor of a wooden house near the edge of London. A heavyset man with brown hair and a look of solid, middle-class respectability waited there.

The smaller man was prompt; he entered the room with his cloth cap in one hand and said doubtfully, "Master Rodgers?"

"I own the name," the heavyset man said, waving the newcomer to a joint-stool beside the table. "And you will be Charles Sledd."

"That I am, sir." Sledd ran his tongue nervously over his lips. "You've a job for me to do?"

Rodgers did not reply at once. His superiors' instructions notwithstanding, he continued to have grave misgivings about embarking on an investigation of Doctor Dee, who received visits from courtiers such as Lord Russell, Sir Phillip Sydney, Lord Walsingham, and even from the Queen herself. He had, however, delayed matters as long as he dared. "I have," he said. "You're to go to Mortlak. There's talk of foul sorcery in the town, and 'tis like that Doctor Dee's work is the occasion of it. Come near him by some ruse, but remember: you're to look and come away, no more."

"As you say, sir," Sledd replied, nodding respectfully. When he raised his head, there was a glint in his eyes. "And the wage, sir?"

Rodgers threw a small cloth bag, tied at the neck with a piece of string, across the table. It landed with a muffled clinking. "There's for you to begin; more will follow, an the word you bring back suits us."

The bag vanished into the recesses of Sledd's clothing. "Thank you, sir; I'll do my best."

"'Twere best you did," Rodgers said dryly, and the small man left.

◆　　　◆　　　◆

John Rimer did not return to the Widow's cottage for nearly a week. Rosamund, who had become accustomed to frequent visits, was first angry and then troubled by his absence. Her mother was not so strongly affected, though the Widow cast occasional frowning glances down the road toward Mortlak when she thought no one was looking. Blanche's mind was almost completely taken up in reworking yet again the spell she hoped would disenchant

Hugh; she commented fretfully that she could use John's assistance, but otherwise seemed untouched by his truancy.

This attitude did not endear Blanche to her sister, and the atmosphere in the cottage had become unusually tense by the time John finally came walking up the road from the village.

"Where hast thou been?" Rosamund demanded as he entered the cottage. Her voice mingled with Blanche's, who said at the same instant, "What news of Hugh?"

"Girls!" the Widow said sharply.

John bowed to the Widow and gave Blanche and Rosamund his most charming smile. "Good morrow, Mistresses. I hope I find you well?"

"Well!" Rosamund said indignantly. "Is that all—"

"Rose!" the Widow said even more sharply than before. Rosamund bit her lip but did not continue. The Widow eyed her daughters sternly until she was sure there would be no further unseemly behavior, then turned an equally severe expression on her visitor. "As for thee, Master Rimer, thou needst not try to cozen me. What is it thou dost want?"

"A favor," John admitted, "and one I'm loath to ask, but that I can find no other way to do it."

"What is it, and why art thou so unwilling to speak of it?" the Widow asked warily.

John looked at Blanche and Rosamund. "You said some time ago that soon you'd visit Faerie to collect your herbs. Do you still intend it?"

"We'd planned to go tomorrow, or the day after if the weather's poor," Blanche said.

"Then this is what I'd ask of you: to take a message with you into Faerie and leave it behind you there."

"No!" the Widow protested.

"I do not ask this lightly," John said. He looked at Rosamund and Blanche again, and then away. "I cannot go to Faerie and seek out the folk who have bedeviled Dee and Kelly. You can visit

Faerie, but the search that's needed is beyond the power of mortal visitors. Yet I still have friends who'd help if they but knew my need, or so I hope. It seems the sole solution. Will you take my message into Faerie?"

"I will not have it," the Widow said firmly, before Rosamund or Blanche could so much as nod. "'Tis dangerous enough to tempt witch-hunters; wouldst have my girls chance Faerie's anger too?"

"Nay, Mistress Arden, that I'd never ask," John said reassuringly. "'Tis why I've spent these last three days in crafting what I hope to send. Look here."

John reached into his purse and with a little difficulty drew out a grey, lumpy-looking, fist-sized rock. "This must be carried through the Faerie border and dropped on the other side, no more. The passage will upset the outer spell that holds this hollow shell together; within an hour, 'twill fall apart. The enchantment inside carries my message, and once free will seek out one who'll listen. There'll be naught left that can be used to trace how it was done."

The Widow looked at Rosamund's determined expression and Blanche's hopeful one, and sighed. "Thou'rt sure?" she asked John.

"I am."

"And I've no need to ask if you are willing," the Widow said to the girls, and sighed again. "Very well. An I forbade it, 'tis likely Rose would steal that lump and do it against both our wills."

John hesitated, then set the rock on the table. "I'll see you tomorrow, when 'tis done," he said. "Afterward I may not visit, lest I bring upon you the very attention I've tried to avoid."

"That's no matter," Rosamund said quickly. "We'll hang the house with rowan boughs and wear hawthorn in our kerchiefs. You've no need to forswear our company."

"I know that you have knowledge enough to guard yourselves from Faerie," John said gently. "But no man's proof against mistakes. 'Tis better that your knowledge be unneeded."

"What of thy brother?" Blanche said. "How shall we have word of him, and how he fares?"

"'Twere best that thou forget him for a time," John answered.

"We'll send word when we're certain it will not bring harm with it."

"Thou mayest think it 'best,' but 'tis impossible," Blanche said, and her eyes filled with unshed tears. "If we're willing to chance Faerie notice—"

"If harm should come to thee or to thy family because of Hugh and me, we'd sorrow for it all our lives," John said soberly.

Rosamund swallowed the indignant comment she had been about to make, and looked at her mother. "What sayest thou to this, Mother?" she asked.

"I think John's wise, and generous," the Widow answered. "Still, he'll be welcome here, whenever he comes. 'Tis his to judge when that should be."

"And we're to have no say in this at all?" Rosamund said in the tones of one who knows the argument is lost. "How can we be of help to Hugh, if we see neither him nor John?"

John sighed. "There's naught more can be done before I've had word from Faerie. Will it content you if I promise to seek your aid as soon as we have need of it?"

Rosamund was far from content, but neither she nor Blanche could persuade John to change his mind. The Widow refused to be drawn into the argument, and at last the girls were forced to accept his decision.

The following day, everything went as planned. Rosamund and Blanche carried the rock into Faerie and left it at the foot of a beech tree, then went on to gather herbs. Rosamund was almost unhappy that things had gone so smoothly; for all their mother's protests, there seemed to be nothing dangerous about crossing into Faerie and dropping a rock. She wanted to pass by the spot on their way home, to see whether John's spell had worked, but Blanche overrode her, and the girls returned home by a different route.

CHAPTER · TWENTY

•

"Some time later, the mother sent the girls to town to buy needles and pins and thread for sewing. On their way, they crossed a meadow, and as they walked they saw a large eagle circling in the air above them. Suddenly it dove toward the ground, and the girls heard a cry of terror. They ran toward it and saw that the dwarf was once again in trouble; the eagle had seized him and was about to carry him off."

•

THE MESSAGE ROSAMUND AND BLANCHE TOOK INTO Faerie brought quick results. Two days after the girls made their expedition, John was walking through a stand of beeches in the forest when something fell out of one of the trees, knocking his hat off. John looked up; seeing nothing, he bent to retrieve his hat. The missile was still lodged firmly in the brim. John stared at it, then said casually, "Thou mayest show thyself, Robin. Or wouldst thou have me believe that chestnut burrs have begun to grow on beeches?"

High in the air, branches rustled. A moment later a wiry youth slid down the trunk of one of the beech trees. He wore a loose green jerkin and brown hose that fit him like a second skin. He tossed his head to shake an unruly shock of black hair from in front of his eyes, and grinned at John. "I see thou thinkest thyself a clever one."

"I never said so," John answered, but he smiled in spite of himself. "'Tis good to see thee, Robin."

"Maybe 'tis so for thee; I'll wait to judge till I've heard thy designs."

"Thou hadst my message, then?"

"Oh, aye, I had it, for all it told me. Thou hast a niggardly way with a tale, John," Robin said in a complaining tone.

"Why, did I not say I had need of thee?" John said innocently. "I knew curiosity would bring thee, if naught else did."

"Thinkest thou so little of my friendship, then?" Robin said indignantly. "Base rascal! I am insulted." He tilted his sharp chin upward in a display of displeasure that was immediately spoiled by his having to toss his hair out of his eyes once more. "Insulted," he repeated. "Aye, and wounded too." He shot John a sly, mischievous look. "Thou must make reparation for it!"

"Oh, indeed," John said with an exaggerated bow. "What dost thou demand?"

"A well-told tale, complete in all its parts," Robin said promptly.

"That thou mayest have, and welcome," John answered. "Save only that thou repeat it not in Faerie. The tale itself will tell thee why."

Robin folded his arms and leaned back against the mottled bark of one of the trees. "I am all attention."

Settling himself in a similar position, John gave his friend a full account of the nine months which had passed since his voluntary exile from Faerie. Robin interrupted frequently with questions, observations, and wry remarks, until at last John commanded him to hold his peace until the tale was told. Robin shrugged, his eyes dancing wickedly, but he did not interrupt again.

"Well?" John said when he finished. "What dost thou make of it?"

"Am I now permitted to speak?" Robin said with wide-eyed innocence. "I was not certain."

"Play not the fool," John said. "This matter's grave, to me at least, and I've no stomach for thy games."

"So I see," Robin said. "But I cannot change my nature. What wouldst thou?"

"I'd have the loan of thy eyes and ears," John answered, taking the question at face value. "Tell me what's toward at court, and the how and why of this Faerie meddling with the human wizards and their crystal."

"I can bore the ears from thy head with gossip of the court," Robin said, "but I can tell thee little of the matter that chiefly interests thee. These days there's little talk of mortals or the mortal world, and none that touches thee or thy unfortunate brother. The Queen likes it not."

"She hath forbidden it?"

"No, 'tis not so bad as that; merely, 'tis writ plain in her manner that talk of thee's unpleasing, and the court, as always, doth follow her lightest whim."

"What of Bochad-Bec and the wight I told thee of, that showed itself in the crystal?" John asked. "Knowest aught of them?"

"Oakmen are sour and solitary, and come seldom to the court," Robin answered. "I've seen Bochad-Bec a time or two, but I know little more of him. As to thy wight—" Robin scowled in concentration, and his hair fell into his eyes again. "I have a thought on that."

"Ring bells and sound trumpets," John said. "What is it?"

"Furgen died ten days ago. It was a grey and scaly water fay, much like to thy description, and it made no secret of misliking mortals."

"How did this Furgen die?" John asked.

"There's the heart of things. The fay was killed by recoil from some spell that seemingly o'erreached the bounds of Faerie. The Queen is furious."

"Well might she be," John said slowly. "This touches her authority. But how hath a water fay contrived the power for such a spell? Or was it one of the greater of its kind?"

"Nay, 'twas rather lesser," Robin said. He brushed his hair from his eyes with an impatient gesture and grinned impudently. "Thou seest why it hath such interest in't. Some stronger fellow needs must have assisted Furgen's work, but who would dare to so defy the Queen? And 'twas not Bochad-Bec, I'll warrant you; that one's no spellmaker of this ability."

"Who, then?" John said, his tone expressing his frustration with all the world. "Who and why?"

"That's the question, indeed," Robin said agreeably. "Wouldst care to wager on how long 'twill take me to discover it?"

"'Tis kind of thee to offer, Robin, but I cannot let thee take the risk," John replied. "It would go ill with thee, an the Queen were to find thee helping Hugh and me."

"Belike it would," Robin said. "And belike not. In any case, how dost thou think to stop me? I am no brown-haired mortal wench, to quail before thy railing and displeasure."

"Do not be a fool!" John said, and was not sure himself what part of Robin's statement he was referring to.

"Tcha!" Robin said. "It is my nature; how can I be otherwise?" He tilted his head to observe his companion, and grinned again. "And thou'st said thyself that curiosity is my besetting sin."

John rolled his eyes. "Thou art as bad as ever mortals be. Well, have a care, then; I've not so many friends of late that I can bear the loss of one."

"Thou art not so bereft as thou dost think," Robin said. "But have no fear for me; I'll find no grief in this."

"That's as may be. Now tell me, ere thou leavest: what news of court?"

Robin's eyes sparkled, and he launched into a witty description of the doings of the Faerie court, liberally laced with gossip. By the time they parted, John had an excellent picture of the state of affairs in Faerie, and he found it somewhat disturbing. The Queen had not put off her mourning clothes, and the atmosphere at court was uncomfortable, at best. Worst of all was the clear implication that Furgen's spells had been employed without the knowledge of the Queen.

John turned his conversation over and over in his mind during the long walk back to Mortlak. As he passed the Widow's cottage, he was strongly tempted to stop and ask her advice, but his promise to avoid drawing Faerie attention to the cottage held him back. Robin might have been followed, or the message spell noticed; if there were the slightest chance that the eyes of Faerie were turning in his direction, he would do nothing that might lead them to the Widow and her daughters.

◆　　　◆　　　◆

In the weeks that followed, John held firm to his resolve. He no longer visited the cottage, and tried to avoid even the most accidental meetings with Rosamund and Blanche. In this he was more successful than he would have liked, and he found himself thinking more and more often of Rosamund's chestnut hair and warm brown eyes while he waited for Robin to reappear with more specific news of Faerie.

Joan Bowes's sharp eyes noticed the change in John's habits, and she rejoiced silently at this evidence of her love spell's success. She had followed Kelly's directions with care, writing "John Rimer" and "Joan Bowes" three times on the cloth with a swan's feather and the magic ink containing John's hairs, steeped in moonlight. For a week following the spell's completion, she waited hopefully for John's head to turn in her direction. When it did not, she took to lingering in the street outside his lodgings whenever she could find an excuse for it. She was sure that sooner or later John would recognize her, and be lost.

John himself was quite unconscious of Joan's peculiar conduct, for Kelly's charm had not touched him at all. This was due more to his mother's distaste for her son's baptismal name than to his Faerie blood. Joan Bowes had had no way to know that the name she so carefully inscribed should have been "Thomas," not "John," and her spell had spent itself on emptiness.

When three weeks had gone by, and her hoped-for lover continued to ignore her, or to respond to her greetings with "Mistress" and an indifferent nod, Joan herself realized that the spell had failed. Stubbornly, she decided to find some other way to trap her chosen victim. Meanwhile, she consoled herself with the thought that at least her charm had put a stop to John's visits to the Widow Arden's cottage, and she spent several enjoyable hours picturing the disappointment of the Widow and her daughters at the disappearance of their suitor.

♦   ♦   ♦

The cessation of John's visits to the cottage pleased the Widow very well, for she was not blind to Rosamund's attraction to him. Had he been wholly mortal, she would have gladly given them her blessing, but she did not entirely trust John's Faerie blood, and she did not wish to see her daughter hurt. It would be as well for Rosamund to have some time alone, to reconsider, or so the Widow reasoned.

Moreover, the atmosphere in Mortlak troubled her. Witchcraft was no longer openly talked of in the market square or gossiped about in the public houses, but the joiner's shop was doing a brisk business in small crosses made of ash, some of the laborers had begun wearing loops of red thread tied to their wrists and ankles, and clumps of rowan berries had appeared above more than a few doorways. These circumstances revived all the Widow's misgivings about her family's involvement with sorcerers and creatures of Faerie; she was certainly not going to encourage her daughters to deepen that involvement. She would have stopped them talking about Hugh, could she have done so.

Keeping Rosamund and Blanche from discussing Hugh was,

however, quite beyond the Widow's power. She had to be content with keeping her daughters away from the forest and the Faerie border, and with filling their hours so full of work that they had little time for other considerations. She hoped that, with their time occupied and John no longer visiting to remind them, her daughters' interest in magic would gradually fade. It showed no sign of doing so, but the Widow knew how to be patient, particularly when she had no other choice.

•   •   •

Patience, even when there was no choice, was not and had never been Madini's strong point. A week after Furgen's death she was primed for action; by the end of July she was ready to explode. Unfortunately, the Queen of Faerie was still watching the border far too closely to allow a repetition of any of the spells that Madini had previously used to influence Dee and Kelly.

Of necessity, Madini turned to other channels. She slipped across the border (there being no ban on traffic to and from the mortal world, only on magical communication), and spent some time searching for a lever with which to pry the crystal free of Dee. She found Charles Sledd and his employers.

It had not previously occurred to Madini to make use of mortal edicts to achieve her purposes, but she realized at once that the witch-hunters were an ideal tool. If Dee and Kelly were arrested, their tools were certain to be confiscated as evidence, and once the crystal was outside Dee's study and the protective spells that surrounded it, Madini would have no difficulty whatever in stealing it at last. With any luck, the witch-hunters would notice something odd about John Rimer, and cause trouble for him as well.

Well pleased with her discovery, Madini began adding fuel to the fires of rumor already running wild in Mortlak. She sent ghostly illusions to dance above the rooftree of Dee's house at midnight, and disembodied voices to whisper Kelly's name among the tombstones beside the church. She left a piece of mandrake root on the doorstep of the house for the maid to find, and tormented those who spoke ill of the wizards in hopes that her victims would think that Dee and Kelly had cursed them. Then she returned to Faerie and waited expectantly for Sledd's arrival.

◆   ◆   ◆

Charles Sledd was not particularly admirable in other respects, but he at least knew his trade. On the first of August, he visited Dee's house, on the pretext of desiring a look at Dee's wooden chest of seals, and was very well received. Dee not only welcomed him, but invited him to come to dinner with the household.

For this good fortune, Master Sledd had the Queen herself to thank. On the previous day she had sent Master Dee a gift of forty angels, and this princely sum had been delivered by no less than the Earl of Leicester. Master Dee was, therefore, in an unusually expansive mood; Master Sledd had only to show a small interest in Dee's work, and the supper invitation was assured. The atmosphere was at first open and relaxed, and Master Sledd was soon deep in conversation with his host.

"They are great achievements," Sledd said, in response to a long explanation of Dee's various mathematical and nautical projects. "But I've heard that you've accomplished greater things still. What of those?"

"Those are not matters for common conversation," Kelly interrupted. He had paid little attention to Dee's guest until then, being more interested in watching Dee's wife as she quietly directed the servants who were bringing in pewter cups and plates to set before the diners.

Sledd, who was a quarrelsome man at best, took exception to Kelly's tone. "Do you call me common?" he demanded pugnaciously.

"I would not say—" Kelly began, then broke off, staring at the little man beside him. "What means this, John?" he said in quite a different tone.

"Why so fierce, Ned?" Dee asked, bewildered. "And what should it mean, but that I've invited Master Sledd to come to dinner with us, as I've done with others before?"

"I know you!" Sledd broke in, staring at Kelly. His voice was a snarl of resentment. "I saw you in York some three years past."

"And I know you!" Kelly retorted. "You're a renegade, a Papist, and an informer." He turned to Dee. "What does such a man at your table?"

"And what do you?" Sledd shouted. "Edward Kelly the forger, Edward Kelly the necromancer, Edward Kelly who had his ears—"

"Out!" Kelly roared, leaping up from the table, his face contorted with anger and the fear of revelation. "Out of this house, you pusillanimous maggot! Had I known 'twas you, I'd ne'er have sat with you. Out, I say!" He reached for Sledd, but the spy dodged too quickly for him.

"You'll rue those words!" Sledd cried. His face was blotched and purple with rage, and he had unconsciously clenched his hands into fists. Kelly, however, was considerably the larger of the two, and Sledd was not foolhardy enough to strike the first blow where he was almost certain to lose. He hesitated, then turned away. "I know when I'm unwelcome; I'll go. But mark me well: I say you'll rue this, and you shall."

"Threats from such as you do not affright me," Kelly sneered. "Get you gone! I'll have none of you."

Sledd threw Kelly one last furious look before departing, leaving a stunned silence behind him. Kelly's shoulders twitched, then relaxed. When the door had closed behind the erstwhile visitor, he turned to Dee and his wife, and bowed. "I do crave your pardon, Mistress Dee, and yours too, John, for causing such an uproar at your table. Would you have me leave as well?"

"Nay, Ned, do not go," Dee answered quickly. "Stay, and explain the meaning of all this."

"As you will." Kelly shook out his scholar's robe and seated himself once more. "The long and short of it is that I have known that wretch, and no word of his is to be trusted. He is a liar and a spy and worse, and I fear his presence means some mischief's afoot against us."

Mistress Dee's complexion turned a shade lighter, and she pressed her lips together. Her husband stroked his beard with one hand, frowning. "I thought him an honest man, but those wild accusations he threw at you give credence to your words."

"You were too trusting, John," Kelly said earnestly.

"Belike." Dee smiled suddenly. "But look you, 'tis all for the best. For he hath seen all I have to show, and can have found nothing wrong, and may so report to whoever sent him."

Kelly rolled his eyes. "Have I not said he's a liar above all else? You heard what he accused me of. He'll have us charged with witchcraft before the month is out; doubt it not."

"Then what are we to do?" Mistress Dee put in.

"Poland?" Dee said to Kelly. "Prince Laski—"

"Perhaps, but 'twould be better discussed elsewhere," Kelly said, with a meaningful look at the servants who were just bringing in five rabbits boiled in wine. On that unsatisfactory note, the conversation ended and the meal began.

CHAPTER · TWENTY-ONE

•

"The girls ran forward and caught hold of the dwarf. The eagle was not strong enough to fly away with all three of them, and at last he let go. The dwarf, once he had recovered a little, began abusing the girls as usual. 'Why weren't you more careful, you stupid clumsy creatures! Look at the holes you have torn in my coat!' He picked up a sack full of jewels, which he had dropped when the eagle caught hold of him, and slipped away into a hole. The girls were used to his ways by this time, and they shrugged and went on toward town to do their shopping."

•

WORD OF THE ROW BETWEEN KELLY AND SLEDD WAS soon all over the village. Dee's manservant told the whole tale to his good friend, Master Townsend's steward. The steward, knowing his employer was a friend of Dee's, mentioned the quarrel at breakfast, in the hearing of both the master and mistress, and that was the end of any hope Dee might have had of keeping the matter quiet.

When the two wizards were not immediately arrested for the practice of black magic, public opinion was outraged. For a fortnight the atmosphere was tense and angry. Master Dee was pelted with moldy bread and wormy green fruit whenever he dared to leave his house, and Master Kelly thought it best to take himself off entirely for a few days.

The initial wave of violence was subdued at last by the necessities of bringing in the harvest, and the town subsided into sullen resentment. By then, the demonstrations of ill-feeling had convinced Dee and Kelly that they would be wise to quit the country altogether, and they began making the arrangements in secret. The Polish Prince, greatly pleased by the genealogy Dee had finally delivered to him, had been urging the two men for some time to bring their skills and knowledge to Poland, where he promised them they would be greatly honored and (more to the point) well paid. Until the quarrel with Sledd, neither Dee nor Kelly had considered the proposal seriously; now, it seemed a quick and effective way of escaping the threat that hung over them. The departure was set for the third week of September, when Laski himself was leaving, and all the plans were carefully kept private so as to avoid interference from Sledd or his employers. Chief among the treasures they planned to bring to Poland with them was the crystal gazing globe that held the Faerie part of Hugh.

◆   ◆   ◆

The uproar in the village gave the Widow Arden yet another opportunity to point out to her daughters the risks of using magic. Her handwritten book of spells had long since been banished back to the bottom of the chest, but she had not tried to stop discussion of methods for disenchanting Hugh. Now even that was forbidden, and the crockery jars of Faerie herbs were hidden at the back of the shelf.

These changes could not have happened at a worse time for Rosamund and Blanche. Their frustration had reached a peak; Rosamund was anxious for action of some kind, any kind, and Blanche worried more and more about the possible effects on Hugh of remaining in bear form for so long. Both of them wanted to know what response John had had to his message, and both of them missed the company and camaraderie of the bear and his brother (though on the rare occasions when the subject arose John's name crossed Rosamund's lips most frequently, while Hugh was Blanche's chief concern). The girls had nearly reached the point of expressing their dissatisfaction to their mother when the rumors began flying around Mortlak and the Widow banned all talk of magic.

Rosamund and Blanche knew better than to argue when their mother spoke in that tone, and for a few days the girls accepted the prohibition. Then one afternoon while they were picking mint and basil, Rosamund pulled one of the basil plants up by the roots and hurled it like a spear at the garden wall.

"'Tis not fair!" she said.

"I see naught to complain of in it," Blanche said, retrieving the abused plant and examining it. "Thou shouldst not have uprooted it so hastily; we might have had another harvest or two from it, an thou hadst left it growing."

"I do not mean the basil, thou feather-brain," Rosamund replied crossly. "I mean this latest notion our mother's taken, that we'll be hung for witches if we so much as speak of Hugh, or John, or Faerie."

"Hush! She'll hear." Blanche cast a glance over her shoulder at the cottage.

"Nay, she's gone to Mortlak to fill her ears with yet more reasons why we must shiver in our smocks," Rosamund said with disgust. "Didst not hear her say so?"

"No," Blanche said, turning back to the patch of herbs, "but if thou'rt sure, then 'tis no matter."

"'Tis matter enough that she's so overcautious," Rosamund muttered. "She behaves as though we're children, without sense enough to take precautions; yet I'll be seventeen ere Christmas and thou hast turned eighteen already."

"She fears for us," Blanche said, clearly trying to be fair.

"What danger's in it for us, if Dee and Kelly are accused as witches? And that seems but little likely, or it should have happened ere now."

"It seems so to me as well," Blanche admitted, and sighed. "But Mother will not be convinced."

"Must we abandon John and Hugh because our mother's fearful?"

"I fear 'tis so," Blanche said very softly, and bent over the mint to hide her face. "'Tis hard, but there's no help for it."

"There is, an thou'st the stomach for't," Rosamund said, watching her sister closely.

"What's that?" Blanche asked, and her tone indicated her doubt.

"To work without Mother's knowledge," Rosamund said. "We've studied all she has to offer; surely we can devise a spell or two without her help."

Blanche's head came up and her expression was a combination of hope and disbelief. "Rose! Thou dost not mean it."

"Do I not? Look thou, in this our mother's wrong, no matter how it ends. For if her fear's unwarranted, then we've abandoned Hugh and John for naught. If she's right to fear that the town will soon be seeking witches to hang, 'tis all the greater reason to work while still we may."

"My heart agrees with thee," Blanche said slowly, "yet even so I do not see what's to be done, since Hugh and John do side with Mother. Nor do we know what's toward in Faerie."

"Dee and Kelly know less of Faerie than do we, yet they made the spell that stole Hugh's shape," Rosamund said, waving a handful of basil as if to brush away her sister's objections. "And Hugh was nowhere near them, yet their spell worked. Come, sister; say thou'lt help me try."

"Dost doubt it?" Blanche said with unusual determination. "There's danger in't, but I'd dare far worse to be of help to Hugh."

Something in her voice made Rosamund look sharply at her sister, and what she saw in Blanche's face caused her to hesitate.

"Thou knowest he's a prince of Faerie," she said, unsure of how to express her sudden suspicion or her warning.

"I know." Blanche dropped her eyes. "And if we are successful, he'll return there," she added softly. "I know that too; thou needst not say it."

Rosamund nodded. Unable to find words, she gave Blanche an impulsive hug of sympathy. Blanche smiled shakily and went on, "It matters not, or not in this, at least. But how shall we keep our trials from Mother?"

"'Twill not be easy," Rosamund said, frowning. "But if we labor in such secret that even Mother does not know, how will others suspect us?"

"And how shall we do that?"

"We'll make a beginning now, while she is gone, and after we'll work and plan in the forest as much as we may," Rosamund said. "We know the places where no one comes, and we can hang valerian and rue on the bushes to keep away the fay. And we'll plan so that if someone does come upon us unawares, 'twill look as though we're gathering herbs for Mother just as usual. 'Twill not be easy, but it can be done."

Blanche had no fault to find with this program, and the two girls set to work at once. In the two hours that passed before the Widow returned, they planned and plotted with all the suppressed energy produced by nearly two months of frustration and imposed inactivity. After some discussion, they were forced to set aside the idea of duplicating Dee and Kelly's spell, since they could not be sure what preparation had gone into making the tools the two men had used. They settled at last on an approach which was familiar to them both: herbery. Both girls had extensive knowledge of the mundane uses of the plants they gathered; their knowledge of the magical properties of herbs was not quite as wide, but it was still impressive. They would see what could be done with spells based on the plants that were their livelihood. In addition, this approach was unlikely to attract attention, either from their mother or from suspicious villagers.

The Widow was pleased by the marked improvement in her daughters' dispositions in the days that followed. She commended their work in the garden, and was more than willing to consent to several herb-gathering expeditions in the woods, once she was assured that the girls would stay away from Faerie. She began to hope that she had been right in thinking that the girls' preoccupation with magic would fade naturally, though she was not foolish enough to believe it had actually done so with such speed. She was more inclined to believe that Rosamund and Blanche were merely restraining any open acknowledgment of their interest, but for the time being she was content with that.

Meanwhile, Rosamund and Blanche took every opportunity to slip away to the forest and perform their trials. They dried rosemary and rue and herb-of-grace and burned them separately, and then together. They sang over some and muttered in Latin over others. They made infusions of boiling water and dried camomile leaves, and collected the essence from rose petals and mint by crushing them and steeping them in cold water for days.

Nothing they tried served their purpose, but they learned a great deal from their mistakes. By mid-September they had made a dark but sweet-smelling ointment of dill seeds pounded with vervain and rosemary leaves, mixed with a strong infusion of thyme, marigold, and powdered witch hazel bark, and thickened with honey and beeswax and the essence of rose petals. The girls agreed that this was the best they could do; they bottled it with care and took it home, to await an opportunity to anoint Hugh with their concoction.

◆　　　◆　　　◆

When it became clear that, love charm or no, John Rimer had no interest in her, Joan Bowes returned to her jealous prying. At first she discovered nothing, for John was still avoiding the Widow's cottage. Then one day she followed Rosamund and Blanche into the forest and watched them for some time from behind a tree.

Joan knew next to nothing of herbery, but she was certain that what she saw went more than a little beyond the bounds of the permissible. Gleefully, she hurried back to Mortlak to consider what use to make of her new knowledge.

At the edge of town she met with a knot of people who had paused briefly to indulge in yet another long complaint against Dee and Kelly. Joan felt obliged to join them and come to the defense of the wizards. She still had confidence in their abilities, despite the apparent failure of Master Kelly's spell, and there was no telling when she might need another love charm.

"Master Kelly's not so bad as that," she broke in, interrupting the baker's diatribe, to which half a dozen men and women were listening and nodding in agreement.

"Aye, he is indeed," the joiner's wife contradicted sharply. She did not like Joan, and was glad of the opportunity to put her in her place. "Why, he's a sorcerer, girl!"

There were murmurs of agreement from others of the group. A brown-haired, heavyset man with a look of ponderous respectability said, "So it seems. Have you cause to think the matter otherwise, Mistress?"

Rather than be drawn into an all-too-revealing discussion of her relationship to Master Kelly, Joan switched tactics. "'Tis but that there's others worse than he about," she said darkly.

"There's none in Mortlak worse than Doctor Dee," the baker said flatly.

"Belike not in it, yet still too close for my liking!" Joan retorted.

"Who is it you speak of?" the heavyset stranger asked mildly. "Or do you but talk at random?"

"Not I!" Joan said, tossing her head. "'Tis the Widow Arden and her daughters, if you must have it."

"Ridiculous!" the joiner's wife snorted, and there were several disbelieving headshakes among the others of the group. The sawyer's daughter and the wheelwright, however, both nodded slightly, which was all the encouragement Joan needed.

"I say that *someone* in the Widow's house dabbles in things better left alone," Joan said. "I've seen the signs of it myself."

"What signs are those?" the baker said skeptically.

"She's kept a familiar, i'the shape of a lamb; last winter when my mistress sent me to her, I saw it with my own eyes."

"It seems it's done you no harm," the joiner's wife said in a sarcastic tone.

"'Tis only because I said my prayers at once when I saw the creature," Joan answered, warming to her tale. "It set a most unnatural fear upon me, which vanished at the Lord's name."

"Fool of a girl," the baker said, shaking his head. "Do you not know that Master Hinde gifted the Widow with a winter lamb last October? It's grown into a fine young sheep, and pastures in the commons with Master Hardy's flock; there's naught unnatural about the animal."

Joan shrugged. "I know what I saw. And there's yet more: from my small window I've seen strange lights in the fields near the Widow's cottage, late at night, and come upon her daughters in the forest burning herbs and chanting in the smoke."

"Thou'rt a foul-minded, vicious wench, to invent such tales about so good and pious a woman as the Widow Arden," the joiner's wife said angrily.

"Believe what you will," Joan answered with an outward show of indifference. "For me, I'm glad the church doth stand twixt Mistress Rundel's house and the Widow's. I'd not sleep nights else."

"I'll hear no more of this," the joiner's wife said, and swept off in a state of high indignation. Her departure signaled the breakup of the little group of gossipers, and Joan continued on her way home, satisfied that she had done what she could.

◆　　　◆　　　◆

The heavyset stranger continued on through Mortlak to the tavern, where he took a room on the third floor. There he sat deep in thought for some time. He had come to Mortlak to follow in the footsteps of the spy Charles Sledd, but in a more circumspect manner. Sledd's report had very nearly finished the investigation into Dee and Kelly's supposed black arts, for it was obvious to his superiors that the spy was both vicious and vindictive. But the rumors and unrest were too serious to ignore, and at last Master Phillip Rodgers had decided to come and see for himself.

Thus far, his investigations had done nothing to diminish his misgivings about the possible prosecution of Doctor Dee. On the contrary, it seemed that the Polish Prince, Laski, had recently become embroiled with Dee and his dubious friend, Kelly. It would never do for a foreign dignitary to become involved in a sordid investigation of witchcraft and black magic.

Joan's remarks about the Widow Arden seemed, therefore, a blessing straight from Heaven. Master Rodgers's superiors would be as relieved as he if Mortlak's witchcraft rumors could be brought home to a penniless widow instead of a learned man with influence at court. The lamb was a mildly unfortunate detail, since it was unlikely that a servant of the devil would choose as a familiar an animal symbolic of the Christ, but a clever prosecutor might do something with the perversion of holy things to evil purposes.

Rodgers therefore determined to turn his attention on the Widow Arden and her daughters, while continuing his investigation of Dee and Kelly only far enough to make it clear that he had done his duty. This decision made, Master Rodgers descended to the serving room to have a pint of ale and listen to more gossip about the various subjects of his inquiries.

Over the next few days, Master Rodgers was nearly everywhere in Mortlak. Ostensibly, he was in search of a suitable place for wool shipping, and few suspected that his evident concern about the rumors of witchcraft in the village was anything more than the prudence of a man who wanted no troubles that might interfere with business. He even found an excuse to visit the forest several times, hoping to catch the Widow's daughters at whatever malevolent activities they performed. By then, however, Rosamund and Blanche had finished their ointment and were no longer haunting the woods, so Master Rodgers found nothing.

♦　　　♦　　　♦

Madini, who had been watching with growing impatience the slow development of matters in the mortal world, was pleased that action of some sort seemed imminent at last. She had been greatly annoyed when Charles Sledd left Mortlak without moving against Dee, but when Master Rodgers appeared to replace him her anger faded. She did not bother to follow the progress of Rodgers's inquiry; his presence was enough for her. So long as Dee and Kelly left their house and took the crystal with them, it made no difference to Madini whether they fled in fear of exposure or were taken out in irons to a witchcraft trial.

She was, however, concerned lest she should miss their leaving, and so it was that, late one cool and cloudy September night, Madini crossed the border of Faerie into the mortal world and made her way to Mortlak. She carried with her a wand of peeled willow and a handful of the enchanted mixture known as Faerie dust. Unseen, she reached Dee's house beside the river. She paused a moment in the street outside; then, soundlessly, she circled the house three times. On the first circuit, she drew an unbroken line on the ground with the willow wand. On the second, she traced a similar circle in the air at the level of her waist, and the wand left behind a faintly glowing afterimage as she moved it. On her third trip around the house, Madini left a trail of Faerie dust across each window ledge and doorsill.

When the third circuit was complete, Madini stood looking at the house for a long moment, studying her work. Then she whispered a word in the most ancient tongue of Faerie, and cast the remainder of her Faerie dust into the air. It spread up and over the roof of Dee's house, sparkling for an instant though there was no light to make it do so.

With a satisfied smile, Madini returned to Faerie, certain that when the crystal left the protection of Dee's house at last, she would know instantly. Behind her the sparkle of the Faerie dust disappeared, leaving only a faint, impossible scent of spring to hang in the fall air.

CHAPTER · TWENTY-TWO

> *"Crossing the meadow on their way home, the girls saw the dwarf again. He had emptied his bag of jewels onto a flat stone to gloat over them, and they shone and sparkled in the evening sun. The glittering colors were so beautiful that the girls stopped and stared at them in wonder."*

WHILE DEE AND KELLY WERE PREPARING FOR THEIR flight to Poland and the Widow's daughters were secretly compounding their herbal ointments, John was waiting for word from Robin. He visited the bear regularly, but he was scrupulous in keeping away from the Widow's cottage. His message into Faerie had not gone unnoticed, and several times he saw signs of Faerie watchers around his house. This served to confirm the wisdom of his decision to avoid Rosamund and Blanche, though as the days grew into weeks John's determination wavered more and more.

Fortunately, Robin reappeared before John's resolution collapsed completely. It was early in September, when the weather was in an uncertain condition—fair and warm one day, damp and cold the next. The chestnut burrs were just beginning to turn from green to golden brown, and the grain stood tall in the fields, waiting for the reapers. John was in the forest with his brother, pondering for the thousandth time what could and should be done before the winter, when Robin popped out from behind a holly bush. His sudden appearance startled a growl from Hugh.

"Is this how thou dost greet thy friends?" Robin said to Hugh with a mock frown. His doublet was a deep green velvet, his hose were silk, and his hair appeared to have been recently cut (though that did not stop it from falling in his eyes). "Methinks that thou must mend thy manners, old bear."

"Robin," John said in a warning tone.

"Thou, too?" Robin said, widening his eyes and almost achieving an expression of innocence. "I am wounded."

"If that be true, 'tis thy own sharpness that has wounded thee," John said dryly. "Pardon our bad tempers; waiting sits ill with both of us, and thou hast been a long time in returning with thy news."

"Not so long as I might have been," Robin said. He shook his hair out of his eyes and gave John a sly grin. "Shall I go away again, and let thee practice patience more?"

"Do so," John invited him cordially, "and by thy actions I'll know thy news was of but little moment."

"Nay, thou hast me there," Robin said cheerfully. "Wherefore I'll tell my tale." He flung himself down on the ground, completely careless of his fine clothes and grinned up at John through a fringe of black hair.

"Say," the bear rumbled. Robin glanced at him in surprise, which changed quickly to a deep, thoughtful consideration. "Well?" Hugh said after a moment.

"I do beg thy pardon," Robin said. "But 'tis a great thing indeed to hear a bear speak, no matter what one has been told. Say something else."

"Robin!" John said, exasperated. "Thou'dst try the patience of whole legions of saints!"

"I doubt it," Robin answered. "Human saints have naught to do with Faerie."

"Robin!" Hugh and John said together.

"Oh, very well, if your forbearance has reached its end," Robin said with an exaggerated sigh. "But I had hoped you would be understanding; I've been to court, where they've but little fondness for my merry ways. 'Tis hard indeed always to behave one's best."

"Thou must speak of theory, for I see no sign of 'best behavior' in thy practice," John said. "Thy tale, Robin, thy tale! What's toward in Faerie?"

"Much that puzzles me," Robin said, abandoning his teasing at last. "Bochad-Bec's withdrawn into his oaks, and has not been beyond them since Furgen's death. 'Tis not surprising, since the two were friends; but that friends they were, or had ever been, surprises many."

"An oakman and a water fay?" John said. "Art sure of this?"

"Aye, and a dislike of mortals was the greatest bond between them, though I doubt 'twas widely known," Robin replied, shaking hair out of his eyes again.

"Hatred," the bear growled, shaking his head emphatically.

Robin looked at him with wide eyes, as if expecting him to continue. Hugh looked at John instead, who said, "Hugh finds speech difficult. I think he means that thy description was not strong enough; 'twas hatred of mortals that bound Bochad-Bec and Furgen, not mere dislike." The bear nodded, and John went on, "Yet even so, why would they meddle with Dee's spells, as seemingly they have?"

Robin shrugged, and his hair fell back into its accustomed position. "I know not, but I can guess." He looked at the bear. "They liked thee not, but they liked mortals less. They'd burn to think a mortal wizard had imprisoned Faerie power."

"'Tis possible," John said doubtfully.

"'Tis but a guess," Robin said, sounding faintly hurt. "But knowing Madini's pride—"

"Madini?" Hugh said sharply, and was immediately taken with the fit of coughing that struck whenever he forced his bear's throat to do too much.

John glanced at his brother, his expression troubled. When the coughing lessened, he turned back to Robin and said, "Who's this Madini?"

"One of the Queen's ladies," Robin said. His eyes sparkled. "Have I not mentioned her before?"

"Not of late," John said, "though I think thou saidest something of her when last I was in Faerie. What's Madini to do with this?"

"Why, she was friend to Furgen too, and for reasons like to Bochad-Bec's. 'Twas not a firm foundation for a friendship; her response to Furgen's death looked more like rage than grief."

"What meaning dost thou find in that?" John asked.

Robin shrugged. "Nothing sure. But if 'twas dislike of mortals bound Bochad-Bec and Furgen, why not Madini also? This meddling with the wizards smells more of her than them."

"No," Hugh said, and shook himself all over in incredulous negation. "She serves the Queen."

"That makes no matter," Robin said cynically. "There's little that's beyond those lasses, if they think 'twill benefit Faerie. And 'tis not always simple to say what is a benefit or no."

"Thinkest thou the Queen's entangled in this?" John asked with visible reluctance.

"Because her lady is? I greatly doubt it. If, of course, her lady is embroiled as I suspect; when all is said, 'tis but a guess."

"Then thou hast no certain knowledge that Madini's part of this," John said, frowning.

"I've said so twice already in plain language," Robin answered in tones of irritation. "Wouldst thou grasp my meaning better if I spoke in riddles?"

"I crave thy pardon, Robin," John said.

"And well thou shouldst," Robin said severely, holding his unruly hair back with his right hand while he rested his chin on his left. The posture robbed his tone of most of its intended effect.

"This is the sum of thy tale, then," John said, "that Furgen, whom I saw in the crystal, may have partnered Bochad-Bec in some mischief aimed at mortals, whose purpose we cannot now know since one of them is gone and the other dead, and that Madini too may have had some part in it."

"'Tis true enough, though 'tis a cold and stingy summary of all my work," Robin complained.

John sighed. "I'd hoped for better news, or more of it at least. Still, I owe thee a favor, Robin; 'twas kind of thee to help."

"Thou talkest as if my part in this were done," Robin said disapprovingly.

"And so should it be," John said. "Thou'st done enough."

Hugh nodded his agreement, and Robin gave them both a disapproving frown. "Nay, I've not done with my inquiries yet. Will you, nil you, you shall have my help; said I not that curiosity was my besetting fault?"

"No," John answered. "'Twas I that said it, and 'twas truer than I knew. Thou'rt near as foolish as the Widow's daughters."

"That's as may be," Robin said, "but 'tis better than being foolish over them."

This brought indignant responses from both John and Hugh, and the discussion degenerated rapidly from this point. Robin left soon after. In his heart John did not expect to see him for another month or two, or perhaps even longer, for Robin's grasp of mortal time was not always a strong one. John was therefore thoroughly surprised when the irrepressible youth turned up less than two weeks later with further news. He had established by some means of his own (into which John preferred not to inquire too closely) that Madini had crossed the Faerie border into the mortal world at least twice since Furgen's death, and that her errands involved the wizards, Dee and Kelly. When pressed, Robin was forced to admit that he had been unable to determine exactly what those errands had involved; he was clearly much disgruntled by this failure.

◆　　　◆　　　◆

Hugh and John talked the matter over for a long time after Robin left. Madini was a power in Faerie; if she were part of the disasters of the past year, they had to know what she was doing. How to discover it was another matter. Hugh favored waiting on Robin's next report, though he had little faith in Robin's ability to discover any more. John, who had long ago used up his entire supply of patience, insisted that the only possible course was for him to follow Madini and find out for himself what her purpose was.

In the end, John won the argument. This left him with the problem of finding Madini and determining when her next foray into the mortal world would be, so that he could follow her. None of the spells known to him or Hugh would do; they depended on the atmosphere of Faerie, and did not have the strength to either trace Madini through the mortal world or to penetrate the border and locate her within Faerie.

It was the bear who found the solution. John had told him of the scrying spell he had sensed nearly a year before, on the night that Rosamund and Blanche had been forced to spend in Faerie, and both brothers now knew that it had been the Widow who had cast it. Hugh suggested asking for her help once more; with John's knowledge of Faerie, the spell could be adapted to be indetectable.

John made a few token objections, but he did not resist for long. He was too anxious for action, and besides, he missed the company of Rosamund and her family. He was confident of his ability to elude at least once whatever Faerie watchers were observing him, and once was all that should be necessary. He let Hugh convince him, and went home to make his preparations. These took nearly two days, so it was early on the morning of Saturday, September twenty-first, the day of John Dee and Ned Kelly's secretly planned flight to Poland, when John finally made his way to the Widow Arden's cottage.

He was fortunate enough to find the Widow and both her daughters in. They gave him a warm welcome, once the Widow had determined that he was not carelessly exposing her daughters to the dangerous interest of Faerie. She even agreed to his request for help, but only if John's suggested changes in the spell were certain to keep Madini from noticing it.

"And not," said Rosamund, "until we've heard the story of these past two months."

John was more than willing to talk, but Rosamund was the only one of his listeners who gave him her full attention. The Widow moved about the room preparing the ingredients for her scrying spell and listening with only half an ear, while Blanche's mind was occupied in trying to think of some innocuous way to mention the small jar of ointment she and Rosamund had made for Hugh. Still, John did not appear to notice any deficiency in his audience.

As usual, it was the Widow who reminded them all that there was work to be done. "If thou'dst have thy scrying done ere noon, 'tis time to begin," she told John.

"I fear you're right," John said. He tore his eyes from Rosamund and looked across at the trestle table where the Widow stood. "Have you finished your preparations?"

"I've yet to mix the herbs; all else is ready," the Widow replied. "I wait only on thy alterations."

"I crave your pardon for my delay," John said, rising from his seat on the hearth. He joined the Widow at the table, and Rosamund and Blanche crowded close around him to peer over his shoulders. "Angelica, juniper, rosemary, eyebright, rue, and yarrow," he said, examining the Widow's herbs. "Do you mix them all together, or add them singly?"

"Together, and crushed into a powder," the Widow answered. "And I speak the charm as the water's poured across them."

"Mmmmm." John stared at them a moment. "'Tis chiefly the angelica that makes this spell so plain to those of Faerie; that, and its pure humanness. 'Twould be best if we could substitute some Faerie herb."

"Would mortal herbs that grew in Faerie do as well?" Rosamund said. "We've rosemary, and rue, and yarrow, at the least."

"'Tis well thought of," John said, smiling warmly at her.

Rosamund blushed, the Widow frowned, and John went on hastily, "Leave out the angelica, then, if 'twill not hurt the charm's potency, and use herbs grown in Faerie for the rest."

"That's all?" the Widow said.

"Not quite; while you work your spell of scrying, I'll cast one of another sort so that even if Madini sees what we're about, and follows it, 'twill be me she finds, not you."

This satisfied the Widow at last. She began measuring herbs into a tin dish on the table, while Rosamund removed the jars of rosemary, rue, and yarrow and replaced them with the Faerie-grown herbs. John paced the room while the Widow repeated the spell she had used to watch Rosamund and Blanche in Faerie so many months before.

As the Widow spoke the last words of the charm and began pouring boiling water over the powdered herbs, John stopped his restless movement. Turning to face her, he spoke a word of warding and drew in the air with the forefinger of his left hand. A faint, smoky shadow followed his fingertip; it hung for an instant in the center of the cottage, then dissipated.

"That's not the most consoling of charms," Rosamund commented to him in a low voice.

"'Twill do what's required," John answered, "and 'twas none of my inventing. What dost thy mother see?"

"Dee's house," the Widow answered, bending over the dish of herb water. "Someone has set a spell upon it, or rather, round about it. The magic still glows golden on the doorsills."

"Faerie dust!" John said. "'Tis Madini's doing, I doubt not. Do you see her there?"

"No," the Widow said. "But I do agree with thee; 'twas her mischief that we sought, and 'tis hers we're shown."

"Canst thou see the crystal, Mother?" Blanche asked.

"'Tis not kept outside the house," the Widow said. "Nor is it of Madini's—no, thou'rt right; I spoke too hastily. The crystal's here, and marked by the same magic as doth guard the house. That's all;

the vision's gone." She straightened with a sigh, and rubbed a hand across her eyes.

"If thou'rt finished, I'll open the door and let the odor out," Rosamund said, and suited her actions to her words. The Widow carried the dish of herbs and water outside and emptied it under the rosebushes; when she returned, she discovered that her daughters had asked John to stay and eat with them. Bowing to the inevitable, the Widow refilled the kettle and sent Blanche to the garden to bring in a few more carrots and onions to add to the supper stew.

◆　　◆　　◆

The hint of Faerie added to the Widow's spell did, indeed, keep Madini from noticing it. Unfortunately, it was just what Dee and Kelly had prepared their own spells to espy. The wizards knew at once when the Widow's scrying spell touched the crystal, and they dropped their other business and dashed for the study. They arrived in time to see a swirl of light flicker and fade in the heart of the crystal itself.

"'Tis done!" Kelly said, after examining the crystal and the table it stood on. "We have them now. Said I not that 'twould be so?"

"What matters it?" Dee asked. "We leave today for Poland; the barge is already half-loaded."

"Do you think that Faerie's bound to England?" Kelly said. "'Tis no more tied so than are Heaven and Hell. We must stop them now, John, else we'll regret it a thousandfold."

"What would you have us do?"

"What we'd planned," Kelly answered impatiently. He muttered a peculiar sentence, half in Greek and half in Latin, then leaned forward and scooped up the crystal. "We'll trace this spell to its source, and put an end to our troubles."

"An you must have it so," Dee said with a reluctant sigh.

Kelly smiled grimly and hid the crystal in the loose sleeves of his scholar's robes. Then the two men left the house. As they crossed the threshold, Faerie dust sparked invisibly, and the crystal flickered in unseen response. Unconscious of anything unusual, Dee and Kelly turned down the street and started for the edge of Mortlak. They could not, of course, walk through the village streets openly carrying the crystal, but they were certain that the source of their troubles lay outside the town, so they were not disturbed by their inability to consult the glowing sphere for guidance during the early part of their trip.

When they reached the edge of town, Kelly paused in the shadow of a building. He checked carefully to make sure they were unobserved, then drew the crystal from his sleeve for an instant. The glow at its heart was brighter, and he smiled.

"That way, John," he said, replacing the globe within his sleeve. "And not too far, I think. We'll reach our goal ere midday."

The two men set off again. As they struck out along the road, heading south toward the forest, they passed the portly figure of Master Phillip Rodgers, traveling in the opposite direction. The three men nodded greetings and went on, but Master Rodgers did not go far. He had been lurking in the forest for the early part of the morning, looking for proof of the nefarious activities in which Rosamund and Blanche were presumably engaged. Now he saw the two men whose magic he had been sent to investigate heading out of Mortlak in the direction of the forest and the Widow's cottage. With the sinking feeling that his efforts to avoid political trouble were about to come to naught, Master Rodgers turned and followed.

CHAPTER · TWENTY-THREE

"'Why are you standing there staring?'" cried the dwarf.
His face turned red with rage, and he began cursing at the girls.
Suddenly there was a loud growl from out of the forest; a
moment later, a black bear appeared among the trees, coming
toward them."

THE WIDOW WAS JUST FINISHING HER STEW-MAKING
when Dee and Kelly arrived at the cottage. The visible traces of the
scrying spell had been carefully cleared away, and Rosamund and
Blanche were busy with ordinary tasks. Rosamund laid out wooden
spoons and bowls on the trestle table and argued with John, while
Blanche sat in a corner, frowning at her mending. Blanche still
had not found the opportunity she wanted to tell John—and her
mother—about the ointment she and Rosamund had made for
Hugh, and it was troubling her. Now and then she patted the
pocket where she carried the vial, as if to make certain it was safe.

The knock at the door surprised everyone, for they were not
expecting visitors, but it did not trouble any of them. Rosamund set

down the clump of spoons she was holding and went to answer it. Her expression of polite welcome changed to shock when she saw who stood outside. "Master Dee! Mother, 'tis Master Dee and Master Kelly!"

"Mistress Arden?" Dee said as the Widow came hurrying forward. His voice was uncertain and slightly apologetic; he was not at all sure how to explain his reasons for appearing so unexpectedly at the Widow's door. The strong smell of cooking onions and the half-laid table made it plain that the inhabitants of the little cottage were engaged in perfectly ordinary activities, not sorcery, and Dee's memory of his strong-willed wife's reaction when he had, upon occasion, interrupted her supervision of the dinner preparations made him dubious about the sort of welcome he was going to receive.

"Good day to you, Master Dee, and what may I do for you?" the Widow said, doing her best to conceal her astonishment.

"You may tell us what you mean by your interference in our affairs," Kelly snapped before Dee could answer her. "And you may cease from it at once. Nay, John, I'll not be silent; this woman's the source of that spell we sensed."

"You're certain, Ned?" Dee said, while the Widow, stunned into silence, stood and stared.

"I'd hazard my life on it," Kelly answered, making a small gesture toward the sleeve in which he had concealed the crystal.

"There must be some mistake in this," the Widow said, finding her voice at last. "What mean you by this talk of spells, sirs?"

"You know as well as I," Kelly growled.

"Belike she doth not," Dee said nervously. "Think, Ned! We know the root of that meddling to which you referred; 'tis hardly possible that Mistress Arden is of such a kind."

"Speak plainly, an you must speak at all," the Widow snapped. Her initial shock was past, and she had had time to realize that Dee and Kelly were the last men in Mortlak who would denounce her for witchcraft, or who would be believed by the townsfolk if they did so. "Have you aught to accuse me of? Then go back to Mortlak and lay your proof before the constable; Heaven will protect the innocent. Or does it please you to rant at helpless women?"

"Perhaps 'tis we who should summon the constable, Mother," Rosamund said. She had come back to stand just behind the Widow's shoulder, where she could study the unwelcome visitors. Blanche, too, had set aside her mending and come to her mother's side, though she said nothing.

"You would be ill-advised to do so," Kelly said. "Take our warning as it's meant, and have done with hindering our work, or you will rue the consequences."

John, who had been standing out of the visitors' line of sight, moved around where he could see them. "It seems Mistress Arden's right in saying you're pleased by threatening others," he said in tones of exaggerated politeness.

"Nay, Master Rimer, this is no affair of thine," the Widow said. "Masters Dee and Kelly will be leaving now; I think they can have no more to say to me."

Dee would have been more than happy to do as the Widow had said. He had been startled and not altogether pleased when Kelly's tracing spell led them to the small cottage outside the forest, instead of to some Faerie haunt, and he was even more disturbed by Kelly's hostile demeanor toward the Widow. John's unexpected appearance in the cottage was the final straw. "Come away, Ned," he said. "'Tis surely some mistake."

"Mistake?" Kelly rounded furiously on his companion. "'Tis no mistake! He's part of it too; look!"

Kelly plunged his right hand into the left sleeve of his gown, and from its loose folds he pulled the crystal globe. It was glowing redly, and heat radiated from its smooth and shining surface. Blanche gasped and took an involuntary step forward, jostling her mother and her sister. John shouldered past the Widow with an absently murmured apology, his eyes fixed on the sphere in Kelly's hand.

Kelly ignored them all. He passed his left hand across the surface of the crystal, barely brushing it with the tips of his fingers. "Monstra!" he said in a clear voice, then he turned and thrust the crystal in Dee's direction. "There; you see? 'Tis no mistake; they are all part of this."

◆   ◆   ◆

In the depths of the forest, the bear's head came up and around. He sniffed the air, his clouded mind momentarily uncertain what it was he searched for or how best to go about finding it. Activated by Kelly's use of its power, the crystal's presence pulled at the bear, and the bear did not resist. Rising, Hugh lumbered on all fours in the direction of the strange compulsion. His pace quickly grew more rapid, until he was crashing heedlessly through the underbrush, heading straight for the Widow's cottage.

◆   ◆   ◆

At the door of the cottage, Dee stepped back, startled by the intensity of the emotion in his friend's voice. He recovered himself quickly, and, with a sidelong look at the tense expressions on the faces of the Widow and her family, he bent over the crystal. In its depths he saw a picture, a miniature portrait of the Widow and her daughters, caught in a web of red light. To one side was another figure, shadowy and hard to distinguish but nonetheless identifiable as the young man standing so protectively at the rear of the group inside the cottage.

Dee looked up in astonishment, surprised as much by the effectiveness of Kelly's spell as by what it showed. "It seems you're right again, Ned," he said in a low, unhappy voice.

"And now we'll finish with this foolishness," Kelly said. He turned back to the Widow and her family. "You see there's no more reason for pretense. Why have you made such mischief with our work? I will know!"

"Because you've taken what you've no right to have," Rosamund said. "Nay, Mother, I'll not be quiet. We've made no mischief that we know of, but 'twas not for lack of wishing!"

"What mean you?" Dee demanded, stung by the anger in her voice.

"She speaks of that," Blanche said, waving at the crystal. "You've stolen what you hold there, and caused much grief and suffering by it, though perhaps you knew it not."

"Impossible!" Kelly scoffed. "You speak of what you do not understand"—his eyes flickered in John's direction—"or else you've been misled."

"'Tis you who're ignorant in this," John said. He looked at the light shifting within the crystal, then back to Kelly's face. "You've trapped some part of my brother in that globe, condemning him to be a beast till it's returned."

Dee shook his head. "That cannot be," he said gently. "'Tis some other spell that troubles your brother, not this; the humors of this globe came out of Faerie."

❖   ❖   ❖

Behind the hedge that partly hid the Widow's cottage from the road, Master Rodgers crouched, grinding his teeth and cursing under his breath. When he had, with much misgiving, crept close enough to hear the conversation between Dee and the Widow Arden, his spirits had soared. Rather than joining the Widow in some arcane ritual, it seemed that Dee and Kelly were accusing her to her face of dealing in magic. With such support, a charge of witchcraft against the woman would be a simple matter.

Then Blanche and John made their accusations, and Rodgers's brief fantasy of a triumphal return to London vanished with a crash. The transformation of man to beast was one of the most heinous crimes possible to witchcraft. Instead of a simple, clear-cut matter, the case was rapidly beginning to look like the sort of nightmare in which charges begat countercharges until nothing was certain except the eventual disgrace of the unlucky man who'd raked it up. With an increasingly gloomy expression, Master Rodgers remembered Joan Bowes's spiteful talk about the Widow, and the equally energetic remarks of the joiner's wife regarding Kelly. There would be witnesses on both sides.

With a soundless sigh, Master Rodgers began quietly twisting the twigs of the hedge to make a hole so that he could see through it. Though he might wish he'd spent the day at the tavern instead of following Dee and Kelly, his duty now that he was here was plain, and if he could say he'd done it well, things might go more easily for him in the end.

♦   ♦   ♦

"An your globe comes out of Faerie, so do I!" John answered Dee fiercely. "Think you I do not know whereof I speak? 'Tis your work and no other that's been Hugh's bane."

"He speaks but truth," the Widow said, responding to the look of incredulity on Dee's face.

"What of it?" Kelly said, and there was a hard undercurrent in his voice. "Would you have us destroy our work for the sake of some soulless Faerie wight?"

"Yes," Blanche said simply.

"'Tis only right," Rosamund added.

"I do not think—" Dee began in a doubtful tone, and once again Kelly interrupted him.

"We will not do it," Kelly said flatly. His eyes were on Dee as he went on, "Even if this is not some Faerie trick, there's more at stake than you know. Our work has just begun; to stop it now would be too great a loss, and not only to us. All the world will benefit from what we learn."

"You have other gazing globes," John said. "I've seen them."

"Indeed." Kelly gave John a sharp look. "It seems you know much of our affairs."

John smiled coldly. "They've been of some interest to me since you stole my brother's form. Return the power you've imprisoned there; it need not stop this work you set such store by."

Kelly was shaking his head before John had finished speaking.

"You know not what you ask," he said. "This globe, and this alone, can show us what we need to know."

"'Tis true," Dee said, nodding. "The spirits who've been drawn to this are wise beyond all telling. The other globes are . . . limited." He shook his head sadly and gave John a sympathetic look. John glared back, and Dee hastily transferred his gaze to Rosamund and Blanche. "The pursuit of knowledge oft requires some sacrifice," he went on in the same kind, explanatory tone. "I fear we cannot grant your request, for 'twould be the end of our work."

"Easy enough to speak of sacrifice when 'tis someone else who suffers," Rosamund said angrily.

"You speak as if Hugh were someone's pet, and not a person!" Blanche said at the same time.

"And so he is, now, and well may it suit him," said a new voice from behind Dee and Kelly. "He'll stay so for long and long, if I'm the one to choose his fate."

The two wizards whirled, and Kelly thrust the crystal out in front of him like a shield. Madini stood just inside the Widow's gate, her face cold and expressionless and her dark eyes bright with triumph. She wore her own form, which she had never showed in the crystal, and neither Dee nor Kelly recognized her as their helpful familiar spirit. Her height and grace and her unearthly beauty proclaimed her Faerie origin to all her observers, and the Widow closed her eyes briefly as if to deny this sudden manifestation of so many of her worst fears.

"Who are you?" Kelly demanded.

"Thou'rt ignorant indeed to ask such a question," Madini responded in biting tones. "Dost thou truly expect me to make a present of my name to such as thee?" Though she would have liked nothing better than to snatch the crystal out of Kelly's hand, caution held her back. The wizards deserved a grave punishment for their presumption, but Madini still remembered that the despised "mortal magic" had forced her to give truthful answers when she first encountered the crystal, and she would not lay herself open to such humiliation a second time, particularly in front of John. Then, too, she was curious about the Widow and her daughters, though she would never have admitted it. So instead of claiming the crystal at once she waited in hopes of learning more, or at least seeing some certain indication that none of the humans was a danger to her.

"I could put a name to you, I think, though we've not met before," John said, studying Madini with narrowed eyes.

Madini gave him a chilling look. "Thou! Thou'rt good for naught save causing trouble to thy betters. Faerie's well rid of thee and thy brother both."

"Then what brings you here?" Rosamund said. "If you do not come to lend John your aid—"

"I've come for that which all of you are greedy for," Madini said, abandoning a caution that sat uncomfortably with her temperament and gesturing at the crystal. "The difference is that I shall have it."

"You see, John?" Kelly said to Dee. "'Tis all one; when their first trick fails, they'll try another."

"What are we to do?" Dee asked, frowning.

"There's naught that thou canst do, mortal," Madini said. She waved a hand almost negligently, and lines of fire appeared in the air, following her outstretched fingers. "Give me the crystal," she commanded Kelly, and flung the web of light toward him.

"Avaunt!" Kelly said, raising the crystal like a shield and ducking his head behind it.

"Time hath laid his mantle by," said John at the same time, and gestured like a man throwing a ball at bowls.

Madini's spell went spinning sideways and disintegrated into flashing motes of light. "Meddler! Dost thou challenge me?" Madini cried, glaring at John.

"Did you truly think I'd let you take Hugh's only hope, and never question it?" John retorted. "What do you mean to do with the crystal, if you can come by it?"

"That she'll never do," Kelly said angrily, and he began muttering over the shining globe he held. Madini and John ignored him.

"I shall return it to Faerie, where it belongs," Madini said. She half lowered her eyelids and smiled. "And then thou, and thy brother, and all these misbegotten mortals may do whate'er you will for all of me."

"'Twill return to Faerie when Hugh does, in his own shape once more," John said, and his voice trembled with the force of his emotion.

Madini laughed. "That is to say, never. There's no charm in all of Faerie to remedy so great a sundering."

"Perhaps that's why John came to us for help," Rosamund put in.

"Rose!" the Widow said sharply. "Hold thy tongue!"

Madini's head turned, and her lips curved into a thin, cruel smile. Before she could speak, Kelly's voice rang out in triumph: "Fiat; fiat; fiat voluntas mea!"

Silence fell like a blanket over the garden, sudden and complete. No one moved. Madini's eyes remained fixed on Rosamund; the Widow's gesture of restraint hung half-completed in the air.

"What have you done, Ned?" Dee quavered after a moment.

"Fixed them like statues where they stand," Kelly answered. His voice sounded breathless, as if he had been running. "Shall we go?"

"We cannot leave them like this!" Dee said, horrified.

"'Twould be no more than they deserve," Kelly retorted. "But 'twill not last above an hour, and so much will do them good, I think. 'Tis but a foretaste of what awaits an you continue meddling, or attempt again to take my crystal," he added, speaking directly to the motionless figures grouped around him.

"They can hear us?" Dee asked.

"Aye, and much good may it do them," Kelly replied. "Come, John; let's away before we're found here. 'Twould be unwise to give substance to the rumors that run so strong in Mortlak."

"I'll come," Dee said, but he did not move to follow Kelly toward the garden gate. Instead he peered in fascination at John's motionless face. "'Tis truly amazing, Ned. I'd no idea you'd made such great advances in the crystal's use."

"'Tis as well I did," Kelly said. "Come away! We've much to do before—"

The roar of an angry bear drowned out the rest of the sentence. Dee and Kelly whirled to see Hugh racing toward them from behind the Widow's cottage, his lips curled back from his strong yellow fangs and every hair in his coat standing on end. "Ned!" Dee cried. "Do something!"

CHAPTER · TWENTY-FOUR

·

"The dwarf tried to run, but the bear was already too close for him to get away. Trembling and in fear for his life, the dwarf said, 'O bear, spare me and I will give you all these jewels!' But the bear came on, and did not heed him. 'You do not want to eat me!' the dwarf said. 'Why, I am too small to make even one good mouthful!'

"Still the bear came on, and now he was drawing very near. Then in desperation the wicked dwarf said, 'See these two girls; they are young and plump and tender, not old and tough like me! Eat them, and let me go!' But the bear did not listen. He struck a single blow with his paw, and the dwarf fell and lay still."

·

THE SIGHT OF A RAGING BEAR RAPIDLY APPROACHing them, just when they thought they had won through to safety, paralyzed both Dee and Kelly for a moment. They had both heard, and both discounted, the stories of a ghost-bear in the forest which had been circulating since Master Kirton's ill-fated hunt. The unexpected appearance of a large, dangerous, and very angry animal identical to the whispered descriptions was more than enough to freeze them both as motionless as the victims of Kelly's spell.

Kelly recovered first. Once again he raised the glowing crystal and shouted, "Fiat voluntas mea!"

Hugh stopped short, shaking his furry head as if there were a bee in his ear. Kelly, at once pleased that his spell had had some noticeable effect and disconcerted to find that the bear could still move, shouted once more, "Fiat!"

The bear's only reaction was to lumber forward once more. In truth, Hugh had only been affected by the casting of the spell, and not the charm itself. The magic of the crystal remained his own; it could not touch him except through the tenuous link that informed him with waves of discomfort whenever the crystal was in use. He was close enough by then to see the motionless figures of John, Madini, and the Widow and her daughters, and though he had been growing more bearish with each spell Kelly cast, he retained enough human wit to connect the state of his friends with the two strangers and the strangely attractive globe they carried.

"Run, John!" Kelly said, suiting his own action to his words.

Dee caught at his companion's arm, all but stopping the flight he had hardly begun. "But these people! What of them?"

"An we're fortunate, the bear will take them instead of us," Kelly said. Unable to free his arm from Dee's grasp, he dragged the older man with him toward the Widow's gate.

The bear broke into a lope as he passed by the living statues, intent on the crystal in Kelly's hand. He caught up with the fleeing wizards as they reached the Widow's rosebushes. With a roar that expressed all the anger, hurt, suffering, and confusion he had felt over the eleven months past, he reared back on his hind legs and swiped at Kelly with one powerful paw.

Kelly recoiled almost, but not quite, in time. The blow, which would have seriously injured him had it struck where the bear had aimed it, glanced off the arm that held the glowing crystal. Kelly's grip was not strong enough to withstand such an unexpected shock. The crystal globe flew from his grasp, struck the gatepost, and shattered into a thousand fragments.

"No!" Kelly said, and his cry was echoed an instant later by Madini's shriek of angry disappointment and exclamations of horror from John and the Widow. Then all four cries were drowned in a howl of pain from Hugh.

It was too much for Dee. The sight and sound of an angry bear rearing above him, having just attacked his friend, was more terrifying than anything his scholarly life had prepared him for. With a moan of fright, the dignified Doctor Dee hauled up the hem of his long black robes and ran through the Widow's gate and down the road toward Mortlak, as fast as his legs could carry him. Kelly barely hesitated before following, one hand clutching his skullcap to keep it from falling off and the other holding his robe out of the way of his flying feet. The wizards were too intent on their own escape to notice Master Rodgers cowering behind the hedge, or to see him scramble to his feet and stumble after them, his only thought to put as much distance as he could between himself and the terrifying animal in the Widow's garden.

The bear did not notice their departure. He was not, in fact, aware of anything but the pain of loss. He stood roaring in agony, while from the shining splinters of quartz around his feet a bright mist began to rise, turning his fur briefly golden in the sun and then dissipating in the warm fall air.

The remaining watchers were momentarily stunned into inactivity by Hugh's loud, angry roaring. Blanche was the only one who moved. She had been facing the gate, and when she felt Kelly's spell dissolve with the shattering of the crystal, she ran forward. She ignored Dee's and Kelly's rapid exit completely; she had eyes only for the bear. As she reached his side, she pulled the little jar of ointment from her pocket, broke the sealing layer of beeswax with her thumb, and dumped it unceremoniously over as much of Hugh as she could reach. The smell of roses and honey spread through the garden.

"Blanche, what dost thou?" the Widow cried tardily.

"All I could," Blanche murmured, stepping back. "Pray Heaven this prove as potent as we hoped, Mother, for I do not think we'll have another chance."

No one answered; they were all too busy watching the bear. For an instant there seemed to be no change; then the glowing mist stopped spreading and began to thicken. Soon the bear was completely hidden in a dense, sweet-scented cloud the color of whipped honey, and his roaring subsided.

"What foolery's this?" Madini said to no one in particular. She started to raise a hand, and John caught her arm.

"You'll add nothing to this spell, for good or ill," John told her, ignoring her furious glare. "Though I doubt not 'twould be for ill, an I left you the choice."

"Thy magic is not strong enough to stop me!" Madini said. She tried and failed to wrench free of John's grasp.

"Belike not, but my arms are," John responded with deceptive mildness. "And believe it when I say that, woman or no, Queen's lady or no, I'll strike you down where you stand if you make the smallest move to injure Hugh."

"Thou'rt a knave and a base-born villain!" Madini snarled. Every line of her body proclaimed her outrage and indignation at being stymied by such crude methods.

John's expression did not change, but there was a sudden aura of danger about him that made even Madini pull away involuntarily. "I think this is no time or place to talk of that," he said.

"Look!" said Rosamund, effectively distracting both the combatants.

Under other circumstances, Blanche's carefully ensorcelled ointment might not have been strong enough to wrest Hugh's power from the crystal where Dee and Kelly had half-unknowingly imprisoned it. With the crystal broken and the power floating free in the air around him, the spell had only to return the power to Hugh. This was not simple, but it was nonetheless the easier part of the task.

The glowing mist that surrounded the bear was thinning; his furry coat soaked it up like a lamp wick soaking up oil. Then it was gone, and the bear stood gazing at them with a puzzled look in his eyes.

Blanche's shoulders sagged in disappointment. John let go of Madini's arm and, after a moment's pause to master his own chagrin, turned to the girl and said, "'Twas a noble attempt, and no fault of thine that it did not prosper."

"I would not say it did not prosper," Hugh said. Everyone turned to look at him, and he ducked his shaggy head and scratched at it with one large paw.

"Thy voice is back!" Rosamund said. She did not add that his wits, too, seemed to have returned. Had Madini not been present she might have mentioned it, but she would not expose any of Hugh's difficulties before a hostile stranger.

"True," said the bear, sounding surprised. "I'd not realized. I meant only that I feel far more myself than I have since this began. Except—"

"Except what?" John said, frowning.

Hugh swiped at his ear again. "Except I itch," he said. He lowered his paw, and a large piece of skin and fur came with it.

Blanche raised one hand to her mouth in horror, and John started forward with a wordless exclamation. Hugh shook his head violently, and bits of fur flew in all directions. John stopped short as his brother's human head appeared beneath the grisly shreds that remained.

"I itch most vilely," Hugh repeated, scratching at his left shoulder. Pieces of the bearskin began to drop away in chunks. John's face lit with relief, and he started forward once again, only to be stopped by the Widow's voice.

"I think this task is thy brother's alone," she said. She smiled shakily at John. "I doubt 'twill take him long."

In this the Widow was entirely correct; by the time she had finished speaking, a naked man with dark, wavy hair stood where the bear had been, studying his hands as though he had never seen such wondrous things before in all his life. The Widow blinked, then said with great presence of mind, "Rose! Go and bring out the brown blanket at once, lest Master Rimer's brother catch a chill."

"Yes, Mother," Rosamund said. She darted into the cottage and was back an instant later with the first large square of cloth on which she could lay her hands (which happened to be a green blanket, somewhat smaller than the one her mother had wished her to use). Rosamund was rapidly recovering from the shock and surprise of recent events, and she did not want to miss any interesting developments. When she returned, Hugh and John were exchanging a heartfelt embrace of relief and joy.

Rosamund waited until John stepped back, then handed Hugh the blanket. Her eyes were dancing, and she dropped a careful curtsy as soon as her hands were free.

"I do appreciate your kindness," Hugh said gravely. He draped the blanket carefully around his shoulders, and though it reached only to his knees he managed somehow to make it appear almost elegant and entirely natural. Then he turned and looked at Blanche. "And my gratitude to thee is beyond the power of words to tell," he said, "and beyond the wealth of all the world to repay thee for."

Blanche blushed red as a rose. Then she went pale as milk and looked down at her feet. Hugh's voice still held a faint echo of the familiar, bearish rumble, but the slender, dark-haired Faerie man before her bore no other resemblance to the animal she had pitied and befriended. He was alarmingly handsome, and even draped in an old blanket he carried himself like a prince. The faint glow of enchantment still hung in the air around him, reminding her of the depth of the difference between them as his bear's fur had not.

"'Tis noble in thee to admit as much, since words are all thou'lt ever have to pay her with," Madini's sarcastic voice broke in. "But it makes a pretty scene, I do admit."

"Whate'er it makes, 'tis no affair of yours," John said. "Get you back to Faerie, and leave us in peace."

Madini's expression did not change, but the eyes she turned on John were dark with hatred. "Peace? I'll give thee peace indeed, as much as a grain of corn between the millstones! Thou hast overset my plans, but I'll see that thou dost rue it, and thy mortal friends as well."

"Thou'lt see to nothing of the kind," the Widow said before John could answer. Her voice was sharp, and her expression angrier than Rosamund and Blanche could ever remember seeing before.

"Who's to stop me?" Madini said, looking contemptuously down at the Widow. "These half-breed exiled bastards? They've not the power to protect thee from my wrath; never think it. I am of the great ones of Faerie."

"Thou mayest be great in Faerie, but thou'rt of small account in my garden," the Widow retorted. "Nor have I ever asked these two for a defense against thy malice."

"Thou hast no need to ask, and well thou knowest it," John said, stung. "Whatever aid we can give thee and thy daughters, thou hast it."

"My brother speaks for us both," Hugh added.

"Thy offer's kind," the Widow said gently, "but 'tis more likely you'll have need of us."

"Thinkest thou that thy mere mortal magic can best me?" Madini said, and this time amusement tinged the contempt in her voice.

"'Twas my daughter's mortal magic that did what thou saidest no Faerie charm could do, and restored Hugh's shape to him," the Widow shot back. "And 'twas mortal magic that stole it away. And however great thy vaunted power, it seems thou hadst not means to wrest the crystal from two mortal wizards. I think 'twere best thou didst not speak so hardly of 'mere' mortal magic. 'Twill serve to keep me and my daughters safe from thee."

Rosamund and Blanche looked at their mother in wonder. Madini gave the Widow a slow, cruel smile. "'Tis not my magic thou needs must fear, but my unwitting mortal servants."

"What mean you?" Hugh demanded sharply.

"Why, only that this day's work has been observed, and by one Master Rodgers, who doth hunt witches for his bread," Madini said, and watched with great satisfaction as the Widow turned pale.

"This is a tale, or trickery," John said quickly.

"No trick," Madini said, and seeing the trouble in his expression her smile grew. She looked at Hugh. "Did thy bear's nose not smell him when thou camest roaring up?"

John made an angry movement, and Hugh put a hand on his arm. "I do recall something like to what you say, but 'twas not my object at the time, and I do not well remember," the erstwhile bear answered mildly.

"Thou'lt soon see all the truth in what I say," Madini said.

Rosamund slipped around behind Hugh and went out through the open gate. She came back a few moments later and broke in on the argument, which was growing more heated. "There are footprints behind the bushes by the gate," she said, "and I do not think they're Master Dee's or Master Kelly's. But there is no one about now."

"You see?" Madini said triumphantly. "He's gone to fetch his constables. You'd best begin your flight, unless you wish to hang, every one of you. And be assured, where'er you go I'll set your own mortal laws against you."

"I think not," Rosamund said, considering. She looked at her mother. "Has not the talk in town been all of Master Dee and Master Kelly?"

The Widow nodded. "But that makes no—"

"Nay, Mother, it makes a great difference," Rosamund interrupted. "For even if this man saw and heard all that occurred, 'twas Master Dee's spell that Blanche unraveled, and the breaking of foul sorcery's no crime."

"Thou mayest well be right," John said slowly. He paused, and looked at the Widow. "And 'tis also true that the greater part of this day's magic can be laid at Kelly's door. 'Twas he who held the crystal and cast the spell that froze us where we stood, and I do not think his past will bear the close examination of the courts. But if you choose to remain and defend your innocence, 'twill be hard for you, no matter what the outcome, and that's by no means sure."

The Widow hesitated. Then she looked at Madini, and her lips firmed. "An we choose to leave, this one has said she'll set more of these dogs to snap at our heels. 'Twere better to stay where we've some chance to win the fight, or so I think."

Rosamund flung her arms around her mother. Madini's smile slipped slightly. "You are all fools," she said.

"That's no problem of thine, is it?" Rosamund said, letting go of her mother.

"How long dost thou think 'twill take this Master Rodgers to return?" Blanche asked John.

"I do not know; does it matter greatly?"

"An we're to stay and face these charges, would it not be best for Hugh . . . for thy brother to be better clad?" Blanche said, blushing slightly.

"Oh, you've time and plenty for such niceties," someone said behind them. The company turned as one, to see a long-legged youth leaning over the Widow's gate and shaking black hair out of his eyes.

"Robin!" said John and Hugh together.

CHAPTER · TWENTY-FIVE

"Snow White and Rose Red had begun to run away, but the bear called out to them, 'Wait! Do not be afraid; I will not hurt you. Stop for a moment, and I will join you.' The girls recognized his voice, and they stopped and waited. As he came toward them his bearskin suddenly dropped off, and a handsome man stood before them, dressed all in gold."

ROBIN PUSHED THE GATE OPEN AND SAUNTERED IN, plainly enjoying the attention he was receiving. He was dressed for court, his doublet so heavy with gold-thread embroidery that he glittered in the sunlight when he moved. Madini's eyes narrowed. "What dost thou here, sprite?" she demanded.

"This and that," Robin answered, widening his eyes innocently. Then he frowned and tilted his head to one side. "Though now I think on it, thou mightest well have phrased thy question with a greater grace. I'm sure my friends here would have put it better." He waved casually toward John and Hugh.

"Place no wagers on it," John said. "If I'd been less surprised by thy appearance, I'd have been the first to speak those self-same words."

"Ah, but thou wouldst not have called me 'sprite,'" Robin said, in tones which indicated that that settled the matter completely.

"It seems this man's a friend to thee," the Widow said pointedly to John.

"Alas, I must admit it," John said, "though 'tis no credit to either of us. Mistress Arden, I present to thee Master Robin; Robin, be at thy best behavior, I pray."

"When am I otherwise?" Robin said, bowing extravagantly to the Widow.

"Always," Hugh said, smiling in spite of himself.

"Never say so," Robin answered, straightening and twisting around. He studied Hugh for a moment. "Thou'st found a tailor since last I saw thee," he said with the air of one identifying an elusive change that had been puzzling him. He leaned forward and said in a confidential tone, "Thou shouldst lose him again, an thou'lt take my advice."

"Cease thy foolery and explain thy presence!" Madini cut in. She was angry as much at being ignored as at Robin's failure to give her any real answer to her first question. Events had slipped from her grasp, if they had ever been in it, and Robin made an excellent target for her frustration.

"Why, I thought I'd done so," Robin said, blinking at her through a fringe of black hair.

"Belike you did, but I did not understand your explanation," Blanche's soft voice put in.

Robin looked to where she stood with Rosamund, a little to one side. His eyes widened, and he bowed even more extravagantly than before. "Roses!" he exclaimed as he straightened up. "One white and one red. Nay, do not blush; thou'lt stain thy petals."

"Robin," Hugh said warningly, and his voice was very near a growl.

"What wouldst thou have of me?" Robin said, ignoring Hugh. "The half my kingdom? 'Tis thine before thou ask!"

"An easy promise, for thou hast none," John commented. "Be not so saucy, Robin."

"Wherefore dost thou command him so?" Rosamund said. "He but matcheth thee; you are a pair of saucy rogues."

"Oho! Is this the way on't?" Robin said, looking gleefully from Rosamund to John. "Thou didst not tell me—"

"Robin!" John interrupted. "Thy best behavior; look thou, remember it."

Blanche was still blushing furiously, in part from Robin's teasing and in part from finding Hugh's eyes fixed gravely on her once more. Seeing no sign that Robin would cease his banter, she ventured, "I would put a question to you, Master Robin."

"Didst hear what she called me?" Robin said in delight. " 'Master Robin'! It has a ring to it; do you not think so?"

"The ring that suits thee would be made of hemp and fitted round thy neck," Madini snapped.

Robin looked wounded. "Thou'rt unkind to say so. But what was it that this lovely blossom wished of me?"

"I would know what you meant when you said we had time and plenty. 'Twas just as you arrived," Blanche said.

"Why, I meant whate'er I said," Robin answered. "So do I always."

"Then give us the reason for thy speech," John said. "Assuming that thou hadst one, more than to cause confusion."

"Oh, very well," Robin said, and grinned wickedly. " 'Tis but that all of you seemed troubled by the large man in brown who watched you from behind the hedge there. You have no need of haste on his account; he'll not see home before mid-afternoon, and I misdoubt he'll speak with sense before the morrow."

"Robin, what hast thou done?" Hugh demanded.

"I think I liked thee better as a bear," Robin complained. "Thou wert not so importunate."

"An thou wouldst reach home thyself with a whole skin, 'twere best thou didst answer," John said.

"Thou, on the other hand, hast not altered by a hair. Oh, very well, but 'tis no great matter. I but did what thou thyself hast done for a bear hunt not so long ago, or so I've heard."

"You've pixy-led this Master Rodgers?" Rosamund asked.

"Did I not just inform thee of it?" Robin said.

"How didst thou dare!" Madini snarled, seeing her hope of a quick revenge on John and Hugh fading.

"Was it daring?" Robin said, frowning. "No, I think 'twas not. But the man was ponderous and full of substance; he fair cried out to be misled. Then, too, there was John's work with Master Kirton's hunt to be surpassed." He contemplated his fingernails for a moment, then added modestly, "In that, at least, I have succeeded."

"How say you so?" Rosamund demanded, springing to John's defense without a thought. "To pixy-lead one man must surely be a lesser task than to confuse a score of riders and their dogs and beaters."

"'Tis no great matter, Rosamund," John interrupted her. "An Robin says his work surpasses mine, 'tis nearly certain that he's right."

"Oh, there's no arguing with it," Robin said. "I'll show thee on the morrow. But 'tis a mark of friendship that thou'lt agree before thou'st seen."

"Braggart! Thou'lt rue the day thou didst ever name thyself a friend to these," Madini said, waving at John and Hugh.

"I doubt it," Robin said, then stopped, considering. "Though perhaps the next time Hugh takes all the dances with the prettiest of the Queen's ladies . . ."

"I think thou hast little need to fear that now," Hugh said with a quick glance toward Blanche.

"For once thou speakest truly, for neither thou nor thy brother will e'er see the court again," Madini said, savoring the words.

Hugh's expression sobered, but Robin shook his head. "I am desolated to contradict thee a second time, but thou'rt wrong," he said, looking rather pleased with himself and not at all desolated. "Hugh will be welcomed back without a doubt. His banishment originated in his bearish form; that remedied, there's naught to keep him from returning. As for John"—he paused tantalizingly— "'tis surely not for thee to say."

"Robin, dost thou have news?" John demanded. "I thought 'twas but thy curiosity that drew thee here!"

"What else?" Madini said loftily. "This puffed-up sprite's no courtier; he knows naught of matters such as this."

"Again I fear thou'rt wrong," Robin said. He looked, if possible, even more smug than before. "In truth, I've but now come from court."

"Speak plainly, then, and tell us what thou knowest," Hugh commanded. "I've little patience with thy prevarications today."

"I see thy change in form hath not improved thy humor," Robin commented. "Well, an thou must have it. The Queen thy mother hath decreed thy brother's exile is suspended for a time, that he may come to Faerie and report his recent sojourn in the mortal world." He shook his hair out of his eyes and looked at John, and for once his expression was serious. "'Tis not certain thou'lt be allowed to remain, look thou, for thou didst cross the Queen's command. But thou'lt be allowed to plead thy case."

"How's this?" Madini cried. "Thou liest! The Queen doth not alter her decrees."

The mischievous look returned to Robin's face. "Ah, but it seems the counsel she received in this was poor, so she hath reconsidered. She'll want to see you all, I think," he added with a negligent wave that included Hugh and the Widow's family. "Oh, yes; you'll cause a great stir at the court. I make no doubt thou'lt start a new fashion, Hugh."

"What does the Queen of Faerie want of us?" the Widow said, swallowing hard.

"Your stories, first of all," Robin answered. He glanced at Hugh. "And I think when your tales are told there'll be rewards for all your services. The Queen likes not to leave a debt unpaid."

"Thou wouldst bring mortals to the Faerie court?" Madini said in tones of mingled distaste and disbelief.

"By the Queen's command," Robin replied. "And I'd advise thee to be circumspect in thy objections, an thou hast any." He hesitated, as if he were about to add to his remarks, but Madini cut him off.

"We'll see who knows best how to persuade the Queen," she said. "And thou'lt regret thy meddling, that I promise thee!" With that, the Faerie woman turned and swept off, vanishing into a shower of sparks before she had gone three paces.

"A pretty trick," Robin murmured, eyeing the spot where Madini had disappeared with a frown, "but dost thou not think 'twas a trifle vulgar to make such a show, John?"

"It matters not," John said. "Robin, how didst thou persuade the Queen to consent to my return? And what good dost thou think to do by bringing Widow Arden and her daughters to the court? 'Tis bad enough to take me back; if matters go awry, thou'lt suffer for it. But to drag unwilling mortals—"

"Have we said we are unwilling?" Rosamund interrupted.

"No, but 'tis plain thy mother likes it not," John said.

"Even so, 'twere better thou didst not put words into my mouth," the Widow said unexpectedly. "I'll hear what thy friend has to say, ere I choose what I'll do."

"I'd thought but to give thee a chance to speak before the court," Robin said, answering John's first question as though no one else had said anything at all. "But that was before I found Hugh so unexpectedly restored. As to how 'twas done, 'twas not so difficult. I told the Queen what thou didst tell me some weeks past, when first we met within the forest there."

"Thou—" Words failed John.

"Thou didst not think," Hugh said to Robin. "If the Queen was sure the fault was John's before, she'll be more certain still since he has disobeyed her."

Robin shrugged. "Howe'er it be, 'tis done, and now the Queen hath summoned thee to Faerie, and thy companions here as well,

that she may hear the story as a whole and thus unravel all this
tangled weaving."

"We'll come," the Widow said. Rosamund, who had been
preparing for a battle, gaped at her mother, her mouth full of
unneeded arguments. Blanche only smiled. Then she glanced at
Hugh, and her expression sobered, and she looked away.

◆ ◆ ◆

They left almost immediately. The slight delay was to allow Hugh to put on his brother's jerkin and rewrap the blanket
about his waist. Nothing could be done about breeches, hose, or
shoes; the Widow had long ago dispensed with every piece of
her late husband's clothing that would bring in a farthing, and
what had not been sold had been remade to serve herself or her
daughters.

Their progress was, therefore, quite slow, but fortunately they
did not have to go far. They were just inside the forest, still within
sight of the cottage roof and barely out of view of the road, when
they saw the faint distortion of the air, like a heat haze somehow
formed in the shadows under the trees, that was the border of
Faerie.

"I've never known it to come so close before!" Rosamund said,
glancing over her shoulder to make sure she could still see the
cottage.

"The Queen's assisting us," John said. "She must be anxious for
our arrival."

The Widow's expression grew more troubled, and Rosamund
edged closer to John as they walked.

"She'll have to wait a little longer," Hugh said firmly. He
indicated the blanket. "I'll not appear before the court like this,
though I be exiled thrice over for my tardiness."

"Thou dost lack daring," Robin commented in a disapproving
tone.

"'Tis not everyone's ambition to set the court by the ears," Hugh answered. "There'll be stir enough to suit me when I walk in as man instead of beast."

They crossed the border and went on. The air of Faerie seemed even brighter than usual, the colors still more vivid, the scents of spring yet more intense. Strange birds sang merrily in the treetops as they passed, or now and again dove across their path in a flash of orange and yellow feathers. John was silent, drinking in the sights and sounds and smells and storing them up against the future. Rosamund, sensing something of his mood, was also quieter than was her wont.

At last they came to a stand of ancient oak trees, their branches scarred and twisted by centuries of storms. In the midst of the oaks stood the palace of the Faerie Queen, its outflung wings and soaring towers blending smoothly into the forest around it. Long green ropes of ivy and wild grapevines decked the palace front, weaving intricate patterns against the ocean-colored marble. An inlay of precious stones arched above the gleaming wooden doors, and the walk that led up to them through the trees was paved in malachite and edged with tiny red flowers.

Robin, Hugh, and John did not give the women much time for observation. They hurried inside, down corridors of rose quartz, amethyst, and agate, through rooms with walls inlaid in yew, mahogany, and cedar. In a white-walled suite that smelled of thyme and rosemary, Hugh left them briefly.

He returned arrayed in a splendor that suited his surroundings. His jerkin and breeches were of velvet, midnight blue embroidered with silver, and the stiff white ruff at his neck was edged with silver lace. His boots were soft and close-fitting, dyed the same color as his jerkin, and his hose were white silk. A velvet hat with a white plume and a white wool cloak edged with ermine completed the costume.

"Robin's right; thou'lt make a stir indeed," John said as he put his own plain wool jerkin back on.

Robin did not give Hugh time to respond, but hurried the little group back out into the corridor and down a hall of milky jade to a set of doors made of carved and gilded wood. He flung them open, and with a flourish motioned to the Widow and her daughters to enter.

CHAPTER · TWENTY-SIX

"'I am a prince, who was bewitched by the dwarf,' the man told the two girls. 'He stole my jewels and forced me to live in the forest as a bear. Now his death has freed me, and he has gotten the punishment he deserves.'"

BEYOND THE DOOR WAS A HIGH MARBLE HALL FILLED with the glitter of the Faerie court. An aisle had been left clear from the door to the crystal throne on which the Queen of Faerie sat, her perfect face expressionless as she watched the mortal women enter. Just beside the throne stood Madini, her face as unrevealing as the Queen's. The Widow sank at once into a profound curtsy, and Rosamund and Blanche followed her example. Behind them, Hugh doffed his hat and bowed in time with Robin and John.

"I welcome you to Faerie, mortals," the Queen said. "My will hath brought you here, and 'tis my will that you leave Faerie safely when my questions have been answered."

A faint stir of astonishment passed over the assembled courtiers, like the ripple of a field of wheat at a puff of wind, which grew as Hugh straightened and they saw him clearly for the first time. Madini stood motionless, her eyes glittering.

"Thou hast been longer at thy task than I expected, Robin," the Queen went on, and there was more than a hint of displeasure in her tone.

"The delay was my doing," Hugh said, stepping forward. "I pray Your Majesty to pardon him."

"Such welcome news as thy return was surely worth the wait," the Queen replied. "But tell us how it comes about that thou'rt restored to us."

"That story properly belongs to Mistress Arden and her daughters," Hugh answered with a small bow in the direction of the Widow.

"So it be told, it matters not who does the telling," the Queen said. "Mistress Arden, if you will, begin."

The Widow stepped forward hesitantly, curtsied once again, and began as best she could with the alarms and uncertainties of the previous fall. She made Rosamund and Blanche recount their accidental eavesdropping on Dee and Kelly's spell on All Hallows' Eve. The girls, together with John, told the story of their involuntary night in Faerie and John's escape by following them, invisible. Then the Widow took up the tale once more, speaking of the vision she had seen in her scrying spell and the first appearance of the bear. She touched lightly on the months of winter work that led to the first attempt to disenchant Hugh. John spoke quietly of his reunion with his brother and the endeavor to combine mortal and Faerie magic in reversing Dee and Kelly's spell on May Eve Day. Hugh described how they had witnessed the beginning of Dee and Kelly's second spell-casting, which had been interrupted by Bochad-Bec's theft of the lamp.

The Faerie Queen listened with particular intentness to Hugh, but she did not ask any questions and no one else dared to interrupt. The Widow took up the tale again, covering the two frustrating months of Hugh's deterioration which culminated in John's invisible invasion of Dee's house in search of the crystal. John and the girls described that inconclusive effort in counterpoint, and again the Queen seemed unusually interested, most notably in John's description of the water fay he had seen in the crystal. John told of the message he had sent into Faerie, and Robin's agreeing to assist him, and Blanche and Rosamund explained why and how they had concocted their vial of ointment.

Finally, the Widow described the confrontation with Dee and Kelly, Madini's unexpected appearance, the smashing of the crystal, and Hugh's resumption of his proper form. She was extremely careful in her description of Madini's part in the scene, omitting most of the Faerie woman's threats and angry remarks and confining herself otherwise to a strict recounting of the actual events. Rosamund stirred restlessly several times, but did not interrupt or contradict her, for which the Widow was profoundly grateful.

"I am in debt to thee and thine," the Queen said when the Widow finished at last. "We shall speak more of that presently. First I would hear what Madini has to add."

"Little enough, Your Majesty," Madini said, sinking into a graceful curtsy. Her voice was low and sweet, without a trace of either anger or unease. "Save that I think the mortals owe more to Faerie than Faerie owes to them."

"Say you so?" the Queen said, frowning very slightly.

"Did not the mortal wizards cause your son's misfortune?" Madini replied. "And these have made their livelihood for years from the virtue of the plants within our borders. They have restored your son by accident as much as by design, it seems, and accidents breed no debts."

"And will you say naught of your part in all these matters?" the Queen said gently. "How you did come so timely on the wizards, and the reason for your interest in their crystal?"

"My tale's of little interest," Madini temporized, "though if Your Majesty commands, of course I'll tell it."

"I do command it," the Queen said sternly. "Say on, but know before you do that Bochad-Bec hath told us much of your conspiracies together."

A murmur of surprise rose from the assembled court, and several of them frowned at Madini. "How's this?" Hugh murmured.

"I know not, but I think 'tis great good fortune for us," John replied in a low voice as Madini, after a startled look, began a slow recitation of her dealings with the mortal wizards.

"Oh, 'twas not fortune, I assure thee," Robin said, smiling slyly.

"What?" John stared at Robin, and shook his head in wonder. "And how didst thou manage *that?*"

"With guile and resolution," Robin said cheerfully. "When thou asked me to discover what was toward in Faerie, he pricked my curiosity. The court's been tense and thick with plots since you two left, and 'twas no easy thing to find their source. And though it seemed Madini was waist-deep in all these schemes, I could find naught but rumor that would say so. So I went to Bochad-Bec, for though he's no courtier I thought from what thou'dst told me that he, too, was tangled in Madini's web. Once I . . . persuaded him to come before the Queen, the rest was certain sure."

"Thou'st gotten Bochad-Bec to speak for John and me?" Hugh said skeptically. "I cannot believe it."

"Not for thee, old bear; against Madini," Robin replied, grinning. "And that was but a matter of repeating certain comments that she's made these past few weeks, regarding the character and habits of oakmen. 'Twas easier than I expected; our Madini's no great one for tact."

"So 'tis seen," Rosamund said, indicating the tableau before the throne. "Hush!"

"And this is all your tale?" the Queen was saying to Madini.

"It is." Madini lifted her head proudly. "I acted for the good of Faerie, so I thought, and still do think it. Would you have Faerie tied forever to the mortal world?"

"That is the question you should have asked ere you began your plotting," the Queen said in a tone like breaking ice. "'Tis I that am Faerie's Queen, yet you have presumed to work against my sons, cast spells that crossed the border without leave, and tried to alter Faerie's very nature because you hate all mortals. Can you deny it?"

"No," Madini said, and was silent.

"Then hear my sentence: you did play counselor to the mortal wizards when you did think thereby to gain their crystal; now shall you be their counselor again, imprisoned in another globe for seven mortal years. You shall be at the beck and call of the mortals whom you so despise, and be a link twixt Faerie and the world that you would have us sundered from."

Madini's sudden pallor was the only outward sign she gave of her reaction to the Queen's sentence. "What of Faerie?" she said after a moment, and her voice was strong and steady.

"Faerie is my concern," the Queen said, and there was no trace of sympathy or softness in her voice. "And I'll have no more talk of separation from the mortal world; such a course would be disaster. Mortal lands are our stability, and without our link to them we'd fade to mist and shadows."

"And so instead you'll have us dwindle till our magic's but a memory," Madini said bitterly. "Will you command us to attend their feasts, and dance at mortal christenings and weddings?"

"It might be no bad thing," the Queen said, glancing at her two sons. John smiled and inclined his head very slightly in acknowledgment.

"Save that Your Majesty command, you'll ne'er find me in such a place," Madini said.

"An that's her humor, she'll not be invited," Rosamund whispered softly in Blanche's ear.

"Have you spoken your fill?" the Queen said to Madini. Madini nodded proudly. "Then thy punishment begins; go, and for seven years be bound."

As the Queen spoke, she traced three lines in the air above Madini's head. They hung glittering, then grew and enveloped the

Faerie woman in a shimmering bubble. The bubble shrank in on itself until it was about half its original size; then it seemed to turn sideways, and for a moment there was a blurred impression of a small room full of books and a polished black crystal. Bubble and image vanished simultaneously, leaving no trace of Madini or the Queen's spell but a rainbow mist of tiny drops like the residue of a soap bubble bursting.

"And now 'tis your turn," the Queen said, looking at John. "You disobeyed my firm command."

"I did," John said steadily. "And Your Majesty knows why."

"I do indeed," the Queen said. "Yet still, my order stands. You have made your choice, and for that choice, you're barred from Faerie. Henceforward, you shall be no more than mortal."

John bowed his head, and did not answer. Beside him, Hugh stirred and said, "Your Majesty, may I speak?"

"No," the Queen replied. "Not until I have done." She paused, surveying the company. "There remains the matter of reward for these four mortals, who have brought my son back here to me. As a beginning, 'tis but just that they have leave to visit Faerie when they will; if they have more requests to make of me, I'll listen, for my debt to them is great."

"*Four?*" Hugh said, just above a whisper. He turned and looked at John, and suddenly he laughed. "It seems thou canst resume thy wandering ways in all regards. Wilt thou be back before All Hallows'?"

"Belike," John said in a dazed voice. The Queen gave him a small smile, while the court murmured appreciative approval.

Hugh shook himself, and looked across at the Widow and her daughters. "Your Majesty, I would request a favor."

"Ask," said the Queen.

"I would have your permission to wed the Widow's elder daughter, Blanche, if she and her mother are willing," Hugh said.

"'Tis an appropriate reward," the Queen said, nodding. "Wilt thou have him, girl?"

Blanche glanced at Hugh and blushed, but this time she did not look down. "Gladly, Your Majesty," she said, and held out her hands to Hugh. "Oh, gladly, indeed."

John leaned over to Rosamund. "And thou, my most uncommon Rose," he whispered. "Wilt thou have me, an I ask for thee?"

"Ask, and thou'lt discover it," Rosamund whispered back, but she blushed as red as her sister while she spoke.

"It seems unfair to leave the younger girl unwed," John said more loudly. "An Your Majesty permits, I'll have her, and make all even."

"Thou hast my blessing," said the Queen of Faerie, and her smile was almost warm. "But what thinks the girl of this?"

"I think he is an impudent rascal," Rosamund said, lifting her chin, "and I'll wed with him or no one."

"Then wed with him thou shalt." The Queen studied the little group before her throne for a moment. "And, I think, as soon as may be. For tonight, you are my guests, and we will feast in honor of my sons."

Hugh and John bowed, the Widow and her daughters curtsied, and the audience was at an end. Over John's and Hugh's objections, Robin took the three women off to the court seamstress to be suitably gowned for the coming banquet. That evening they feasted royally with the Faerie court, and the following morning the preparations for the weddings began. They were so busy that it was several days before any of them thought to wonder what might be happening back in the mortal world.

◆　　　◆　　　◆

True to Robin's prediction, it was late afternoon when Master Rodgers finally staggered into Mortlak. His doublet was unlaced and full of weeds; his boots were muddy, his hose torn, and his brown wool cloak and hat completely missing. His eyes were dazed, and he mumbled constantly beneath his breath. At the edge of the market, his legs failed him and he collapsed into a shuddering heap, still mumbling.

Such an apparition quickly drew a crowd. "His wit's been turned," the saddler said, nodding sagely.

"He mumbles of the Widow Arden," the chandler said with a frown. "And Doctor Dee as well, but to what import I cannot tell."

There was a murmur of anger from the assembly, and then Joan Bowes pushed her way to the front of the expanding crowd. "'Tis the Widow's doing!" she cried. "Her witchery has brought him to this state!"

"Witchcraft," Rodgers said clearly. "Admitted sorcery. The bear . . ."

"You see?" Joan said triumphantly. "He confirms it as best he may. The Widow Arden's done this!"

The humming of the crowd grew louder, and then a clear, no-nonsense voice from the rear said distinctly, "Done what?"

A low voice muttered an explanation, and an instant later Mary Hudson thrust her way in among the inner ring which surrounded Master Rodgers.

"Belike the girl is right," the baker said importantly. "He came from the south road, where the Widow's cottage is."

"The Queen's palace at Richmond is to the south as well," Mistress Hudson snapped. "Will you lay this to her?"

The baker returned a shocked negative, and Mistress Hudson turned to Joan. "You're a spiteful, jealous girl," she said contemptuously. "I might have guessed 'twould be more of your mischief."

"I?" Joan said, her eyes widening in shock. "I've naught to do with this!"

"And 'tis plain to see you've done naught, neither, or by now this man would be in a sickbed where he belongs," Mistress Hudson retorted. She picked out three stout yeomen with her eyes. "You, carry him to his lodgings and see that someone stays with him until the doctor comes."

"The doctor!" Rodgers said, rousing and looking wildly around. "Dee? Nay, 'twas Kelly brought the bear!"

"Hurry, lest he stir up trouble with his words," Mistress Hudson said to her chosen assistants, and together they bundled Rodgers hastily away.

But the damage was done. Too many in the crowd had heard Rodgers's final words, and instantly coupled Kelly in their minds with the terrifying phantom bear that prowled the forest. The anger that had simmered all summer came to a head at last, and the crowd became a mob that surged through the streets to Dee's riverside home. Joan Bowes screamed frantically that it was the Widow, not Dee and Kelly, who was at fault, but she was shoved aside and all but crushed against a doorway as the throng hurried by. Badly battered, she limped home after the mob had passed, only to find that Mistress Hudson had stopped by and she was without a position. For Mistress Rundel credited the Widow Arden with saving the life of her small daughter, Elanor, and having been told of Joan's malicious comments refused to have her in the house a moment longer.

Dee and Kelly were already on their way to Poland with their families when the mob arrived; their house was empty. Balked of its prey, the mob threw stones through the windows, then broke in the door and poured in a strong, untidy stream through all the rooms. They smashed or scattered anything they found that seemed to smack of wizardry, beginning with Dee's books and astrolabe. The gazing table with its arcane diagrams was reduced to a pile of splinters. They passed on to breaking stools and crockery, and in the end set fire to the house itself.

By the time Master Rodgers had recovered from his ordeal

sufficiently to understand what he had set in motion, John Dee's home was a smoking ruin. Wisely, Master Rodgers decided to say nothing more of the strange scene he had observed in the Widow Arden's garden. He had no wish to be declared a madman. In any case, Dee and Kelly had fled the country, the Widow Arden and her daughters were gone, and there was no one left to prosecute. Rodgers departed for London on Monday morning, and confined his report to an account of Dee's mysterious disappearance and the violent reaction of the mob.

News of the destruction of his home did not reach Dee for many months. By then, he and Kelly were well established in Krakow, with their wives, children, and servants. They had brought with them the things most necessary to their experiments, chief among them their original gazing crystal. When they were settled enough to begin their work once more they were amazed and delighted to discover that their helpful spirit had accompanied them.

Madini's presence in the gazing mirror did much to reconcile Dee, at least, to the loss of the other crystal, and he never again attempted to meddle directly with Faerie. He and Kelly spent several years in Poland and Bohemia, though relations between them grew more and more strained as the differences in their goals became more apparent. In the end, Dee returned to England alone, bringing the crystal with him, but by the time he found another man to act as scryer Madini's sentence had been completed and the crystal was empty.

When the Widow returned home at last, late in the week following the sacking of Dee's house, she was profoundly thankful that she and her daughters had missed the preceding events. For Mistress Townsend's benefit, the Widow spun a tale of illness among distant relatives, who had urgently summoned her to help. To Mary Hudson she told a story somewhat nearer to the truth; then she packed up her Bible, her prayer book, and her book of spells, and left again. In time, most of Mortlak forgot that she and

Rosamund and Blanche had ever lived in the tiny cottage at the edge of the forest.

♦   ♦   ♦

♦

"Snow White married the prince and Rose Red his brother, and they divided the dwarf's treasure between them. They all went back to the prince's kingdom, where they lived happily for many years. The girls' mother lived with them, and she brought with her the two rosebushes from her garden. She planted them outside her window, and every year they bore beautiful roses, white and red."

AFTERWORD

I don't know why I have always been so attached to the fairy tale *Snow White and Rose Red*, but I have. As a child, it was one of my favorite stories, and as an adult it remained a fond memory, though it had been years since I had read it. When Terri Windling told me about the Fairy Tales, it seemed a natural choice, and I was a little surprised to learn that no one else had already claimed the privilege of rewriting it.

When I finally reread *Snow White and Rose Red*, I began to understand why. The story told in the fairy tale was not nearly as smooth as my memory had made it. It was episodic and unconnected; characters appeared and disappeared without explanation, and the motives of nearly all of them were unclear, at best. Even if I chose to use the fairy tale as a loose framework for my own story, rather than as a kind of outline, I had a lot of work ahead of me.

Despite the fact that *Snow White and Rose Red* is one of the tales collected by the Brothers Grimm and therefore of German origin, I chose to set my story in England. The Elizabethan atmosphere seemed to suit the "feel" of the fairy tale; furthermore, it was an era that for me combined reality (or perhaps history) with magic. If the American colony of Virginia was named in honor of Elizabeth I, so was Spenser's *Faerie Queen*, and it was not thought at all odd or irrational for a serious mathematician to make an equally serious study of astrology and magic. (Dangerous, certainly, but not irrational.)

Once the setting was determined, John Dee and Edward Kelly were the obvious choices for the role of the dwarf. From then on, the writing process focused sometimes on history, sometimes on the fairy tale, and sometimes on the story I was inventing, but it was always driven by the same two questions: "What on earth do he/she/they think they are doing?" and "Why in heaven's name would they want to do it?" My goal was to tell a story whose general outlines and events would be true to the original fairy tale, while explaining the disconnected scenes and elements of the tale and integrating it with the rich background of the time and the actual events of 1582–1583.

How well I succeeded, you must decide for yourself.